UNFAIR
catch

A TEXAS KISS NOVEL

KELSIE STELTING

Copyright © 2017 by Kelsie Stelting

All rights reserved. This book is a work of fiction, created from the author's imagination. Names, characters, places, and incidents either are the product of the author's imagination or are used fictitiously. Any resemblance to actual persons, living or dead, events, or locales is entirely coincidental.

No part of this book may be reproduced, transmitted, downloaded, distributed, stored in or introduced into any information storage and retrieval system, in any form or by any means, whether electronic or mechanical, without express written permission of the author, except by a reviewer who may quote brief passages for review purposes.

For information address Kelsie Stelting by email at kelsie@kelsiestelting.com.

Cover design by Kelsie Stelting.

Editing by Theresa M. Cole and Yesenia Vargas.

To my beautiful sister, Savannah, who teaches me to stand up for what's right and say to hell with everything else.

And to my first roommate, Madison, a best friend and soul sister who lets me enjoy the single twenties life vicariously through her.

TABLE OF contents

CHAPTER ONE	1
CHAPTER TWO	4
CHAPTER THREE	7
CHAPTER FOUR	10
CHAPTER FIVE	17
CHAPTER SIX	24
CHAPTER SEVEN	41
CHAPTER EIGHT	51
CHAPTER NINE	53
CHAPTER TEN	57
CHAPTER ELEVEN	63
CHAPTER TWELVE	74
CHAPTER THIRTEEN	81
CHAPTER FOURTEEN	84
CHAPTER FIFTEEN	88
CHAPTER SIXTEEN	97
CHAPTER SEVENTEEN	109
CHAPTER EIGHTEEN	113
CHAPTER NINETEEN	120
CHAPTER TWENTY	128
CHAPTER TWENTY-ONE	139
CHAPTER TWENTY-TWO	147
CHAPTER TWENTY-THREE	149
CHAPTER TWENTY-FOUR	153
CHAPTER TWENTY-FIVE	160
CHAPTER TWENTY-SIX	166
CHAPTER TWENTY-SEVEN	169
CHAPTER TWENTY-EIGHT	184
CHAPTER TWENTY-NINE	189

CHAPTER THIRTY	196
CHAPTER THIRTY-ONE	206
CHAPTER THIRTY-TWO	208
CHAPTER THIRTY-THREE	210
CHAPTER THIRTY-FOUR	216
CHAPTER THIRTY-FIVE	227
CHAPTER THIRTY-SIX	237
CHAPTER THIRTY-SEVEN	245
CHAPTER THIRTY-EIGHT	254
CHAPTER THIRTY-NINE	266
CHAPTER FORTY	271
CHAPTER FORTY-ONE	280
CHAPTER FORTY-TWO	288
CHAPTER FORTY-THREE	292
CHAPTER FORTY-FOUR	304
CHAPTER FORTY-FIVE	315
CHAPTER FORTY-SIX	320
CHAPTER FORTY-SEVEN	326
CHAPTER FORTY-EIGHT	334
CHAPTER FORTY-NINE	343
CHAPTER FIFTY	347
CHAPTER FIFTY-ONE	352
CHAPTER FIFTY-TWO	356
CHAPTER FIFTY-THREE	361
CHAPTER FIFTY-FOUR	364
CHAPTER FIFTY-FIVE	367
CHAPTER FIFTY-SIX	377
CHAPTER FIFTY-SEVEN	379
CHAPTER FIFTY-EIGHT	383
ONE YEAR LATER	388
ACKNOWLEDGEMENTS	389
AUTHOR'S NOTE	391
ABOUT THE AUTHOR	393
WHAT NOW?	394

CHAPTER one

AGAINST MY BETTER JUDGMENT, I OPENED THE ex-files on the absolute worst day of my life. I sat in an empty corner of my room while my family and roommate loaded our things into a moving truck and flipped to my most frequented page. On the left side, I saw myself and Hudson McAllister in a grain cart, both our grinning faces red from days spent harvesting in the Texas sun.

I slammed the photo album shut when I heard my brother's voice behind the door.

"I'll see if it's in there," he called and pushed it open.

I hoped the stacks of boxes would hide me, but

no such luck.

"What are you doing in here?" he asked, catching sight of me.

Turning away, I wiped at my nose. "Nothing."

His eyes fell on the album I failed to hide in my arms.

"Oh," he said, and he moved to sit by me.

He folded his hands over his knees and waited quietly.

"I don't want to go back," I finally said.

"You know what you need to do?" he asked, putting a hand on my knee.

I shook my head.

"Find a reason to go home—make it feel like your choice. Otherwise, you'll feel trapped as long as you stay there."

"I lost my job, Monti. How could I possibly turn this into a good thing?"

"Cheaper cost of living? Closer to Grammy? I'm not sure. But I know you can figure it out. You always have." He looked pointedly at the photo album and back to me. "But it's hard to move forward when you're stuck in the past."

Without waiting to hear my answer, Monti stood back up. "Any idea where the old blankets are? We need some padding for Cass's vanity."

"Over there," I said, inclining my head toward the closet.

He gave me a final nod before leaving the room with a stack of weathered quilts. After the door latched behind him, I thumbed back to the page and examined the photo on the right. Sixteen-year-old me posed with Rhett Lane at prom. I looked so young with my hair curled in delicate ringlets and braces decorating my ecstatic smile. My heart ached for my younger self, knowing the disappointment I had faced only weeks after that picture was taken.

A tear dripped from the tip of my nose onto the page, distorting the corsage I'd worn so proudly on my wrist. Wiping away the spatter and closing the album, I still didn't know my reason for going back home. All I wanted was to go back and start all over with Hudson, before I could fall in love with Rhett. Again.

CHAPTER two

"HEY."

I looked over to the man sitting on the tailgate of a silver Dodge. He leaned back against the side of the bed with one foot up. From under the brim of his cowboy hat, hazel eyes more familiar than my own shined in the rodeo arena lights.

"Hey," I tried to sound casual and kept walking. I knew all about Rhett and his game—enough to know I had to stay as far away from him as possible. Besides, I was supposed to meet Cassidy in the stands to watch the bronc riding and check out the cowboys.

Gravel crunched behind me as he got up and followed.

"So how are you tonight, beautiful?" Rhett trailed along behind me.

"Fine, thanks." I somehow managed to keep walking, despite the fact that my heart was river dancing on my stomach.

He caught my elbow in his calloused hand.

I turned around to fire off some excuse about needing to get back to Cass, or maybe a snarky comment about how I had no intentions of being his last "eight second ride" of the night. Instead, I found myself just as dopey as I had been my sophomore year of high school, my elbow warm under his touch, my eyes caught in his.

"I heard you moved home," he said, a slight smile playing along his full lips.

Of course he had.

"I've been back for two weeks," I said.

He nodded and moved his hand to rest on the small of my back. "We should catch up."

I patted his arm and stepped away. "I thought we just did."

Savannah-1, Rhett-0. I could play his game, too.

"Where are you working?" he pressed, not deterred in the slightest.

"At Viv's," I said, only because I knew he'd find out someway or other.

His smile got a little brighter, and he pulled his

hat off his head. "I need a haircut," he said as he put the hat back over his short brown hair. "Maybe I'll see you there."

I stood there, still trying to formulate a good reason as to why he shouldn't come to the salon when he gave me a broad smile, dipped his head, and said, "Well, I better let you get going."

Without waiting for my reply, he turned around and sauntered back to the pickup. After a couple of steps, he turned back to me and said, "Oh, Sav?"

"Yeah?"

His eyes slid a path from my curled hair to my new boots. "You look good."

Before he could get the satisfaction of my reddening face and clenched fists, I unrooted my feet and made my way around the arena toward Cass, but not before I heard him laugh.

Chapter three

"I SAW THAT." CASSIDY WAGGLED HER eyebrows. "White cowboy hat. That's always a good sign."

I groaned and sat down next to her. "It was Rhett."

Her eyes got wide. "Oh. Crap."

I nodded.

"His great aunt lives in the nursing home," she said. "Delpha. One of the CNAs says he visits her during med pass every Friday."

The seat became uncomfortable, and I shifted my weight. I hated learning things about Rhett that made him seem like a totally different person than I knew him to be.

"He's really sweet with her," Cass added. "Yesterday he brought his friend and his mom brought games, and they all sat around and played until Delpha was ready for bed."

"Has he made a pass at you yet?"

"Not since I said I moved here with you. I got his friend's number, though."

So that was how he knew I'd moved back to town. "Great."

Cass bumped my shoulder. "Rhett seemed extra interested in you."

I shrugged and looked at the cowboy riding a bronc. My palms got sweaty when the announcer called his name.

"That's Hudson," I said, gesturing at the man clinging to the bucking horse.

Back in high school, Hudson had been one of those string-bean kids with long arms and legs he couldn't quite figure out how to work. Now, things were different. When I'd last seen him during a weekend visit home, I could hardly believe my eyes. He'd filled out to become wiry instead of scrawny. Cords of strong muscle roped his arms, and Wranglers only helped the situation.

Cass pressed her lips together and tipped her head from side to side like she was commenting on curtains rather than a man. "He's not bad."

"Not bad?" I still hadn't told Cass about my half-baked plan to make him fall in love with me because it sounded crazy, even to myself. Out of all the guys we'd seen so far, Hudson was still the only rider I actually wanted to get a dance with that night, but after the way things ended between us, he probably wanted nothing to do with me.

She smiled a little bit. "He's not bad."

CHAPTER four

CASS AND I STROLLED INTO THE DANCE around half an hour after the rodeo. People were already drinking pretty heavily and couples two-stepped to an old, warbling country song.

I grabbed a couple of beers out of an unattended cooler, and we sat down, scouting the crowd.

Rhett sat around a folding table on the other side of the room with some of his friends. He didn't seem to notice me looking, but I hurriedly shifted my gaze, just in case. My sight fell upon Hudson a few tables down. He looked directly at me and tipped his cowboy hat in a gesture that made my stomach twist like the couples on the dancefloor.

Somehow, I managed a small smile and a nod.

He got up out of his seat, moving in my general direction.

Mid-prayer that he was on his way to ask me to dance, Cass poked my side. I saw her doe eyes shifting from me to a point over my shoulder.

"What does a guy have to do to get a dance around here?"

Rhett.

I glanced back at Hudson, who'd changed directions and had already found another girl to chat up.

"You won't decide you want to dance with someone else while we're dancing?" I asked pointedly.

Rhett's smile faltered, but only for a second. "I'm not about to make that mistake twice."

He waited with his hand out, and I had to choose—put my hand in his or run.

I stood up.

"Okay," I said, putting my hand in his and trying not to get lost in his grin.

Rhett guided me out into the fray of pairs dancing. Once we'd reached a clear spot, he pulled me too close to him and started leading me in a quick two-step. However much I hated to admit it, Rhett danced well. He held my hand firmly in his, and there was no doubt that he was the one in charge.

"So, what did you think of the rodeo, beautiful?" he asked.

UNFAIR CATCH

If I hadn't been so focused on ignoring the smell of his cologne, I would have blushed. "Fine. How was that fall?"

Instead of the annoyance I hoped to see on his face, I found a smirk instead. "I've had worse."

Was it just me, or was he talking about more than bull riding?

He broke apart from our two-step and spun me around him; I did my best to hold on.

"So, what do I have to do to get a date?" he asked after he tucked me back into his side and we had resumed our shuffle around the other couples.

"It's not happening," I said, the resolve I attempted to force into my voice made it sound like a razor blade.

He surprised me again by smiling. "Playing hard to get?"

"I'm not playing."

This time, he even chuckled at me. I tried to pull away, but he kept a firm hold on my waist.

"Neither am I," he whispered in my ear.

The shiver sliding down my spine definitely didn't come from disgust, and that scared me. Shouldn't I know better by now?

Much too slowly, the song came to a close. I wanted to get away from him, get out of the room and catch my breath, but he held me for an extra second.

"Trust me, Savannah." In his drawl, my name

sounded like an old song I used to listen to on the radio over and over. "This isn't a game to me."

With that, he tipped his hat and left me in the middle of the dancefloor in a stupor while fast-paced bluegrass music blared over the speakers.

"Would you like to danshhh?" one of the drunker men asked me, and just to prove I wasn't interested in Rhett, I took part in one of the sloppiest two-steps I'd ever attempted.

He thanked me by placing a wet kiss on my hand, which I wiped off after he wobbled to the cooler.

As I walked back to where Cass and I had been sitting, I caught Rhett looking directly at me with his trademark smirk. I returned it with a glare.

He smiled even wider.

I found our table and half-empty drinks, but no Cass. After searching for a few seconds, I saw her dancing with Rhett's friend Vox. Guessing he must have been the one who gave her his number, I sat down and finished my beer, then started on hers. She'd probably be occupied long past the time her beer grew warm.

"Didn't think you were that much of a heavy-weight," said a rough voice from behind me.

Hudson stood with his thumbs hooked into the pockets of Wranglers that fit him just right. He sat down across from me with his cowboy hat still on, sexier than I remembered him.

UNFAIR CATCH

I could have said a million things to him. How sorry I was I broke up with him for a chance with Rhett. How glad I was to see him. How well his ride went. That he'd been more than just a high school crush; he'd been my best friend. Instead, I wrapped my lips around the opening of the bottle and took a drink.

He considered me for a second, then took the beer out of my hand and set it back on the table. "I think it's about time we danced."

A flush not entirely due to the drink found my cheeks.

"Okay," I agreed, fighting to keep my voice at a normal octave.

He took my hand and guided me to where I'd danced with Rhett only moments ago. Confidently, he held me against him, but not in the suggestive way Rhett had. I leaned my head back to gaze up at him; he was so tall now.

"You look great, Sav," he said finally.

My face felt even warmer than it had been before. "You don't look too bad yourself."

"Thank you," he said.

"Good ride tonight."

He smiled slightly and thanked me, but didn't say anything else.

"Dating anyone?" I blurted.

I could have kicked myself! The combination of seeing Hudson up closer than I had in years and one beer had flustered me. All the lessons Cass had taught me about making guys work for it had flown the coop.

He let out a deep, sexy chuckle and met my stare. "Not really."

"What does 'not really' mean?" I pressed, not able to put my curiosity to bed.

Instead of answering my question, he asked, "Are you seeing anyone?"

"Not really."

Cass would be proud.

"You and Rhett looked pretty friendly." He lifted an eyebrow.

He was challenging me.

"Rhett? No. I—he's the last—absolutely not."

So much for poise.

Hudson laughed like I was some sort of a comedian. "Things cooled off, huh?"

Ouch. "You know they did."

"Sure." His voice was light, but he stared over the top of my head into the crowd, making a point to look anywhere but at me.

Though I never would have thought it was possible before, I actually felt relieved when the song ended.

To drown my sorrows from my lukewarm dance with Hudson, I went to the cooler and grabbed two more beers before heading back to the table where Cass and I had been sitting. Of course, instead

UNFAIR CATCH

of finding her there, I caught sight of her in a corner making out with Vox. At least one of us had good luck with guys.

CHAPTER five

"UGH." I ROLLED OVER IN MY BED AND SAW Cass snoring softly on the other side.

The last thing I remembered was Rhett asking me to dance a second time and thinking that I was going to need more beer. Now, I was regretting that thought.

I rubbed my eyes, then got up to make coffee—black. When I looked around my kitchen, I saw a single wild sunflower, my favorite, sitting on my table.

A ripped piece of lined paper sat underneath.
Thanks for the great night, beautiful.
-Rhett
My stomach turned. Everything after my dance

with Hudson got a little bit blurry until it faded to black. Ugh, that dance with Hudson… That was one thing I wished I would have forgotten.

"Cass, what do you want to eat?" I called to the bedroom.

"Aarrgghhhh," she groaned.

"Cass!" I yelled at her, hoping she could stay awake and distract me.

"Doughnuts," she said through her pillow.

I didn't have any doughnuts in my house, but I knew I owed her for being DD last night. I did my best to look like I wasn't hungover and drove to the grocery store to pick up a box for her. Feeling a bit guilty about the less than healthy breakfast sitting in my basket, I walked toward the produce aisle and began sorting through bananas until I found some that weren't over or under ripe.

I dropped a bundle of bananas when I heard Rhett's voice an aisle over.

Crap.

I grabbed the bananas off the floor and strode toward the checkout line before we could accidentally bump into each other.

Please don't find me, please don't find me, I begged silently, wishing the woman at the register would hurry up and decide whether to pay with a check or credit card.

"Thanks," Rhett sounded closer. "Yeah, that bull

was rank. I was lucky to get a ride on him."

"Well, ya did good, son," the man said in an old, withered voice.

"Thank you, sir," Rhett said. The thought of him tipping his hat to the man, acting like a good ol' boy made me sick. He thought he could play all nice and pretend he wasn't the biggest womanizer in McClellan. Well, if I ever had the chance to tell him what I really thought, he would be in for it. He wouldn't think he could get away with being such a two-faced—

"What's the prettiest girl in the county doing this morning?"

Great.

"Oh, you know, hunting elephants."

I turned to face him, even more upset than I had been before. Dressed in a pair of dark, starched jeans and a green plaid shirt that brought out the mossy colors in his hazel eyes, he looked like a country music star. And I looked like… a hungover girl on a doughnut run.

He chuckled. "You always were funny."

I rolled my eyes. "Thanks."

I set my bananas and doughnuts on the counter—the woman ahead of me having finally paid—but he took a step closer, and I couldn't bring myself to move. Rhett stood much too close. The scent of his cologne poured over me, and even with a million things in the store to look at, I only had eyes for him.

To say my self-control was waning quickly would have been a lie—it was nowhere to be found.

"Let me get this for McClellan's best elephant hunter," he breathed. "It would be an honor."

I started to smile, but stopped. "I can pay for myself."

"And deprive me the privilege?" He sidestepped me, pulling a leather wallet out of his back pocket.

"Whatever floats your boat," I sighed.

The cashier, a beaming high school girl not immune to his charm, bagged both his and my groceries, and handed him the receipt with a Tony the Tiger style, "Have a grrrreat day!"

Rhett refused to let me carry my bag out to my car, even though he already held three full of his own groceries.

"You know what would float my boat?" he asked, a mischievous, little twinkle in his hazel eyes.

"What are you talking about?"

"Earlier, you said, 'whatever floats your boat.'"

I opened my trunk. "Yes, Rhett, it's a common expression."

"Well, don't you want to know?" he asked, keeping a firm grip on my breakfast.

I raised my eyebrows but decided not to encourage him.

"A repeat of last night," he said with a smirk.

My tough-girl barricade came crumbling down at the reminder of the flower and the note. I did my best to hide my nerves at the thought of what a girl had to do for Rhett to leave a flower. "What happened?"

He touched my chin with his thumb in a gesture that made my stomach flop like a dog waiting for its belly to be scratched.

"I can't give all my secrets away," his voice slowly drawled over the word "secrets."

"We both know all about your 'secrets,'" I snapped.

He shrugged, unfazed. "I guess you don't want to know."

I took the bait. "What happened?"

"I have to get something in return."

"And that would be?"

"A date. With you."

My eyes narrowed. "If you think we're ever going on a date again, you're out of your mind."

"One date. Please," his tone was more earnest than I'd ever heard him.

The back of my eyes stung with tears I thought I'd ran out of. "After everything?"

If he was going to be serious with me, I was going to be serious with him. Not that he deserved it.

He frowned. "You don't think I'm the same guy I was then, do you?"

UNFAIR CATCH

I took my bag out of his hand.

"Why wouldn't I?" I dropped the bag in the trunk and slammed it shut.

"Just one date, Sav," he widened those attractive hazel eyes, and I closed my eyes against all the memories that came flooding back. "I'm a different man now. Just get to know me again. Please?"

Between his pleading tone and earnest expression, I was thrown back into a time when he was all I wanted. I was different now, too, but not enough to say no.

"Coffee," I said. "Nothing more."

"You won't regret it," he said and helped me into my vehicle before I had a chance to change my mind.

While I cussed myself on the way home for even entertaining the idea of a date with Rhett, I had one of the best realizations: he had never told me when or where. Hopefully it would be one of those things where we always planned to go out but "the timing was never right" or some other line that excused me from dating him.

I told Cass about the encounter when I got home.

"How have you already had an emotional mini-drama?" Cass yawned. "I'm pretty sure I'm still drunk from last night."

"Cass! You were supposed to be DD," I

chastised. "How did we get home?"

She shrugged. "Rhett and Vox drove us home."

"But they didn't stay?"

"I'm pretty sure I'm the only one who slept in your bed last night." She laughed. "He's just playing games with you."

"I hope so."

"D'you think he's changed?" she asked through a mouth full of doughnuts.

"Does it matter?" I asked. "I don't know if I could ever get past it."

"Well," she swallowed, "things didn't go very well with Hudson."

I put my face in my hands. "Don't even remind me."

CHAPTER six

CASS AND I HUNG AROUND UNTIL THAT evening when she had to go home to get ready for work.

My house felt so quiet without her in it. This was the first time I had a place without roommates, and even though I'd already been there for two weeks, I still hadn't unpacked all the boxes. Mom kept offering to come over and help me, but I feared what her Pollyanna touch would do to the decor. I wanted the home to feel like mine, and now that I lived in McClellan again, I was determined to keep my personal life separate from my parents.

Instead of unpacking like I should have, I

decided to soak in a bath. Mid-soak—bubbles, candles, and all—I heard the doorbell.

Pass, I thought. I'm taking a bubble bath.

I smiled at the thought and leaned back in the tub. If they wanted to talk to me that badly, they could come back later. Or call.

Whoever it was knocked.

I put a wet washcloth over my eyes and waited for them to give up.

For the third time, the knocks came at the door.

Persistent asshole.

They knocked for the fourth time, and now I starting worrying something bad had happened. Covered in suds, I got out of the tub and hastily wrapped a towel around myself. I hurried through the living room to see who was there. Of course, whatever incompetent handyman installed the door forget to include a peep hole, so I had to edge it open to check.

The second I saw Rhett waiting on my doorstep, I shut it.

"I'm busy!" I yelled.

"What about our date?" he asked through laughter.

Preparing to tell him off for showing up unannounced and ruining my bath, I flung the door open, giving him the dirtiest look I could muster. What I didn't count on was the door swinging into his face.

He yelped in pain, and stumbled backward over

my step until he landed on his back.

With a groan, he moved into a sitting position, rubbing his forehead. "When I called you a knockout, I didn't mean it literally."

The cogs in my mind spun into place, and I moved to check on him. In my fluster to run out and check if he was alright, I lost my grip on the towel, and it slid to the ground, leaving me butt naked. On my front porch. In front of Rhett.

Rhett's jaw dropped, but he quickly replaced his gaping mouth with his trademark smirk.

I snatched up the towel, covering myself up as fast as I could.

"The first date, Sav?" he asked through a laugh. "Most of the girls I know wait 'til at least the second."

If it was possible, I gave him an even dirtier look than I had earlier. For the second time that day, he'd seen me dressed down, and I didn't like the deficit that put me in. "I'm sure the girls you go with would put out in the first five minutes if you asked."

He quirked an eyebrow at me. "Who says I have to ask?"

I rolled my eyes. "Please."

He stood, dusting off the seat of his pants. "I've already seen you naked, and it hasn't even been five minutes."

"Rhett!"

Raising his hands, as if in surrender, he said, "I

know, I know. I'm lucky just to get a date with a girl as beautiful as you."

I readjusted my towel so I had a firmer grip on it. "Use your lines on someone they'll actually work on."

"Had to try." He shrugged. "So, can I come inside?"

Without an answer, he walked past me and looked unabashedly about my house.

"Um, no?" I said.

"Too late." I heard the smile in his voice.

"Seriously, Rhett, I'm taking a bath." I said, exasperated. "Go home."

"I said I was taking you on a date, and I keep my word." He ignored my scoff. "Go take your bath. I'll wait here."

Without getting a response, Rhett picked up my remote, turned on the TV, and started flipping through channels. What a surprise it was when he stopped on the rodeo station.

I groused back to my bathroom and got in the tub. The realization that the water had gotten cold did nothing for the anger burning in my chest.

This was going to be a nice, long bath, I decided. After draining out some of the cooler water, I turned on the tap to hot and warmed the tub back up. Rhett would be waiting for quite some time.

When I finished with my soak, my fingers were wrinkled and all the bubbles were gone. A small part of me hoped that Rhett would have given up and left by then, but when I checked my living room, he still lounged on the couch, eyes glued to the TV. I sighed heavily, and he laughed.

In an act of retaliation, I went back to the bathroom and took my time to look nice. I was not going to stay in this deficit with Rhett. The girls he'd "dated" since me were absolutely stunning, and I wanted him to know what he had been missing.

"Okay, are we taking your truck?" I asked, making my appearance in the living room.

Rhett's eyes grazed over my body, but he didn't say anything about my tight jeans or off-the-shoulder blouse.

"Of course we are, silly," he said.

Even the way he said "silly" made me mad.

"Fine," I replied and followed him outside to his pickup.

No one locked their houses or vehicles in McClellan, so when I reached to open the door to Rhett's pickup it was already unlocked.

Rhett shut the door I had just opened, paused a second, and then opened it again.

"What was that about?" I demanded.

"You will not open your door whenever you're on a date with me, whether it's the first or the fiftieth. Okay?"

"So you're a gentleman now?" I asked, a rough

edge in my voice.

"Something like that."

He offered a hand to help me into his pickup, but I grabbed the handle and hauled myself in. It smelled like hay, dust, and my sophomore year of high school.

Once he got in on the driver's side, he fired up the truck. It made a low rumble distinct to diesel engines, and he pulled out of the driveway.

"Just coffee," I reminded him.

"Just coffee," he repeated, but the way his lips pulled up at the corners told me he thought otherwise.

We drove past the more popular diner in town, making me assume he wanted privacy so he wouldn't run into whichever girl he was seeing that week. I tried to convince myself I didn't care, as long as this date was over, and soon.

Rhett drove out of town and turned onto a rarely traveled dirt road. It clicked. We were going to his house. My heart sank a little bit. Did he just want to see if he could sleep with me?

"Swallow some piss and vinegar?" he asked, looking over at me.

"No," I muttered and continued to watch fields blur out the window.

The sun balanced on the horizon, making for another beautiful Texas sunset. Bright reds and oranges smeared the sky, punctuated by small tufts of blue clouds. I loved it here… Well, Texas. Not sitting in Rhett's stupid truck.

"Savannah." He had one hand on the wheel and two eyes on me.

"Yeah?"

"Give me a chance."

He glanced back at the road and then to me again.

For a second, the only sound was soft country music.

"Okay."

After fifteen minutes of dust billowing behind us, we pulled up to the Shilling Ranch where a few clapboard houses for hired hands sat close to the corrals.

He parked in the driveway of a small, white one with a patch of irises and wild sunflowers along the front porch. My teenage self would have seen the flowers as a sign, hoping they'd been planted especially for me. My twenty-two-year-old self knew better.

"Don't get out," he said, pointing a finger at me.

I smiled after he closed the door behind him so he wouldn't see.

He hurried around to my side of the truck, giving me just enough time to observe him in his Wranglers. Rhett filled them out better than Hudson, no matter how much I hated to admit it.

After I got out of the truck, he led me up the

cement steps and put his hand on the door handle.

"Now, it's not the Ritz," he told me.

"You saw my place," I said. "Yours can't be that bad."

"I liked it," he said. "It felt like you."

"Directionless and messy?" I shifted my weight to my left leg, and before he could say anything, I asked, "Are you going to open the door or not?"

"Okay, just don't expect too much," he said.

Was Rhett nervous? Surely he'd had plenty of girls over before, but I guessed the inside of a house doesn't matter if the lights were off.

He pulled the screen door open, then a white door, and led me into his house.

"What were you worried about?" I asked.

He shrugged and finished taking off his boots using a boot jack.

It was nice. A pair of worn leather couches with mismatched afghans, pine end tables, and a coffee table filled the living room. In his dining room sat a small wooden table with a vase of sunflowers.

The walls were sparse, though, with only a barn wood cross in the living room, a livestock calendar in the dining room, and a clock in the kitchen.

"Do I get a tour?" I asked.

Unable to stifle my curiosity, I started walking toward the back of the house.

"Absolutely not." He slid in front of me.

"Let me write this down," I said. "Rhett Lane not letting a girl go in his bedroom?"

"'Just coffee,' remember?" He winked.

I rolled my eyes at him. "Well, get on with it."

He walked into the kitchen and started a pot of coffee before opening the freezer door and pulling out a blue package.

"I said just coffee." I was not about to hang around and eat supper with Rhett. Just being in his house put me in this limbo stage of remembering the good times we had together and the heartache I'd felt when the good times were over. Even though he didn't let me see the whole place, it felt like him—simple, warm, masculine.

He turned the package so I could read the wrapper. "You have something against chocolate chip cookies?"

I fought off a smile. "No."

"Well, alright then."

Within fifteen minutes, we were eating gooey cookies and sipping at sugary coffee, and it was one hundred percent awkward. Not because we didn't have anything to talk about, but because of the things we couldn't talk about.

"How's work going?" he asked.

"It's going," I said. "I actually gave Rachel's kid her first haircut the other day."

He used his sleeve to wipe a stray bit of

chocolate chip at the corner of his mouth. "She's a cutie, huh? I just realized I never asked why you decided to move back."

"It's a long story." I took a sip of my coffee, and soon the words were spilling out. "I've worked at a small salon in Austin ever since I graduated cosmetology school, and I loved it."

Rhett nodded and waited for me to go on.

"My Aunt Darla owns a salon in Austin, but she never had an open seat the whole time I lived there… including when I got laid off a month ago. Mom told Aunt Viv about it, and she offered me a seat at her salon here."

"That's tough," he said. "And Cass decided this would be a good place?"

I shrugged. "I honestly think Cass didn't want to look for a new roommate, and it was easy for her to get a job here. Plus, I might have begged a little."

He smiled at me over his lifted cup of coffee. "I'm glad you did. She's great with Delpha."

I nodded. Cass had this way with older people. They gravitated toward her, and I was jealous of the way older women took her under their wing so quickly.

"And I'm glad you're back," Rhett added.

Our eyes met, and it struck me how alone we were out there in the country. "Yeah?"

His hand found mine on the table, and he gripped it. "Really. I've missed you."

At a loss for words, I pulled my hand away and took a bite of cookie, staring at the vase of sunflowers.

Following my gaze, he reached out and twisted a stem so the flower rotated in the vase. "These were always your favorite."

"Everyone likes sunflowers."

He gave me a small smile and let his hand fall to the table.

"So, how's Monti?" he asked.

My older brother Monti had been a year ahead of Rhett in school. I'd gotten to know Rhett from the times he came over to our house with the other guys after games. "Good. He's got a good job and been dating the same girl for five years."

"Are they engaged yet?"

I shook my head. "Might as well be, though."

"Date anyone in Austin?"

"A couple of guys. Nothing too serious," I admitted.

He looked wistful, and his eyes glanced over me. "I always thought you were the marrying type. Figured some guy would sweep you off your feet right away."

Under his stare, I felt naked again. "I guess not."

I didn't know what he was thinking, but thoughts about Rhett and marriage filled my mind and threatened to overflow. He'd been my dream guy, and I had been the marrying type. Until I learned that some people didn't keep promises.

He shrugged, and we sat in silence for a minute.

"Can you take me home?" I asked. I'd finished my coffee and eaten way too many cookies, plus I had to work the next morning.

His face fell, but he recovered quickly.

"Yeah, of course."

He picked up our cups and plates and set them in the sink, then walked over and slipped on his boots.

I stood with my thumbs in my back pockets as he put a ball cap atop his head—despite it being dark out—and held the door open for me.

"Wait," he said when I was halfway out the door. "You do have a jacket, don't you?"

"At my house." A jacket didn't really go with the flimsy top I wore.

"Well, hold on," he said.

I stood in the threshold. "What?"

"Come in for a second."

I put my hands on my hips.

He raised his eyebrows. "Come on."

I stepped inside his house again, and he lifted a dark red sweater from a rack hooked over his front door.

"Here," he said and handed it to me. "If I can't keep you warm, then hopefully this will."

There was the Rhett I knew.

He led me out of the house—for real this

time—and opened the door of his pickup.

Nights got pretty cool in Texas, even in the summer. I had goosebumps, but I still didn't want to put on his sweater.

When he got in and saw me rubbing my arms, he said, "Cold?"

"Nope," I lied and spread the sweater over my lap.

He chuckled and started his pickup. I loved the sound of a diesel pickup—like the one Hudson drove.

Hudson.

I hadn't thought about him all night, a fact that upset me. Now, Rhett and I had been seen together at the grocery store, his pickup sat outside my house for the better part of an hour, and no doubt someone had seen us driving out to his place together. If it got back to Hudson, what little progress I'd made with him at the dance—if I'd made any—would be ruined.

"So, are you gonna come watch me at Parke next weekend?" he asked.

"I'm going," I said, "but not to watch you."

Cassidy and I had been planning to go to all of the rodeos in the area over the summer, something we'd wanted to do ever since we knew she was moving back home with me.

He smirked. "Close enough for me."

"The dance afterward?" he added.

"I think so." I pulled my knees to my chest.

"That's so cute," he said.

I looked down at my knees. "What?"

"You know what."

I resented being "cute." I wanted to be sexy, irresistible, curvy—anything but "cute." Maybe if I had been less "cute," Rhett wouldn't have gone looking for more with someone else when all I had thought of was spending summer evenings with him, driving around the country or curled up watching movies in my parents' basement.

"Do you want to ride with me to Parke?" he asked.

"Cass and I were gonna go together."

"Vox is riding with me. It looked like they were pretty cozy last night."

"Speaking of…" I put one of my legs down and turned so I could see him better. "That note just meant you dropped me off, right?"

Rhett tipped his head back and started laughing.

"What?"

"Yeah, I drove you home."

"Why are you laughing about it?"

He glanced at me with a small lingering on his lips. "You're a lot nicer when you're drunk."

I put my face in my hands. Of course I was.

"Actually," he went on, "you told me you missed getting flowers from me. And some other things about my butt."

I groaned. The part about his butt was embarrassing, and the part about the flowers was true. No one had bought me flowers since my sophomore year unless you counted a corsage from prom dates and a bouquet from Grammy at graduation.

Something didn't quite make sense, though.

"You just happened to have a sunflower with you?" I asked.

"I always keep one on hand, just in case."

I rolled my eyes.

"Why do you think I came to town this morning?"

"You came all the way into town to give me a flower?"

For the second time that night, he looked nervous as he ran his hand over his neck.

"Well… yeah."

I looked out the window so he wouldn't see my smile. "Thank you."

"You're welcome."

I found it difficult to process my feelings and what he said when he sat only feet away from me. It had been five years since he cheated on me. As a sophomore in high school, and him a senior, we'd been children. But I had been a child with her heart broken by her first love, and some wounds just didn't heal, no matter how many times you stitched them up.

"Do you still like country?" he asked.

I saw his finger hovering over the radio dial. "Yeah."

He turned up the music and started singing along. My heart felt like an anvil in the center of my chest, waiting for the next strike of hot iron. He used to sing to me all the time—in the pickup, on the phone at night, in my ear during a slow dance at prom… He had a voice good enough to perform professionally, and I'd always felt special to be the one he sang to.

"I missed this," he said between songs.

I couldn't bring myself to tell him that I missed it, too.

A song about love and second chances came on, and as he sang deeply, I felt my heartstrings match every chord. The song ended before we reached my house, but the feelings stayed until we reached my driveway. Like before, he offered his hand to help me down. This time I took it.

"Thanks for coming out with me," he said when we made the short walk to my door.

"Thanks for the coffee and cookies."

He lifted his shoulders for half a second. "It was my pleasure."

I reached to hand his sweater to him, but he pushed it back to me.

"Keep it," he said.

"See you around, I guess." I reached in my purse

UNFAIR CATCH

for my keys, forgetting that I'd left the house unlocked.

"Alright." He tipped his head to me and started walking to his pickup. Just before he got in, he stood on the running board with his head between the open door and the cab and called, "I'll pick you and Cass up here at four on Saturday."

I wanted to protest, but he'd already sat down and shut the door. Before he pulled away, he met my confounded stare through the windshield with a grin that said he'd won, and part of me was glad he had.

Chapter Seven

"WE HAVE TO GO WITH THEM!" CASSIDY SAID when I told her about my date with Rhett and his proposition for the rodeo.

Every Thursday night, we went out to eat, ordered supper with coffee, and had an hour-long girl gab followed by a night of movies, ice cream, and Mike's Hard Lemonade. Now that we lived in McClellan, we kept up the tradition at a local diner.

"We don't have to do anything," I said from behind my big, laminated menu. "Especially not with him."

"We never do anything new." She pointed at my menu. "Why are you even looking at that? You know you're gonna get a crispy chicken salad."

I sat my menu down and refrained from grumbling. Cass was spot on, and now I would have to order something different just to prove a point. "So, your idea of a good time is riding to a rodeo with them, not being able to meet anyone else at the dance because we're already there with two guys, and getting home God knows when?"

I saw her eyebrows lift into her bangs over her menu. "He was the one who got you home last weekend."

Good thing she was hiding her face. Otherwise, she'd've seen the glare I sent her way.

"Only because you wanted to spend more time with Vox."

"What can I get you two?" the waitress asked, appearing at the table.

Cassidy ordered the special and then gave me a pointed look.

"The turkey club," I said. "With fries."

She took our menus and walked over to the bar where she handed the cook our orders.

"Does that mean we're riding with them?" She looked a little too eager.

"I—"

"Well, look who we have here!"

I twisted in my seat to see Hudson's dad followed by none other than Hudson himself.

Mr. McAllister was no contest one of the nicest men I'd ever met. He had long, bowed legs, a perpetually red face, and almost always wore a huge, crooked smile. Under the tan lines and weathered skin, he was a good looking man, and I should have known Hudson would turn out the same.

"Mr. McAllister!" I said as I stood to give him a hug.

I'd worked with them one summer over harvest, driving grain cart, and Hudson had taught me to drive the tractor. That summer, as his dad hauled the last load of wheat to the grain elevators, Hudson asked me to be his girlfriend. And I said yes.

"You know it's Chuck," he said.

I leaned back from the hug. "Old habits die hard, I guess. You've met my friend Cassidy? She was my roommate in Austin."

"You work in the nursing home, right?" he asked her.

"That's right, just started a couple weeks ago," she said with a sweet smile and shook his hand. "Do you guys want to sit with us?"

It always surprised me how ballsy Cass could be, though it shouldn't have anymore.

Chuck turned to Hudson to ask him, and I shot Cass a look.

She winked.

"I'd never turn down an invitation to sit with

Savannah," Hudson smiled at me.

My knees wobbled.

"Then it's settled," Chuck said.

Hudson slid into the booth next to me, and Chuck sat next to Cassidy. For a moment, I felt bad that she had to sit next to a man she didn't know, but it was her own fault.

The waitress came back over and took their orders. Chuck ordered the same thing as Cass, and Hudson got a cheeseburger with fries.

"Hudson gets the same thing every time," Chuck said.

"I know what I like." Hudson settled back in the booth.

"Exactly!" I said, pointing at Cassidy. "We were just having this discussion."

"I finally got her to order something new," Cassidy said.

I felt Hudson's knee brush against my leg under the table, and my entire body snapped to attention.

"Good for you," Hudson said. "This one's a tough nut to crack."

"What do you mean?" Cassidy asked, leaning forward.

"What if I told you that I used to have the biggest crush on this pretty gal right here?" Hudson said.

"Of course you did," Chuck said. "She's

beautiful."

"Hey now," Hudson said, "I don't need any more competition."

"More competition?" I repeated.

"From what I hear, you and Rhett are getting pretty cozy," Hudson said.

My heart pounded that uncomfortable tap dance it always did at the thought of Rhett, and I tried to settle it so I could come up with something smooth to say.

"Is that Howard's son that was at the rodeo last weekend?" Chuck saved me.

Hudson nodded.

"Works at the Shillings' ranch?"

"Yup."

Chuck laughed. "He'd make a better hired hand than a bull rider from what I saw last weekend."

Why did that make me mad?

The waitress brought out our meals and filled our cups, and I thanked her out loud for the drink and silently for the few seconds she gave me to think about what Hudson had meant by "more competition." Did that mean he was interested? Or was he joking? I found it hard to focus with him sitting so close, his shoulder occasionally bumping against mine and sending heat straight to my core.

Cassidy made small talk about her job as an LPN at the nursing home, and Chuck talked about wheat prices. I knew just enough about both to chime in from time to time without looking ignorant.

Hudson's arm kept sliding against my shoulder. Sometimes, his hand glossed over my thigh, just slowly enough to make me question whether or not it had been an accident.

"Let me take care of the check," Chuck said when the waitress came back.

"Oh, please don't," I said. "I have a big-girl job now. I can cover it."

Chuck lifted his ball cap and pointed at his balding head. "I don't have a need of a haircut, but maybe you can give Hudson a deal."

I'd give him more than that.

"Of course," I said instead.

"And you," he said to Cassidy, "better still be working there when they check me in. Lord knows with this one I might be there in a couple of months."

We laughed.

"Never, Dad," Hudson said.

We made our way to the parking lot, and Chuck got into his old pickup, giving us a quick wave before pulling into the street.

Hudson must have parked closer to us, the rusted blue Ford if I guessed right.

Cassidy's phone rang, and we kept walking toward the cars while she talked. It was a short conversation.

"Hey, Hudson?" Cassidy said.

"Yeah?"

"Could you give Sav a ride home?"

"You're not coming over?" I asked.

She shook her phone at me. "There's something going on with a med schedule at the nursing home, and I need to get there now to check it out. I'll come by when I'm done."

"I'll give her a ride," Hudson offered.

Did I hear an innuendo in his tone?

"Thank you so much," Cassidy said. "I'll see you soon, Sav."

Hudson started walking to the driver's side of an old Ford pickup, and I looked over at Cass.

"You're welcome," she mouthed.

I opened the passenger door and got into his pickup. Empty pop cans littered the floor, and farming magazines covered the passenger seat.

"Let me get those," he said and shoved them to the middle.

"Thanks," I said. "Cass picked me up from work earlier, so…"

My sentence trailed off. We'd been such good friends over that summer I'd worked with him, but things seemed so strained now.

"Not a problem," he said and moved to put his arm over the seat as he backed out.

I suppressed a shiver as his hand grazed my

chest.

"Sorry," he said, twisting around so he could see behind him. "Accident."

"Sure," I said, thinking it hadn't been.

"Where's your new place?" he asked.

"Twelfth and Thurston."

"Okay."

My house was only about half a mile from the diner, and I probably could have walked, but I much preferred riding with Hudson. I was definitely eager to get a second alone with him and make up for my pitiful performance at the dance on Saturday.

"Do you want to come inside for a bit?" I asked when we pulled up.

He paused for a beat, but then he turned off his truck.

"Sure," he said.

I led him to my house, silently thanking myself for unpacking the living room the night before. When we walked in, I flipped on the lights.

"Want anything to drink?" I asked.

"What do you have?"

He wasn't looking around like I had expected him to. Instead, his eyes followed me.

"Beer, wine, water, coffee"—I peered in my cabinet—"and I think my mom brought over some old Kool-Aid packets if that interests you."

He let out a small laugh. "Beer's good."

I went to my fridge and pulled out a couple of bottles for us.

"Here," I said, handing him one. "You can sit down."

I gestured at my couch and tried to forget the memory of Rhett comfortably sprawled out on my couch like he belonged there.

"This is nice," Hudson said.

"Thank you."

He sat down and looked up at me with a mischievous gleam in his eyes. The same look he'd had when he used to play pranks on me at work.

"What?" I asked.

He grabbed my hand and pulled me down next to him.

A small squeal escaped my lips. "What?"

"You're so sexy," he said, sitting his beer on the end table and then my own before lifting me onto his lap. "I've missed seeing you around."

I didn't have a chance to catch my breath, much less ask him how he'd come around to missing me, when his lips covered mine and he wrapped an arm around my waist.

In his arms, I turned into a liquid, conforming in every direction he needed to go, letting him lead the way. His lips moving over mine, and the roughness of his calloused hands on my hips made my stomach contort in ways I didn't know possible.

UNFAIR CATCH

It could have been thirty minutes we made out, it could have been five, but it was everything I'd been hoping for since coming home.

Well, almost.

"I want you," he said, as if reading my mind.

"Have me."

CHAPTER eight

"THAT WAS... UNEXPECTED," I SAID AS WE SAT together on the couch after we were done.

He used the arm he had around my shoulders to pull me closer and kissed me. "You liked it."

I blushed. "Yeah. I just thought you were seeing someone."

He shrugged.

My chest felt just as much turmoil as a fork in a garbage disposal. Was this some sort of karmic retribution for something that had happened before I even knew how to use eyeliner correctly?

"Well," he said, "I better get going."

He lifted himself from the couch and started

walking toward the door, and I had no idea how to tell him I just wanted him to stay and cuddle and talk about all the things we'd missed in each other's lives since we graduated from high school.

"Thanks for the ride," I said instead.

He looked back at me and winked. "It was about time."

I laid back on the couch, closed my eyes after the door shut, and listened until his pickup fired up and drove away. I tried to battle the bad feelings crowding my mind. The Hudson I knew wouldn't sleep with a girl if he didn't want anything more. He was the kind of guy who sat in the tractor with me extra rounds just to make sure I wasn't nervous and texted me the night after a basketball game to tell me good job. A few years wouldn't change that… would it?

CHAPTER
nine

"YOU DID WHAT?!" CASSIDY SQUAWKED when she came over, only minutes after I'd texted her. I hadn't even waited until she sat down for me to tell her, so we stood together right inside my door.

"Yep."

"He must be pretty special."

I blushed. "I know. I never do that sort of thing. I waited six months before I slept with John."

"You've kind of waited six years with Hudson, if you count from when you started dating," she pointed out then gave me a cheeky smile. "You're welcome."

"For?"

"For getting him to give you a ride home. I'm

sure it was a piece of cake from there. The guy had his eyes all over you during supper."

I moved to the couch and sat with my legs tucked underneath me. "I'm not going to tell you where we did it."

Her eyebrows flew up into her bangs. "Here?"

I nodded, grinning.

She picked up a throw pillow and hit me with it.

"Stop!" I cried. "You're going to spill the popcorn."

"You haven't even gotten it out yet."

"So?"

She flopped onto the couch, giggling.

"So what does this mean for you and Rhett?" she asked after she caught her breath.

"What do you mean 'me and Rhett'? We had one date."

She tilted her head down and looked up at me under her lashes. "We're riding with him on Saturday for starters."

"Maybe Hudson will offer to take me."

"Well, he better pony up before Saturday."

I moved to pick up my phone from the coffee table, and Cassidy reached out and grabbed it.

"Do not."

I looked at her in surprise as she put it in her purse and zipped it shut.

"What?"

She raised an eyebrow at me. "You are not going to text him first. I know you don't do this kind of thing, so I will be your guide."

"My guide?"

With an evil grin, she flipped her hair over her shoulder. "Your guide to the world of playing hard to get."

I returned her smile. "I'm already doing that with Rhett."

"Yeah, because you are actually hard to get for him. You're putty in Hudson's hands. Hence what happened tonight," she said.

I frowned. "You don't think I did it too soon?"

"Vox and I already slept together."

"Well… Wait. What?"

I didn't ask for the logistics because I didn't really need them. Cass didn't move slow with guys, and she'd had a few one-night stands of her own, but that was always with some guy I didn't know. Vox had been a fixture in Rhett's life for as long as I'd known them.

She nodded with a sheepish smile.

"Do you like him?"

She pulled her lips into a line and shrugged. "Maybe."

That was the only thing jarring enough to distract me. For as long as I'd known Cass, the only relationships she'd had were the kind that went fast and ended even faster. "Maybe" meant something entirely new in Cass's language.

"You think you could date him, like, long-term?"

"I don't know," I saw several expressions warring behind her storm cloud eyes as she chewed the inside of her cheek. "But you and Hudson—I mean, you've known the guy since high school."

"Yeah…"

"And you like him."

"Yeah."

"Well, then," she said with a conspiring smile, "It wasn't soon enough."

CHAPTER ten

HUDSON DIDN'T TEXT ME THAT NIGHT, OR Friday night, or Saturday morning, and, at Cassidy's advice, I didn't text him. So, on Saturday, I found myself in the truck with Vox, Cassidy, and Rhett on the hour-long drive to Parke.

When they picked us up, Vox acted like he wanted to sit in the backseat with Cassidy, but in one of her best friend moments, she told him maybe on the way home.

"You look beautiful," Rhett said, as he held open the back door for me.

"Thank you."

After I had climbed in and buckled myself in,

he put a hand on my knee. "I'm going to try and make this a good night for you."

He didn't have that dumb smirk, but instead that honest, nervous Rhett was showing again. It unsettled me.

"I can have a good time on my own," I said, fiddling with the seatbelt strap over my chest.

He started snickering. "I bet you can."

I scowled at him as he shut the door, which just made him laugh more.

None of us talked much on the way. Rhett turned the country music up loud and mouthed along with the lyrics. Vox thumbed through his phone, and Cassidy and I whispered back and forth about our plans for the night. I told her I wanted to get out of the truck as soon as possible, so Hudson wouldn't think Rhett and I were together.

Cassidy raised her eyebrows at me like I was naive. "Are you kidding? This is the perfect chance to make him jealous."

"What?"

"Sav. Come on. If he sees you with Rhett, he'll know you haven't spent the last three days waiting for him to text you."

"But I have."

"He doesn't need to know that."

I pursed my lips, conflicted. How could I tell her it felt wrong to use Rhett when he'd made such an effort to be kind to me? When my own heart had to fight the urge to fall back into his arms and beg him to be mine forever.

"What are you two whispering about back there?" Vox called back to us.

I could have smacked him. Vox wasn't bad-looking, but he also wasn't the smartest cowboy at the rodeo. Cassidy said that didn't matter as long as he could dance and was good at... well, other things.

"Just some cute cowboy," Cassidy said sweetly.

Vox smiled back at her and then spit into an empty can. Gross. "Thanks kid."

She reached up and put a hand on his shoulder. "You're welcome, hon."

I looked in the rearview mirror and saw Rhett's face staring back at me. He made a gagging face, and I tried not to laugh too loudly.

Rhett parked the truck in a grassy area near the arena, and when he got out, he opened the door for me.

"Do I get a good luck kiss?" he asked, his face almost too hopeful.

I checked out the surroundings and spotted Hudson leaning up against a pickup about a hundred yards away, chatting with a group of guys in cowboy hats.

"Sure."

Rhett shut the door to the pickup and pressed my back up against it. His face stalled millimeters away from mine, and a slight smile lifted his lips, but his eyes burned with passion. If I was being honest with myself, I wanted this kiss too much, regardless of whether Hudson saw or not. Could I come back from this?

"Are you positive?" he mirrored my thoughts.

His breath smelled like mint, not chew like Hudson's had.

I nodded, not trusting my voice.

With one hand on my waist and the other cupping my neck, he leaned in and put his lips on mine. A warm, familiar tingle went down my neck and settled in my stomach, stilling it for the first time since Hudson left my house.

It was like I was back in high school again, our lips pressed together, my chest melting into his, never wanting to see the moment where we had to break apart.

"Get a room!" Cassidy called from the end of the pickup.

We separated, but Rhett kept my gaze. It made me want to squirm—in a good way.

"Thanks," he said, and then he broke eye contact.

Rhett and Vox started walking toward the arena, and Cassidy came over and put her arm through mine.

"That was convincing," she whispered.

I blushed and looked down at the trodden

buffalo grass.

A little too convincing.

Cass and I took our place in the stands and went about our usual routine of checking out the cowboys. We knew most of the guys from McClellan, but there were a few strangers.

When my phone vibrated, I pulled it out, hoping that Hudson had decided to message me.

Rhett: You look beautiful up there. 7:11 p.m.

One part annoyed, one part disappointed, and one part flattered, I hit the lock button and dropped my phone back in my purse. Hudson and I had hooked up. That had to mean something. It had to.

I watched as Hudson, surrounded by other men in cowboy hats and gaudy leather chaps, settled atop a bronc and gripped the hack rein so he could hold on. Time always seemed to slow down right before they let the bronc and rider into the arena. His fingers flexed around the strap, his chest lifted and lowered, his jaw set, and then, he nodded.

The gate burst open, and time returned to normal.

He rode for eight seconds.

When the bronc riding ended, Cassidy and I went to the bathrooms and locked ourselves in a stall where she finally let me check my phone. Of course, Hudson still hadn't texted me. Rhett hadn't, either.

"Why hasn't he texted me?" I whined.

UNFAIR CATCH

Cassidy pulled out a ribbon of toilet paper. "It hasn't been long enough."

"What do you mean?"

"He won't want you if you're too available. Trust me. Just wait."

"I shouldn't have had sex—"

The door banged open and some girls came in giggling.

"—with him," I whispered.

Cassidy stood up and sucked in her stomach so she could button her jeans.

"Was it good or not?" she asked.

I sat down on the toilet. "It was really good."

"Then he's going to want more. Make him work for it this time."

Chapter eleven

I LEANED BACK AND LET THE EDGE OF THE bleachers press against my back.

What a mess.

Hudson hung out by the corrals with the bull riders, his long, lean arms slung over the fence, one foot resting on a higher rung of the paneling.

I'd had the chance to be with him. Date him. Go to prom with him. The whole thing. I'd passed up a good relationship for some dumb idea of what love should look like—or more specifically, what a man should look like. To see him now, every bit as handsome as the type of guy I imagined I should be with, made me feel my poor decision even more acutely.

UNFAIR CATCH

Back then, Rhett personified my dream guy. Handsome, smooth, fit… other girls wanted him, hell, I wanted him. I was so jealous of his prom date freshman year. So excited when he told me he'd date me if I didn't have a boyfriend…

"There they are," Cass said as she pointed.

Rhett and Vox reached the stands and climbed a few rows to get to us. Vox slid into the seat next to Cassidy and pulled her into a kiss.

I didn't know how she did it. They never said they were dating, or exclusive, or anything at all, yet there they were. She could have a guy she barely knew wrapped around her finger, tight as a bow, and I couldn't even get a guy I'd known my whole life to text me after having sex with him.

Rhett settled beside me, rested his elbows on his knees, and looked me over. A line formed between his eyebrows, and his lips fell into a frown.

"What?"

He shook his head. "Let's get something to eat."

"At the concession stand?"

He got to his feet. "Nope."

I took his proffered hand, but stayed seated. "You don't want to watch the rest of the events?"

His face took on a thoughtful expression for a minute. Then, "Screw 'em."

Rhett gave my hand a little tug, and I stood up, but Cassidy and Vox stayed put.

"Are you coming?" I asked Cass.

She exchanged a look with Vox.

"I want to watch the roping," Vox said. At my frown, he added, "I'll take care of her."

He pulled Cass under his arm and rubbed her head until she pushed him off, laughing.

"See you at the dance," Cass said and pointed her thumb at Vox. "No promises he'll make it, though."

"See ya'll there," Rhett replied and started walking away again.

I waved at her over my shoulder, but she and Vox already sat head to head, holding hands. Rhett let go of my hand as soon as we got out of the stands, and didn't say anything to me until we got into the pickup.

"Is there even anything in Parke?" I asked.

He raised his eyebrows in surprise. "You've never eaten at Tommy's?"

I shrugged. "Not yet."

"Well, then, you're in for a treat."

We drove down the one paved road in town and pulled up to a metal building with a peeling, hand-painted sign.

"We're eating here?" I asked, thinking the place looked more like an abandoned storage shed than a restaurant.

He nodded. "Yep."

I'd rather have eaten stale chips and nacho cheese at the rodeo, but I was hungry, so I reached down to unbuckle myself.

He placed his hand over mine where it rested on the buckle. "Just wait here."

We'd been out of touch basically since he graduated, but I never knew Rhett to be so moody. I guessed he probably hurt himself when he fell off the bull, and I didn't want to ask him about it and make him more upset about his failed ride. Instead, I nodded, and scrolled through social media on my phone until he came back, not knowing whether or not I wanted Hudson to text me anymore.

After fifteen minutes, Rhett came back with a sack full of takeout boxes.

"Are we eating in the pickup?" I asked. "Because I smell barbecue, and I'm a mess."

"No." He reversed the pickup and got back on the blacktop. "I've got a better place in mind."

"How long?"

"Maybe fifteen minutes."

"I'm not going to sit here smelling this food for that long and not eat."

"Hold your horses," he said, a smile finding its way back to his lips for a fraction of a second.

I went to open one of the boxes to see what he'd gotten us.

"Stop it, piggy!" he said, finally grinning.

His smile brightened his whole face, from his tan cheeks to his shining eyes. I liked it so much I almost forgave him the joke. "My name's Savannah."

He laughed then pushed up the tip of his nose and started making snorting sounds.

"Pay attention to the road, you goofball!" I closed the box and sat back in my seat, laughing. That was one thing I always used to love about him—his sense of humor. "Just take us to the troughs."

Rhett drove us out of town, and after a few minutes of me asking where we were going and him telling me to be patient, we pulled off the blacktop onto a trail that butted up against a barb wire fence. Rhett got out and opened the gate to a pasture.

Walking back to the pickup, he looked like something out of a movie with his cowboy hat, dusty jeans, and what my grandpa would have called a "shit-eating grin." The green expanse and orange sky framed him perfectly.

"Okay, not too far now," he said, shutting the door behind him.

Rhett rolled down the windows and steered the pickup over well-worn tracks that cut through the swaying grass. The beauty made my heart swell with an appreciation of Texas. A soft breeze drifted through the cab, bringing with it the scent of earth. The orange sky looked so expansive over the rolling hills it seemed like we could have fallen in.

I still wanted to ask him why we needed to go all the way out of town to eat when we had friends waiting for us at the rodeo, but we crested a hill, and I understood as a canyon that went on for miles came into view.

He put the truck in park, and for a few seconds we let a chorus of crickets serenade us.

"What do you think?" he asked, chewing on the inside of his cheek.

"It's beautiful."

"This is my favorite place in the world." Rhett picked up the boxes and sat them on his lap. "I always come out here when I have something weighing on my mind."

Before I could ask what kinds of things he needed to drive an hour from home to think about, he opened his door, then mine, and walked to the back of the truck. On his way there, he'd opened his tool box in the back and pulled out a big wool blanket.

"A picnic," he said over his shoulder.

I climbed into the bed after he'd dropped the tailgate and spread the blanket out. He opened one box and handed it to me—barbecue pork, green beans, and a baked potato. I used a plastic fork sitting in the box to take a few quick bites.

"What kind of things do you come out here to think about?" I asked before I lost my nerve. This was dangerous territory. I knew that. Keeping my emotional distance was the only thing that had kept me from falling back into his web the night of the McClellan rodeo. But the thought of something affecting the perpetually happy man sitting across from me provoked my curiosity. Whether it was family, sports, or the ranch, he seemed unshakable. And he didn't have to worry about rejection since girls practically fell all over themselves to be with him. What on earth could bother a guy like him enough for him to need a special place?

"Oh, you know… life, work"—he nudged my arm—"girls."

I rolled my eyes and stared out over the waving prairie grass. "You mean you take girls out here to hookup."

Part of me was joking, but part of me meant it. I didn't want step back into the trap again, now that I was old enough to know better. I hated the idea of being a notch on his bedpost or a conquest he bragged about to his friends.

"Look at me," he said, his voice husky.

Folding my arms across my chest, I shifted to face him. "What?"

A muscle in his cheek flexed, and he looked over my shoulder until it relaxed.

Then down at the worn blanket.

Then to the little part of the sun clinging to the horizon.

"I'm trying with you," he said, finally looking back at me.

"Just like I'm sure you try with everyone else," I muttered, not confident enough to meet his gaze.

"That's bullshit, and you know it."

I raised my eyebrows. Hot rage, resentment, and rejection simmered together in the pit of my stomach.

"I like you. Okay?" he snapped. "I like you. I want to date you and you say yes, then you act like no."

"Just like you wanted to 'date' me in high school?"

His mouth fell open and closed again.

My eyebrows flew even higher before my eyes narrowed. "You acted like you loved me, and I broke up with Hudson for you! And then you slept with Cheyenne three days before—"

"I know what happened!" His voice rose. "That was high school. Do you not think I've changed since then? Even a little bit?"

"Oh please." My voice rose to match his. "Every summer, I've seen you at these stupid dances, and it's always with a different girl on your arm, some stupid rodeo bunny in denim underwear and cowboy boots."

"And you're not here every weekend trying to find some guy to sleep with?"

"I'm trying to find someone to date," I spat.

"I'm not allowed to date people?"

"That's what you call your one-night stands?"

"Alright!" he yelled.

I flinched.

"Alright," his tone quieted, but his jaw muscle flexed away. "I've been with a lot of girls."

"We've already established that."

"Damn it, Sav. Let me finish."

I bit my tongue.

"I slept with Cheyenne after I asked you out because I was young and dumb, and you wouldn't sleep with me, and it's the worst mistake I've ever made. I wish I could take it back, but I can't."

I looked down at my half-finished meal. "The worst mistake you've ever made?"

"The worst."

"And why's that?"

I looked back at him to see him staring at me.

"Because now I don't know if I'll ever get another chance with you." He lifted his hand and ran his thumb over my cheek, causing goosebumps to rise from my shoulders to my forearms, despite the warm evening.

I didn't know what to think, much less say. I'd been so excited when Rhett had asked me out in high school. He'd been a good bull rider, even then. Funny, popular, older, tall, and oh-so handsome. Hudson and I had been together for eight months when I broke up with him to be with Rhett. And Rhett and I had been together for three days short of a year when he cheated on me with Cheyenne. I'd given up a great guy only to have my heart broken.

Wasn't one of my goals in coming home to rectify the mistake I'd made?

And for what? Hudson had slept with me and wasn't even enough of a gentleman to call or text or even acknowledge my existence more than three days after the fact. Rhett was making an effort at least, being chivalrous, asking me out…

I still didn't know what to say, so I kissed him—hard. I ran my hand up to his hairline and knocked the cowboy hat off his head. He coiled his arms around my waist and pulled me close until takeout boxes fell aside and the distance between us disappeared. Our breathing drowned out the crickets, and our eyes closed to the world around us.

"Wait," he said.

"What?" I whispered against his lips.

"I want to do this right this time." He pulled away and held both of my hands in his.

My heart dropped, and I closed my eyes imagining all the reasons he wouldn't want to kiss me. "You don't want to be with me anymore?"

Rhett pulled me back to his chest. "Sav, I'd like nothing better than to be with you… in every sense of the word. To be your boyfriend, have you on my arm at dances, lean you over and take you right here—just, you know, jump your bones, blow your skirt up." A smile played over his lips, followed by a laugh I couldn't help but echo.

"Butter your bread," he added.

"Okay, okay."

"Check you for ticks."

"Stop!"

"Give you the ol' Johnny."

"Rhett!"

He tossed his head back and laughed, and it was so light and free, I joined him.

"But I want to be with you right now, and not sexually. Yet. Is that okay?"

I stared out over the pasture, seeing memories more than the landscape, then looked back at him, his eyes matching the darkening sky. How could I promise him what he wanted when I'd slept with Hudson only two days before and was still holding hope that he would want to be with me? Even if I wanted to be Rhett's girlfriend, I'd have to give up Hudson before I told him yes, and I wasn't sure I could.

"Rhett, I'm not ready to be your girlfriend yet."

"I'm not asking you to be. Just for the chance to try."

"Okay."

CHAPTER twelve

WE WALKED INTO THE DANCE TOGETHER, MY arm looped through his. Other guys immediately assailed Rhett with greetings, so I went to get a drink and find Cass. I had a lot to tell her, and I didn't feel like being known as Rhett's girlfriend even though I assumed that's where I was heading.

Cass wasn't anywhere inside the Quonset-building-turned-dance-hall, but Hudson was. Some girl hung on him as they danced together, him murmuring into her teased hair. A hot twinge of jealousy stabbed the pit of my stomach.

I picked up a beer from one of the coolers and walked outside. The air felt fresh on my face, but my cheeks flamed. How could Hudson sleep with me and then ignore me for days?

Admittedly, he hadn't promised anything, but wasn't sex a promise? Didn't it mean one person liked another person enough to engage in one of the most intimate acts a person could perform? Wasn't it at least special enough to text or call?

I suppressed a groan when I found Cassidy and Vox glued together against the building.

I loved Cass but didn't understand how she could find a guy, get with him, and then let it all go so quickly, just to move on to the next one… How did Hudson do it? How did Rhett do it?

A small voice in my head asked me how I did it.

I hated Hudson for putting me in this situation, and I hated Rhett for coming back into my life and making me doubt all the assumptions I'd used to protect myself over the years.

If I was being honest, I hated myself, too.

When I got inside, I saw Hudson lounging in a folding chair, the girl with the ridiculous hair's hand resting on his arm. Averting my eyes from that side of the room, I took a drink from my beer and scanned the crowd for Rhett. I found him sitting across a table from two girls and some guy in a cowboy hat. One of the girls talked with her hands flying all over, and Rhett nodded, listening intently. The green fire in my stomach burned a little hotter as I marched to join them.

"Hey," I said when I reached them, trying to inject some cheeriness in my voice.

"Hey," Rhett said, sticking his hand out for me to take.

When I did, he pulled me onto his lap, which made me a little less jealous—that was until he continued with his conversation without introducing me.

The guys talked a while longer about an encounter with a savage mother cow, and I examined the girls. They were both pretty. One was more of a typical beauty, while the other looked athletic with a harder edge. The guy had one arm draped over the back of her chair, making me think the prettier one had to be a tagalong. Something seemed off about her, though. Every time Rhett's friend told a joke, she laughed a little too hard, smiled a little too large, and made too much of an effort to avoid looking at Rhett and me.

After they left, I gave Rhett a questioning look. "Who was that?"

"My buddy, Steve."

"And?"

"And his girlfriend and her friend."

"Her friend?"

Rhett shrugged and tipped his cowboy hat back so it sat a little higher on his head.

"Ex-friend?" I pressed.

He gave me a look. "Savannah."

Great.

It was easier to think I could get past Rhett's promiscuity in the middle of a pasture when it was just us two. Surrounded with girls, AKA possible conquests, made it much more difficult. How long would I have to wonder if every female acquaintance of Rhett's was a friend or something more?

"Let's dance," Rhett said and started lifting me off his lap.

Voicing my concerns without sounding clingy and jealous would have been next to impossible, so I agreed to the dance without insisting on taking the conversation any further.

He led me to an empty space where Hudson had danced with that girl only minutes prior. I closed my eyes against the image.

Rhett took me through every step and spin, and held me close to his chest when the music permitted. I wondered if Hudson would be watching us like he had last weekend—I hoped so, if only so he would feel some small imitation of the jealousy I felt.

At the close of the song, I started walking back to our seats, but Rhett held firm to my hand and stayed stationary.

"What?" I asked as opening chords played over the speakers.

"I only get one dance?" he asked, his grin

spreading.

I couldn't help but smile back. "Maybe one more."

He guided me through a spin and then pulled me to him again. This time, we didn't bounce along in a two-step or swing dance; he swayed with me in slow circles around the dancefloor.

I felt his mouth against my forehead. "You're beautiful, you know that?"

"You don't look half bad yourself."

"I'm serious. You're the prettiest girl here."

I knew it wasn't true, but I thanked him anyway and pretended for a second that it might be.

After a couple more songs, we left the dancefloor in search of Vox and Cassidy. We hadn't seen them dancing, but the place had gotten packed in the last half hour.

We walked around the room, my hand in Rhett's, and found them sitting at a table, deep in conversation, which seemed rare for the relationship aesthetic they'd developed thus far.

"Where have you two been?" Rhett asked, making "where" sound sharp, but his smirk belied the tone. "We've been worried sick about you kids all night."

Their heads snapped up, and Vox's cheeks grew red.

Cass regained her composure first, and with a smug smile, she said, "Didn't look like it. Sav hasn't even been checking her phone."

She gave me a look that only she and I understood.

I nodded to show I understood, but played it cool. "Did you miss me?"

"Of course."

"So, what's up?" Rhett asked as he pulled out a chair for me.

I rolled my eyes at him. "Thank you."

"Anything for my girl."

Cassidy's eyebrows disappeared into her bangs.

Neither Cass nor Vox volunteered to share about their conversation. As we waited, Cass opened her mouth, but Vox cut in. "We're wondering when Rhett's going to plan a trip to the lake."

The ranch Rhett worked on was actually owned by his maternal grandpa, a retired banker who owned several ranches throughout the south, a hotel franchise, and God knew what else. He'd bought a lake house for family reunions and occasional trips, and he let them use it whenever they wanted, as long as they planned it with each other. Every summer, Rhett's family had a big shindig there. Rhett and I had parted ways before I ever got to go to one, but Rhett's sister, Harleigh, and her friend Cheyenne, were in my class and always bragged about how much fun they had.

Rhett shrugged. "Go ask Mom if you want to go."

Vox got a dopey, lopsided grin on his face. "I'll ask her more than that."

Cass hit his shoulder.

"And I know she'll say yes." Vox doubled over laughing, and Rhett fought a smile.

It was one of those evenings where I felt so grown up and so juvenile all at the same time. There I was with a group of friends, drinking beer, thinking about Rhett and Hudson, and knowing I had reached an age where dating wasn't just something to do to pass the time; it was real… but I felt just as lost as I had when I was leaning in for my awkward first kiss.

Chapter thirteen

AT TWO IN THE MORNING, WE FINALLY PULLED up to my driveway. McClellan was silent except for a few vehicles cruising up and down Main Street. With nothing to do in town except eat and catch a movie on the weekends, teens cruised around as late as their parents would let them, and usually later. A part of me smiled nostalgically at breaking curfew just to drive the half-mile stretch over and over again.

"I had a good time," Rhett said after he put the truck in park.

His face came into relief as a pair of headlights panned over the vehicle and then went dark again as they drove on by.

"Are you sure you're feeling okay?" I asked.

"Yeah, why?"

"You took a pretty good spill earlier."

He looked down, and the green light from the radio revealed a corner of his mouth quirk up. "Didn't I tell you? I'm made of stone."

"Sure."

He lifted a hand and brushed my cheek. "Except when I'm around you."

My stomach swooped as he leaned closer to mine. Every kiss felt like our first—new, exciting, and I never knew what would happen next.

He hooked an arm under both of mine and slid me closer to him, then I moved to straddle him on the seat. I hit the steering wheel too hard and the horn sounde,d causing him to laugh against my mouth.

I bit his bottom lip. "Don't laugh at me."

He smiled. "I won't." Another kiss. "Promise."

"Good." I slid my hand under his shirt and ran it over his stomach, following the trail of his hair under my fingers.

Headlights flooded his truck again, and I snapped my hand away.

When the lights passed, Rhett said, "I think I better take you home."

"We are home," I said, even though I knew what he meant.

He had his hands on my hips and drew small circles above my hipbones with his thumbs. Everywhere Rhett touched me, he left a trail of burning skin and desire. I tried to bury the piece of me that wondered if he'd be even better than Hudson.

"This is going to be great," he said.

"When?"

"When it's perfect."

He pulled his shirt back down, and I took my cue to scoot back over to my side of the vehicle. Rhett opened his door and walked around the truck. He held my hand all the way to the front door where he kissed me again.

"Want to come in?" I asked when we broke apart.

"I'm not moving past that door," Rhett said, leaning against the front of the house.

I looked up at him. I could see him as my boyfriend, but I didn't know whether that scared me or thrilled me. Maybe both. I cracked the door open, reached inside, and turned on the living room light.

"I'll see you tomorrow?" he asked.

I tried to smile. "Sure."

He bent over and kissed me on the cheek. "Sweet dreams."

"Good night."

When I got inside, I dropped my purse on the floor and collapsed onto the couch. I couldn't imagine what the high school me, who cried for weeks when she found out about Rhett and Cheyenne, would have thought of this.

CHAPTER fourteen

ONE OF THE THROW PILLOWS PUT MY BACK AT an awkward angle, so I threw it on the floor and pulled a crocheted blanket over me. My eyes were only closed for a second when I heard someone knocking on the door.

Had Rhett changed his mind?

Whoever it was kept knocking louder and louder.

"Savannah!"

Was that…?

"I know you're in there!"

"Hold on! I'm coming."

The knocking stopped for the few seconds it

took me to cross the living room to the front door. When I opened it, there stood Hudson, dirt stains and all.

"What are you doing here?"

He leaned against the frame, like Rhett had only moments earlier, but Hudson wore an entirely different expression.

"I texted you."

"My phone's dead," I said, not adding that I'd used all its battery checking for messages from him. "What are you doing here?"

"I've been driving around for half an hour waiting for him to leave."

"Hudson, why are you here?"

He stepped forward and slid his fingers through my hair until his rough hand cupped my neck. "I couldn't spend the night without you."

My stomach dropped, with excitement, happiness, confusion, frustration. "Why didn't you text me sooner?"

"Like I want to be in high school again. Chasing you around while you're drooling over Rhett."

My mind flashed back to the pickup and the sunset with Rhett.

"Reasons why you should have texted me sooner," I snapped. "You think you can just have sex with me and pretend it didn't happen for an entire week then just expect me to come crawling back?"

My voice rose with all of the hours I had spent looking at my phone, waiting for him to acknowledge that I existed.

"You're running around with Rhett like it didn't happen! Do you even remember what he—"

"Yes, I remember! I also remember you with some girl tonight. You're probably just done with her and figured you could come on over here and get some more!"

"Come on!" Hudson yelled, bending his knees with each word. Then his voice dropped. "I just want you. I've always wanted you."

"Don't you dare say that if you don't mean it."

He reached out and pulled me to him, electricity crackling between us. I searched his face, examining the peak of his nose and the valley where his lips came together. They crushed against mine, and for a second I got lost in the kiss, thinking it was everything I wanted in that moment. Except it didn't feel right.

I pulled my head away. "Rhett and I are…"

But I didn't know what we were, and it was even harder to remember with Hudson kissing his way down my neck.

"Hudson," I said, trying to get a second to defog my mind.

"Savannah." It was a wish, a promise, a plea—every way I had ever wanted him to say my name. And I fell back into the same feelings from the week before.

Letting him have his way with me, wanting every second of his skin on mine.

When we finished, he stood up and pulled his pants back up.

My heart tightened in my chest.

"Stay over," I said.

He walked back over to me and dropped a kiss on my forehead. "I have to feed tomorrow morning."

"Oh."

"Savannah," he drew it out like a song. "I have to. Otherwise, I would stay here all night long… maybe even have a round two."

I let out a quiet laugh that didn't feel happy at all and tried to be reassured. Still, I felt like the cans rolling around on his pickup's floorboard—dirty and long-forgotten.

He leaned over again and kissed me on the lips, and I tried to make it good so he'd want to stay.

He didn't.

CHAPTER fifteen

I WOKE UP AT EIGHT, AND NINE, AND TEN, until I finally decided to get out of bed around eleven and charge my phone. When it powered on, I started getting all of the texts from the night before.

    Cassidy: U and Rhett looked cozy. ;) 8:02 p.m.
    Cassidy: Were going 2 the dance 9:18 p.m.
    Cassidy: Were here 9:27 p.m.
    Cassidy: Were inside now. 9:45 p.m.
    Hudson: Where are you? 1:45 a.m.
    Hudson: Are you home? 1:47 a.m.
    Hudson: I'm sorry I didn't text sooner. 1:52 a.m.
    Hudson: I need to see you. 2:04 a.m.
    Hudson: I'm coming over. 2:06 a.m.

Hudson: I'm here. 2:09

Hudson: Tell me when he leaves. 2:15 a.m.

Hudson: Please tell me he's not staying the night with you. 2:21 a.m.

My heart fell when I saw that he hadn't texted me yet this morning.

I took in a breath and decided to send him a message. The Hudson I remembered didn't ignore a girl he liked. The year we dated, he'd gotten up early and driven to my house with flowers, just so he could tell me happy birthday before anyone else at school got the chance to. He hadn't played games, and I shouldn't either.

Me: Hey. :)

That was good, right? I knew Cassidy had told me to wait to text him, but she had never told me what to do in case he came over in the middle of the night—or when he left right afterward.

I felt like a child all over again. Sure, I'd been intimate with boyfriends after high school, but out of all my boyfriends—and admittedly, there weren't many—none had made me feel as pathetic as I did spending the afternoon watching TV and waiting for Hudson's name to show up on my phone.

Even though I sent the text again, just in case it didn't go through the first time, Hudson never texted me. My phone did go off around five when Rhett asked me if I wanted to see a movie with him, Vox, and Cassidy.

How could I tell him that I was seeing Hudson?

Sleeping with Hudson, the small voice in my mind corrected.

I had told Rhett I wasn't ready to be his girlfriend and never promised him exclusivity, only a chance to get there, but it felt sleazy to lead him on when all I wanted was a do-over with Hudson. Maybe that wasn't all I wanted though. Maybe I wanted a guy who would treat me like Rhett had ever since he saw me. Someone who would fight for me.

I said okay to the movies, not because I particularly wanted to face Rhett, but because I didn't know what else to do. If I said no, he'd start asking questions, and it dawned on me that I didn't exactly want him dating other people either.

Even though my stomach churned with fear and indecision, I forced myself to eat a little bit and then started getting ready. Rhett wanted to pick me up, but I insisted I drive myself to the movies and left ten minutes late so we wouldn't have extra time to talk when I showed up.

Still, Rhett was waiting outside the theater when I arrived. He hugged me like he hadn't seen me for weeks and gave me a swift kiss when I reached him.

"Sorry I'm late," I said.

He swatted his hand though the air. "You had the right idea. Previews are awful."

I tried to smile, but it was hard when he looked at me like I was the happiest part of his day.

"I already bought you a ticket, and Cass and Vox are waiting inside," he said.

"Thanks."

The McClellan theater only had one screen, so Rhett showed our tickets at the teenager behind the cash register and led me into the dark theater.

Cassidy gave me a side hug with her free arm, and I returned the favor.

"Crap, I forgot. I want popcorn," I said.

"I'll get it for you," Rhett offered, standing up.

"No, let me go get it. Please?"

He reached into his back pocket and handed me a folded bill.

"I can pay for it," I said, pushing it back.

"So?"

I rolled my eyes at him as he put the money in my hand and elbowed Cass in the arm. I attempted, in the light flashing from the screen, to convey the chaos raging in my heart and mind.

"I'll come with you," Cass said, and unthreaded her fingers from Vox's hand.

As we started making our way toward the aisle, Rhett whispered, "Will you get me a root beer?"

I nodded. "Sure."

When we reached the concessions, I walked past and continued to the bathroom. It was only a single room, but Cassidy came in behind me like she usually did.

"What's going on?" she asked when she saw my face.

"Hudson came over last night."

Her mouth fell open. "What?"

I nodded vigorously. "At 2:30. He came right after Rhett left and was banging on the door. I yelled at him for not texting me, and he…"

"And he what?" Her brows now knitted together forming a line over her blue eyes.

"Well, he kind of, we kind of…"

"You slept with him?" she yelped.

"Shh!" I said, hoping no one heard outside the door.

"You slept with him?" she whispered only slightly more quietly.

I cringed, closed my eyes, and nodded.

"Sav!"

I groaned. "I know."

"What are you going to do?"

Tears burned my eyes. "I have no idea. Hudson hasn't even texted me back all day."

"You texted him?"

I nodded and took out my phone so I could show her his messages from the night before.

She scrolled through the texts, and the line between her eyebrows became progressively deeper. "Sav, I know you like him, but he just made you a booty call."

Every part of me rejected that statement, and I felt embarrassment morph into anger. "I am not a booty call."

"To Hudson you are."

"No, I'm not."

"Then why hasn't he texted you?"

"He probably didn't get the message… The signal's not very good on their ranch."

She raised her eyebrows.

"Or maybe he lost his phone this morning," I said, staring at the threadbare carpet and thinking I was being just as dumb as the person who'd decided carpet would be a good idea in a bathroom.

She shook her head. "Sav—"

I took my phone back and interrupted her before she could say anything that made me feel worse than I already did. "Hudson's not like that. He can't be. He said that he didn't want to be like he was in high school, just following me around. Well, he doesn't have to anymore."

"If he wanted to date you, he could have asked. He didn't have to come by in the middle of the night after you'd just been out with another guy."

I put my hands over my face and drug them

over my cheeks. "God, this is a mess."

"Rhett really likes you," Cassidy said softly.

"I know. I know."

"No, Sav, like, he really, really likes you."

I gripped the sink and looked at myself in the mirror. "I don't know why."

Cass put a hand on my back and rubbed small circles. "I know you like Hudson, and he used to be a great guy, but maybe it's time to let him go."

My heart formed a lump in my throat. He'd been the one bright spot of my move back home. Without a chance to make things right with him and date him seriously, I was just another failed cosmetologist moving back to my hometown because nowhere else would take me.

"I'll see you in the theater," I said thickly.

"You're sure?"

I nodded, and she walked out of the bathroom. I took deep breaths until, eventually, I calmed myself enough that I thought I could face Rhett again.

When I took my seat and passed Rhett his pop, he set it down and stuck his hand out so I could hold it.

My hand slid easily into his, and he gripped it, lifted it to his mouth, and kissed it lightly. He looked over at me and flashed a smile that brightened the entire room before directing his attention back at the screen.

We held hands the entire movie, his thumb dancing slow circles over my skin. Without the warmth of his grip, I felt lost, like he'd been my gravity and in his absence I'd drift away.

Cassidy had to work the night shift so we said goodbye after the show. She gave me a squeeze and then sent me a look that lasted a fraction of a second. It said everything we couldn't in front of Vox and Rhett, and then some.

Vox helped her into the car, and I couldn't believe how much had changed for her in the month since we'd moved to McClellan. She'd had boyfriends before, but I couldn't remember the last time one had lasted this long or she'd seemed so happy.

"So, I guess this is goodbye?" Rhett asked after they'd both left and we'd arrived at the driver's side of my car.

I glanced down at the handle and scrutinized a rusting scratch. "I guess so."

"Look at the moon," he said.

Streetlights rendered the stars invisible, but a full pink orb hung in the sky over the town's horizon.

"Harvest moon," he said, his face still turned up at the sky.

When was the last time I had taken a minute to look at the sky? Definitely not since I'd moved home, and maybe even before then. He was making me see the world in a whole new light, and I wasn't sure I liked the new view of myself. But I sure liked the new Rhett he brought to light.

I stood up on my tiptoes and kissed him on the cheek.

He squeezed me around the waist for the briefest of moments and then let me go.

"So, you're heading home?" he asked.

"Yeah, I need to catch up on my sleep."

I felt my phone vibrate in my back pocket, and my heart leapt into my throat.

Rhett frowned at the sound. "I tried to wait to text you so you could get some sleep."

"That was sweet of you. I didn't sleep very well."

"Warm milk. That always works for me." He rubbed my shoulder.

"I haven't done that since I was little."

"You're never too old for a glass of warm milk."

I ran my finger over the ridged edge of my car key, halfway wishing I could be young again and let my parents tuck me into bed and talk my worries away. "Okay. Well, I'll see you later."

"See ya, gorgeous."

I made my best attempt at a smile and got in the car. As I drove away, I looked back and saw him looking up at the moon.

Chapter sixteen

THE NEXT MORNING, I GOT UP, GOT DRESSED, and went to work. On the drive, I thought about calling Hudson and asking him why he hadn't texted me. Or at least asking him if Cassidy's booty call allegations were accurate. Apparently, holding out and not talking to him hadn't worked. Sure, he came over and acted like he wanted me, but now, after all the sheets had been washed? Not so much.

Work proved to be a welcomed distraction. I wasn't naturally extroverted, so being able to meet people at the salon and talk to them from behind the chair was great for me. We could chat about hair or life—whatever the client wanted—or not talk at all.

Both suited me. I especially liked working with the elderly women who came in once or twice a week.

They always asked me about my life, and most of them were keen to offer advice—or at least give me a compliment and speculate at why I didn't have the perfect boyfriend. Although now, I could have one if I wanted. Rhett was handsome, chivalrous, athletic, and he made an honest living. If my parents met him now and didn't know about him cheating on me in our teen years, they would be happy to have me bring him home. But they knew about him, and I did too.

I had appointments through the lunch hour, which normally bothered me, but today, I was grateful to have something to occupy my hands other than dialing Hudson's number. But on the drive home, without anything to keep my mind off Hudson, I finally called him.

"Yello," he answered with the familiar whir of a tractor in the background.

His casualness really ticked me off.

"Yello yourself."

He laughed, apparently not picking up on my anger.

"What's up?" His voice sounded so light, happy even.

"I texted you."

"Oh shit! I saw that and I meant to reply, but I didn't have service."

"How did you get the text if you didn't have service?"

"You know how it is out here. Might have signal at the top of the hill for just long enough to get a text but not long enough to send one back."

"Oh." It sounded like a lousy excuse.

"You should come out."

"What?"

"Yeah, come out. I'm baling, so you can ride with me."

"The hay's not too wet?"

I knew enough to know hay had to be dry when baling, or it could cause fires or equipment failure. Usually hay got wetter as the evening progressed and they had to shut down around eight or so.

"Nah, we've got a few hours left 'til quittin' time."

"Oh." A million reasons not to go formed an untidy pile in my mind. What if Rhett saw? What if we had sex again? What if he just wanted me to go out there so he could tell me that there wasn't a future for us besides a friends-with-benefits relationship?

"Are you coming?"

One reason to go stood out amongst the chaos: Hudson.

"Sure."

He gave me directions to the field, and within thirty minutes, I was waiting at the edge of a mowed-down pasture. A tractor with a baler on the back of it crawled toward me, stopping periodically to spit a big round bale out the back. When he got close enough for me to see him in the cab, he grinned, and memories of working with him during summer harvest flooded my mind.

Back then, we'd been friends, confidants, coconspirators. With sweaty hands in the grain cart, he'd asked me on our first date, and I'd said yes. A week later, while Chuck drove a load of wheat into town, Hudson had shut down the combine, come over to the grain cart, and asked if he could kiss me before his dad got back. Boy, how things had changed.

The tractor's engine throttled down, and then the door popped open. He took the first step down the ladder then jumped to the ground with grace only acquired from years of practice.

"Hey," he smiled, teeth bright against his dusty face.

"Hey."

He spat on the ground, then closed the ten-yard gap between us and pulled me into a hug, which quickly turned into a kiss.

"Well, that's one way to greet a girl," I said, and he laughed.

"Come on," he said, waving his arm behind him and walking back to the tractor. "We're burnin' daylight."

I followed him and helped myself up the ladder and into the cab. After I settled into the small side seat, Hudson reached over me and slammed the door shut. Something about the warmth of his body over mine sent my heart into a frenzy. He throttled up the engine, turned the music up so we could hear it over the din, and started driving over the rows of shredded grass.

"This reminds me of some good summers," he said, one hand on the wheel, the other resting on the back of my seat. Apparently I wasn't the only one frequenting memory lane.

"Reminds me of your mom's cooking." I thought back to all the times his mom had brought coolers stuffed with meals fit for royalty out to the field during harvest time. That woman knew how to pack a lunch.

"Check out what she made me for supper." He pointed at an old red cooler in the corner of the cab.

I leaned over, picked it up, and looked through the contents: a roast beef sandwich, beans, candied pineapple, and a chocolate pudding dessert. "I wish my mom still made me suppers."

"I bet she would if you went to visit her."

I shrugged, not sure what to make of that comment. "Not every day, though."

"Guess I'm lucky."

I turned around to watch thousand-pound bales being dropped out of the baler. I always marveled at how the machine could pick up a line of loose grass and transform it into a perfect cylinder in a matter of minutes.

"So, how's work?" he asked.

"Pretty good. You?"

He raised one of his shoulders in a half shrug. "Same ol', same ol'."

"Getting ready for harvest?"

"Trying to, anyway."

"Who's driving grain cart?"

I wondered who would take my spot. Ever since Hudson and I broke up, I spent summers lifeguarding to avoid the awkwardness that had grown between us. A few people had taken the job over the years, from family to friends.

"One of my cousins from Abilene is gonna stay with us."

"Cool."

"Nah, he's a little shit. I don't think he knows what work is."

I remembered crawling into bed after working the fifteen-hour days with them during harvest, then falling asleep only to dream about wheat for the next six hours, and having to get up and do it again the next day. Harvesting definitely wasn't a job for people who weren't work brittle.

"I guess he'll learn," I said.

Hudson made a noncommittal gesture

somewhere between a shrug and a nod and fell silent. I couldn't understand how he could sit with me in a cab when there were a million unanswered questions between us and not say anything. I wanted to ask him what we were. If our nights together meant anything, or if this was just something he was doing for fun. Most of all, I wanted to ask him if he could see me as more than just some girl who broke his heart when we were both still learning how to love—if he could see me as his girlfriend.

Instead, Hudson pulled out his supper and shared it with me. We talked about what a great cook his mom was and remembered funny stories from high school and working together.

"Do you remember after prom freshman year?"

I put my hand over my forehead and ducked down. "I try to forget it."

His laughter echoed the rumble of the machine. "You looked so cute trying to change a tire in your prom dress."

I groaned. I'd begged and begged my parents to let me take my own car to prom. Our school was small enough that everyone got to go, and since a lot of girls my age didn't have dates, I didn't worry about getting one either. But, at one in the morning, alone on my way home from prom, my tire went flat. I had been too proud to call my parents for help and couldn't walk the two miles home, so I got out of my car and jacked it up wearing my heels and sparkly strapless dress. Of course, Hudson happened to drive by.

"Nat wasn't too happy," he said.

That comment made me laugh out loud. "You spilt pop down the front of her dress! You're lucky she even got in the car with you."

He cringed. "Yeah, I basically assaulted her trying to wipe it off."

We both laughed at the memory of Hudson fumbling with napkins trying to clean cola off the front of Nat's off-white dress.

"And she"—I laughed—"she just sat there while you changed my tire. Didn't say hi or anything."

"She couldn't get out of the truck fast enough. Didn't even get a kiss good night."

"That makes two of us."

He looked over at me and smiled. "You know, I'm glad you were my first."

As my stomach knotted itself into a bow, I imagined a future with Hudson, sitting on our front porch, talking about the day's work or funny stories from our past, knowing that we would be each other's first and last kiss. I wondered if Hudson could picture it, too.

When the sun brimmed the horizon and it reached that time of evening where even turning the headlights on doesn't make a difference, Hudson throttled the tractor down and turned it off.

I tried to open the door to get out, but Hudson reached over me and shut it.

"Where do you think you're going?" His eyes washed over my face and then down the rest of my body.

"Home, I guess," I said, not quite ready for what might happen next.

He ran a hand over my leg. "Now why would I let you do that?"

"I don't know," I breathed.

He edged even closer to me.

"Me neither." His lips landed on mine, and soon, I felt the soft glance of his tongue in my mouth. My body snapped to attention, remembering the last time we'd been together, how he'd touched me in ways that made my body part ways with my mind. He knew what to do, and I was more than willing to let him.

When we were done, I curled on his lap and rested my head against his shoulder.

As he ran his hand through my hair, I whispered, "That was great."

After a beat, he asked, "Better than with Rhett?"

I recoiled at the question, almost not believing what I'd heard. Hudson didn't sound insecure, and it definitely wasn't an honest question—it was a dig, and I was pissed.

"Oh my God." I got off him, furiously tugging

my clothes in place.

He gripped my forearm. "Come on, Savannah. I was just kidding."

I jerked away from his grasp and got out of the tractor as quickly as I could, skipping the last two steps as he had earlier that night.

"Savannah!"

I stormed the twenty-yard span between the tractor and my car; I couldn't get there fast enough.

Hudson caught up and slid between the door and me. "Savannah."

I tried to reach for the handle, but he stepped in front of me again.

"Stop!" He grabbed my shoulders.

I used my hands to pull his off me, and his face got hard.

"What? You're still running around with him, even after Saturday night!"

I glared at him. "You wouldn't even stay the night!"

"What am I? Just some stud at your service?"

"You never texted me. I thought I was just a booty call to you." I spat the last words.

"I. Didn't. Have. Any. Service." He beat his hand on the hood of my car, and I tried not to flinch.

"Bullshit."

"Bullshit? No, bullshit is you sleeping with me and then going out with him before you even changed the sheets."

"Or, maybe, it's leading someone on when you have no intentions of anything more than a two a.m. call."

"Like you did with me?"

My eyebrows knit together. "When?"

At the tilt of his head that said I should know what he was talking about, I asked, "Are you talking about sophomore year?"

He pressed his lips together and nodded slowly like I was stupid. "You picked him. Even then, you picked him."

"We were children then, Hudson!" I yelled, unable to keep my voice down. "You don't think things have changed since then?"

With a quick jerk of his head to the left, then right, he said, "Apparently not."

"At least Rhett takes me on dates and doesn't just come around when he wants a quick lay!" My voice echoed off the hills, and I heard, rather than saw, a bird's flapping wings.

Hudson stared at the ground now. "You wanted it. Why else would you come out here."

It wasn't a question. And it was too true to argue.

"You're an asshole."

"Yeah, and you're a whore."

I watched, my entire body turning to stone as

UNFAIR CATCH

he strode to his pickup, got in, and slammed the door behind him. The tires spun, kicking up bits of dirt and grass and leaving a cloud of dust floating in the red haze cast by his taillights. By the time I got in my car, all I could see of his truck was two small specks of red shining in the inky sky.

Chapter Seventeen

"SO, DO YOU THINK WE CAN INVITE THE Guys to movie night?" Cass asked on Wednesday over lunch. It was the first day since moving home Cass had gotten up in time and I had a lunch break, so we took advantage of the time to eat together.

"Why?" I hedged.

I'd avoided texting or talking on the phone with Rhett for the last couple days using work and family time as an excuse. My parents and I went to visit Grammy in the nursing home Tuesday evening, and we'd spent the night playing Phase10, her favorite game. In between rounds, she hinted about a "handsome young cowboy" that went to her Catholic church in Roderdale, but I put a stop to that one real quick. I already had more cowboys than I could handle. Besides, I hadn't even gone to a Baptist church since I stopped living with my parents, preferring late Saturday nights out and sleeping in until noon on Sunday.

"Sav?"

I snapped out of my thoughts and realized Cassidy was waiting for me to reply. "Sorry, what did you say?"

"We thought it would be a fun date night if the guys came over," Cass said through a mouthful of hamburger.

I raised my eyebrows. "We?"

"Me and Vox."

"You're a 'we' now?"

As she made every effort to focus on her grease-stained paper plate, I saw her cheeks redden. Cass never blushed.

"I guess so," she said, fiddling with a napkin.

"Wait. You're, like, an item?"

She met my eyes and nodded, unable to hide her smile.

"You? You're exclusive?"

She laughed. "Stop! Yes, we're dating. I told him we couldn't make it Facebook official until I told you."

I rolled my eyes at the term, still trying to wrap my mind around Cass's newfound exclusivity. "Okay, I guess they can come over. But I'll make supper."

There was no way I would risk running into Hudson and his dad again, especially not with Rhett by my side. I still fumed at the thought of my fight with Hudson. He hadn't texted me since, and I hadn't texted him, either.

"Great," she said. "I'll text Vox and let him know."

"I guess I'll tell Rhett."

"Did you get things sorted out with Hudson?"

I frowned.

"What?"

I finished chewing and sat my hamburger down. "If you count having sex, getting in a huge fight, and being called a whore 'sorted out,' then definitely."

Her eyes flared open. "You're kidding."

So I told her about calling Hudson and driving out to ride with him in the tractor and how everything had seemed like it used to. How he'd been the guy I knew he could be, and then ruined it with our fight.

She folded her arms across the table. "Sav, you've got to ditch this guy."

"You think I haven't figured that out by now?"

"Well, I just—never mind." She tucked a French fry in her mouth and chewed it slowly.

"What?"

"Well, you don't seem to make the best judgments around him."

"Like I wanted to get in that fight."

"I meant driving out there after that crap he pulled last weekend."

My chest tightened. I already knew I'd made a whole host of mistakes regarding Hudson—the first of which had thinking Hudson would still be the same person he'd been in high school—and I didn't need Cass rubbing it in my face.

"I'm going back to work," I said, standing up. "See you tomorrow."

chapter eighteen

RHETT HAD BEEN EAGER TO COME TO GIRLS' night and showed up fifteen minutes early, which I both expected and dreaded. He offered to cook, but I told him I wanted to prove to him I could make a meal. He reminded me of the time I tried to make supper for him while we were dating in high school and started a grease fire in my parents' kitchen. I'd taken care of it back then—with the help of an outdated fire extinguisher—and I told him I could manage this time.

"Just sit at the table and look good," I said.

He laughed and rubbed the back of his neck, his plaid shirt pulling tight around his muscled shoulder. "I am pretty good at that."

UNFAIR CATCH

I agreed.

While I finished cooking and we waited for Cass and Vox, we talked about his work, and then he brought up the big family trip.

"To the lake?" I asked, even though I already knew.

"Yes." He had his chin tilted down and his eyebrows lifted, making the most "duh" expression he could muster.

"With your family?"

"Well, yeah."

"All of them?"

He nodded slowly.

"For a whole weekend?"

"It's not like you don't know them."

I opened the oven to check the French fries. They squealed in the heat of the oven. "I don't think your mom likes me."

His eyelids fell half over his eyes. "Come on."

Okay, truthfully, I didn't like her. She was one of those ladies who still had feathered bangs, wore turquoise eye shadow, always looked down her nose at other people, and never hesitated to spread a rumor. And Rhett's sister wasn't much different.

"And your dad doesn't talk... like ever," I added.

Rhett came into the kitchen, wrapped his arms around my waist, and pulled me into an embrace. "I bet he'd talk to a pretty thang like you."

My stomach swooped twice—once with that giddy butterfly rush and once with guilt. "Well, this pretty 'thang' hasn't ever heard him talk."

"So?"

I pulled away from him and reached into the fridge for the bag of salad.

He trailed two steps behind me. "We'll cook out and go tubing and fish on the boat and go out on the jet skis."

"Will your sister be there?" I closed the refrigerator.

Harleigh was a topic we usually didn't touch with a ten-foot pole. Of course Rhett loved his sister, but I'd rather walk around with feathered bangs for the rest of my life than spend ten minutes with her.

Rhett took the bag of salad away from me, buried his head into my shoulder, and mumbled something that sounded a lot like "yes."

"What?"

He wiggled his head in my collar bone until his chin rubbed the spot he knew tickled.

"Rhett!" I grabbed his hair and tugged his head away so I could see him.

"Could you please give me a haircut?" he asked. "It's really getting too long."

"Rhett," I said, half amused, half exasperated. "Is she coming?"

He sat the bag of salad on the counter. "Yeah."

He coughed. "And Cheyenne."

My heart dropped. "You're shitting me."

"Savannah." His voice held a tone of finality. "She's her best friend. I couldn't tell Harleigh not to bring her."

"Like hell you couldn't."

"Sav, what happened with Cheyenne, that was a long time ago," he said, addressing the elephant in the room.

"Maybe the first time was." The acid in my stomach boiled with anger and feelings of rejection I'd worked so hard to bury.

Cass and Vox chose that minute to show up. She walked in without knocking—like she usually did.

Like we'd planned it, I turned to the cabinets so I could clear my expression, and Rhett walked over to greet them.

"Food's ready," I said after I'd dumped the bag of lettuce into a bowl and took the fries and chicken out of the oven. "Plates are on the table, so help yourselves."

Things started off awkwardly. Even though I managed to put on my poker face, I couldn't talk with all the turmoil I felt in my gut. But Vox got onto the topic of rodeos coming up, so the conversation started flowing.

"How far away is Freeburg?" Cassidy asked Vox when he mentioned the one on Saturday.

Tucking his food in his cheek so he could talk, he said, "'Bout four hours."

"You guys are driving four hours to a rodeo?" I asked, shocked.

"Well, yeah," Vox said like it was a nonissue.

"It'd feel a lot shorter if you came," Cass added.

"You're going?"

Never had I been out of the loop with Cassidy, but apparently things were different now.

She squeezed Vox's hand. "Yeah. Gotta support my man."

Rhett wiped his hands on a paper napkin. "Will you come? I don't know if I can live another day without your cooking."

He tried to keep a straight face, but his lips broke into a smile, and I smacked him on the shoulder.

"This is delicious." I took a bite of the overcooked chicken to prove it.

"So, will you?" he asked.

It wasn't like I had anything better to do, and Hudson was definitely out of the picture, so I agreed to go along.

Rhett squeezed my knee under the table.

"Do you guys have a hotel already?" I asked.

A shared look between Vox and Rhett made me nervous.

"We've got something better," Rhett said.

"The stabbin' wagon," Vox added, his fleshy lips

spreading into a dopey grin, and Cassidy giggled like it was the funniest thing she'd ever heard.

"Don't listen to him," Rhett said. "It's just a camper we take to rodeos."

I let the subject of their camper drop, but wished I wouldn't have agreed. Campers usually weren't big enough for four people under the best of circumstances. I couldn't imagine what one in the care of two bachelors would look like.

Once everyone had finished their meal, Cass got up and started taking plates to the sink.

"What movie are we watching?" she asked.

We debated about the movie for about ten minutes until Cass gave into Vox. Folding wasn't in Cass's nature. In fact, she prided herself in getting her way and was a self-pronounced steamroller. Is this what a long-term relationship looked like for her?

They sat together on the loveseat because Vox said he wanted another reason to sit closer to his woman. His words, not mine.

I made popcorn, divvied out candy, and then joined Rhett on the larger couch. It crossed my mind that only a few weeks ago, Hudson and I had been naked right where we sat. The thought disgusted me enough to set my popcorn aside.

No matter how angry I was with him, I still had hopes for making peace, even if we couldn't be together. But my phone was still annoyingly silent, and if I knew

Hudson, it would to be a battle of wills to see who caved first. If I knew Hudson. I was starting to think I didn't know him at all.

"What are you thinking about?" Rhett rubbed my shoulder with the hand around my shoulders.

"What?"

"You look distracted."

"Oh… no, just spacing out."

"Is this about the lake trip?"

Thankful for the out, I nodded.

"Please come," he whispered against my cheek before kissing it. "For me?"

In that moment, he looked so hopeful, so nervous, so vulnerable, that I couldn't say no. I never wanted Rhett to stop looking at me like that.

"Okay," I said. "I'll go."

He gave me another soft kiss, on the lips this time. "Thanks."

I pulled up the corner of one side of my mouth in a half-hearted smile. "Sure."

Rhett linked his fingers with mine and turned his attention back to the movie. I tried to do the same. Unfortunately, there were just some things I couldn't push out of my mind.

CHAPTER nineteen

RIGHT AFTER WORK, THEY PICKED ME UP, AND we made the two-hour drive to the lake. Cass and Vox had insisted that we start the trip to the rodeo a day early, and Rhett agreed on the condition we spend the night at the lake, and I agreed because anything would be better than lying in the bed I'd shared—however briefly—with Hudson, who I'd lost as both a love interest and as a friend.

    Rhett had parked the camper, but we were staying in the Lanes' cabin as a "preview to the greatest weekend of my life." (Rhett's words, not mine.) Admittedly, the cabin was nice; it had a rustic yet modern look that made it feel like an upscale country retreat. We'd gone out on the water for a couple of hours on the canoes, and then Rhett took wood from the pile to start a fire for s'mores.

Fire crackled in the cinderblock pit, threatening to engulf my marshmallow.

Country music floated from Vox's phone speaker and fireflies danced around spindly branches in the sparse tree coverage. Being outside at the lake felt like entering an entirely different world where Hudson was only a faded memory—like a bad dream, Cassidy was gooey-eyed in love, and there was a strong, country man who thought the world of me.

I couldn't help but feel a mixture of revulsion and envy when Vox held his s'more out for Cassidy to bite. She got chocolate all over her face, and he leaned in and kissed it off.

"Get a room," Rhett joked and took a sip from his beer before sitting it back in the canvas chair's cup holder. He seemed so at ease slouched back in the chair with his hat tipped back on his head and his marshmallow dangling above the fire.

"The world is our room," Vox said, popping the rest of the s'more in his mouth.

"Yeah, yeah," Rhett said.

Only red embers glowed in the fire pit when Vox called it a night. He and Cass walked into the cabin, and I stayed outside with Rhett.

He found an old five-gallon bucket and walked

to the water spout to fill it.

"What do you think about those two?" he asked.

"They seem happy."

Truthfully, I'd never seen Cass this happy in a relationship, but I also hadn't ever seen her act less like Cass. We'd hardly talked the few weeks since she met Vox. Granted, I'd been preoccupied with Hudson and moving, but back in Austin, we always chatted throughout the week. Not to mention Cass had never admonished me about relationships before. Only a few weeks ago, she would have been asking for all the dirty details on Hudson.

I frowned. "She's different."

"I see that."

"Yeah?"

"She used to push you around more."

My frown grew deeper. "What's that supposed to mean?"

"Forget it." He picked up the bucket and started lugging it back to the fire pit.

"Tell me." Even though he had a bucket of water to slow him down, I still trailed behind him.

"You just let other people call the shots sometimes."

I wanted to say he was wrong, but I couldn't. Wasn't that what had happened with Hudson? I'd wanted to yell and fight and demand answers about why he hadn't stayed, but we'd done exactly what he wanted. Or what Cass assumed he wanted anyway. And wasn't I in this whole mess because of Cass and her advice? Things might have developed differently if I'd been upfront and called him after we slept together the first time.

"So?" I said instead of sharing all the reasons he was right.

"So, you're an adult."

"And I still don't have it together, so why not listen to someone who does?"

Smoke flew from the fire, and a sound like heavy, flapping wings reverberated as he dumped the bucket of water.

"Can I tell you a secret?" he picked up a shovel and started working the dirt beneath the coals.

"What?"

"Nobody has it figured out, but if you keep letting other people tell you what to do, you're gonna end up in a world of hurt."

Like I wasn't already. When I'd made that promise to myself to make things right with Hudson, this wasn't exactly what I'd pictured. I thought for sure Hudson and I would be together by now. I never imagined he could be the kind of guy that could sleep with someone and move on the next day.

My throat burned with unshed tears, and I tried to swallow back the unignorably large lump that had formed.

With his free hand, Rhett put his arm around me and rubbed my shoulder. "Let's go inside."

Unable to speak, I nodded.

As we made our way toward the house, I was faced with a gripping fear about what would happen next. "Rhett Lane" and "take things slow" didn't go in a sentence together unless you added "doesn't" in between. I had more questions than answers. How long had it been since I slept with and woke up next to a guy? Were Rhett and I going to sleep together for the first time? Did I want that?

He dropped the bucket by the shed then led me into the house. True to form, he picked up both of our bags from where we'd left them in the living room and led me back to a bedroom. I happily noted that it was across the house from where I'd heard Cass and Vox's voices slipping through the crack under a bedroom door.

"Will it do?" Rhett asked, stepping into the spacious but simple room.

A lone queen-size bed with a white comforter took up most of the room, as if echoing my questions from before.

"Of course."

"Did you want your own room, or are you okay with staying with me?"

It seemed like a silly question. After the rodeo

the next day, we would be spending the night in the "stabbin' wagon," which, while bigger and cleaner than I had imagined, barely left us enough room to sleep without lying on top of each other.

"Yeah, it's fine," I said.

"Don't make me twist your arm," he smiled and pulled his shirt over his head.

Taking him in, I said, "Well, now you definitely don't have to."

He lifted an arm and flexed, his muscles dancing on his arm.

Farmer's tan aside, Rhett was sexy. I knew he had to be fit to ride bulls and work outside all day, but I hadn't anticipated the way seeing him without his shirt would make my back stiffen and pulse race.

I whistled at him, and he flexed some more. "Who would have guessed you were hiding that under all that plaid?"

He shrugged and took off his pants so only a pair of black boxer briefs covered him.

"Your turn," he said with a wink.

"Ummm, no." I walked over to my duffel bag and rifled through its contents until I found the T-shirt and shorts I'd packed for the night. "I'm gonna put on my PJs."

I took them and my makeup bag into the bathroom and closed the door behind me, battling the nerves that settled on me with all the subtlety of a thunderstorm.

Why was I so nervous?

I reached in my bag, took out makeup remover wipes, and started cutting through layers of foundation, eyeliner, and mascara until I was a slightly red, blank canvas again. Then I looked at myself.

The brown eyes that I usually widened with makeup seemed narrow, my nose a little too big for my face, and my chin a little too pronounced. I wasn't fat, but my stomach couldn't pass for flat, either. The only tone I had was from occasional spurts of I've-got-to-get-my-butt-into-gear workouts with Cass or standing all day at the salon.

I'd never disliked my body, but I knew from cosmetology school how to accentuate what I wanted to showcase and hide what I didn't. I knew how to cut my hair to keep my chin from seeming so masculine and how to highlight my eyes to make my features appear more balanced. Baring all of that to Rhett seemed an act of excessive vulnerability.

After a final glance in the mirror, I went ahead and used the bathroom and changed.

When I walked out of the on-suite, I saw Rhett lying on the bed, under the covers, only his muscular shoulders and head showing. He seemed a lot less intimidating there than he had in his half-naked glory.

"Could you turn off the lights?" he asked.

"Sure."

With the room cast in darkness, Rhett was only illuminated by the muted night sky showing through the window.

He rolled to one side and patted the empty half of the bed.

I smiled and slid in under the blankets, facing him.

"You look good without makeup," he said.

"It's dark."

"I saw you. You look good."

"So do you."

He chuckled and moved, pressing close to me. "I'm serious."

My breath caught in my erratically pounding chest. "Me too."

His calloused fingers traced circles on the soft skin of my thigh.

I reached out and touched the side of his face, feeling the invisible facial hair growth.

"God, you're sexy." He gripped my thigh and pulled me closer so my hips were against his.

I bridged the gap between our lips. It felt right, natural, and he reacted like he felt the same way. We didn't have sex, but things went farther than they had before, and if I said I didn't want to find out how Rhett and I fit together, I would have been lying.

CHAPTER twenty

AN ALARM ON RHETT'S PHONE WOKE US UP at six in the morning. I woke up with my head on his chest and his arms around me.

"Good morning, beautiful," he said in a rasping morning voice, leaning his head up to kiss me where my forehead met my hair.

"Morning."

He untangled himself from me and the sheets and sauntered into the bathroom.

After the door had clicked shut, I leaned over the bed and searched through my purse until I found a pack of mints and popped one in my mouth.

I heard water hit the plastic bottom of the

shower and then the stream get interrupted as Rhett got in. The thought of him in the shower made me shiver, and I considered getting up to join him, but something stopped me.

Hudson.

I still felt guilty about sleeping with him. I'd never promised Rhett anything more than a chance, but I'd never dated two guys at the same time before, and it felt dirty. Any chance I'd had or wanted with Hudson had sailed after the fight we'd had.

Every part of my body wanted Rhett, that much was clear after last night, but part of me wondered how I could give up on Hudson. He'd been perfect for me and I'd missed it.

I pulled the blankets up under my chin and looked around. From the yellow light streaming in through faded white curtains to birds chirping softly out the window, the peaceful ambience of the lake house cooled my thoughts. My head settled into the pillows and blankets, making it feel like a nest that smelled overwhelmingly of Rhett and country air. The rhythm of Rhett's shower lulled me into a peaceful trance less consuming than sleep.

Rhett came out of the bathroom with a frayed green towel wrapped around his waist and made his way to his bag where he pulled out his standard weekend attire: fitted jeans, a white T-shirt, and a western button up.

"Shower's all yours," he said. "But the handles are opposite, so the right one is hot, and the left one is cold."

"I think I might hang around here." I winked sleepily at him.

He smiled a crooked smile and started fiddling with his towel.

"Tease," I said, moving to a sitting position on the bed.

His mouth fell open in playful disdain. "Rhett Lane is no tease."

"He says from across the room, behind a towel."

A small thud sounded as his towel fell to the floor.

I bit my bottom lip to keep from asking him to come over.

"Like what you see?"

I nodded.

"Good." He slipped on a pair of underwear after giving me a seductive smile.

I stuck out my hand, and after a moment, he took it in his.

"Come cuddle with me," I said, knowing I wanted so much more than that.

"I gotta make breakfast for you and the lovebirds."

I rolled my eyes and pulled on his hand. "Come on."

He acted like he was putting up a great fight, but he lifted the covers, laid under the blankets with me, and we did some of the things we did the night before.

"I can't wait to sleep with you," he said against my neck.

My stomach flopped in agreement. "Me either."

We all ate breakfast together—eggs and pancakes that Rhett made from scratch—and then Cass and I did the dishes while Rhett and Vox cleaned up the house.

"What did you guys do last night?" Cass whispered, waggling her eyebrows.

I turned away from her and worked on scrubbing the spot on the pan where eggs stuck to it. "Nothing."

"Your voice went up!" She jabbed a soapy finger at me. "What did you guys do?"

I blushed. "What did you guys do?"

A sly smile crossed her face. "You mean what didn't we do."

I don't know why it was so funny, but it was. We laughed until we were clutching our bellies with wet hands and tears were dripping out of the corners of my eyes.

The door opened from a bedroom, and Vox came out. "Sounds like a pair of hyenas out here."

That made us laugh even harder. By the time

the intermittent fits of giggles died down, the boys had finished cleaning and were ready to go.

Their mood changed when we got about an hour down the road. Cass and Vox shared the backseat, and Cass had fallen asleep, snoring within the first thirty minutes. Her head rested on Vox's lap, and he absently stroked her hair while staring at the pastures blurring by.

I sat in the center seat just to be closer to Rhett. He had one hand on the steering wheel and the other around my shoulders. The music was just loud enough to drown out any possibility of conversation, so I flipped through one of the magazines I'd brought, turning the corners on pages with hair and makeup styles I liked.

Even when we stopped to eat lunch, things were quiet and tense, the anticipation almost palpable among our small group. For the last hour of the trip, I noticed Rhett had produced a rosary from somewhere and silently mouthed the prayers, rubbing the worn turquoise between his thumb and forefinger. I hadn't known he still practiced Catholicism, especially judging by his promiscuity over the last few years.

He stowed it away and hopped out after we pulled into an RV park. Vox told Cassidy he would show her around the campground, so I crossed my legs and picked up a fresh magazine to read while Rhett got the camper ready.

"Wanna learn how to set up a trailer?" Rhett asked, leaning his head through the window.

"Do I have to?"

The door opened and he waved his hand at me. "Come on."

Rhett taught me how to stabilize the camper with blocks of wood and unhitch it from the back of the pickup. He helped me hook up the hoses and showed me where to attach the cord for electricity. Watching Rhett work made me like him more. His hands were as sure with the trailer as they had been with me the night before. Although the tightness in his jaw revealed his tension, his eyes were soft and kind in his instructions, and he never laughed at me when I asked what might have been stupid questions.

A small bit of pride ballooned in my chest when I extended the pop outs and saw it finished. Rhett fished two bottles of water out of a cooler in the back of his pickup, and we sat on the tailgate while we waited for Vox and Cass to come back from their walk.

"How are you feeling?" I asked.

He tipped his hat up and rubbed his face with condensation from the water bottle.

"Just hoping I do a little better than last weekend." He pulled his hat back in place.

"At least you were safe."

He looked over at me and lifted one side of his mouth in a half-hearted smile. "I guess." He gripped the edge of the tailgate on either side of his legs. "I'm just glad you'll be here either way."

My heart wrenched. If he only knew how close I had been to not coming.

"Of course," I said, putting my hand on top of his.

The midday heat kept me from holding his hand much longer, but I sat next to him in an easy silence until we heard our friends' voices and the crunch of gravel under their shoes.

Vox said he wanted to get to the rodeo early to watch the kids ride steers, so we loaded back into the pickup and drove to the rodeo grounds. Even though it was still midafternoon, vehicles filled the grassy lot. Dust curled in small clouds from the arena, and people—mostly with their children—meandered the grounds.

When Rhett stopped and parked, he said, "Okay, we're gonna go register, and then we'll come and watch the show with you."

I nodded. "Okay."

By the tight way he kissed me on the cheek, I could tell his nerves were even worse than before, but I didn't know what I could do to help him, so I just said, "see you soon" to their backs.

Rhett lifted a hand without turning around, and I heard him call, "See you."

I would have watched him walk away—half in

admiration, half in consideration—but Cass looped her arm through mine and started toward the stands. Everything she said on the way there centered on Vox.

"Vox washes his hair with bar soap. Can you believe that?"

"The only thing Vox can cook is steaks."

"Vox said he was thinking about taking me to meet his niece and nephew."

"Oh, well, Vox loves action movies, but I just want to watch a chick flick every now and then, ya know?"

Vox. Vox. Vox.

I tried to listen and nod politely, but her obsession with a guy she'd only known for three weeks was driving me up a wall. I knew I should be happy about Cass finding love and actually being in what seemed to be serious relationship, but I was annoyed. They'd only dated for such a short while, and I already felt like I was losing her to him.

Where was my Cass? Shouldn't we be talking about how to break the news about Hudson to Rhett in a way that wouldn't make him hate me? Couldn't we complain about how Vox talks with his mouth full and makes smacking sounds when he chews? Or how kids were literally running around everywhere?

Little girls who barely fit in their saddles were taking horses much too large and powerful for them around a pattern of barrels. I could tell that the parents had trained the animals well enough that they really didn't need a rider to know what to do. I thought back to the time Hudson took me for my first horse ride on their family horse, which was so old and docile it could barely walk let alone trot, then tried to shake the memory.

The steer riding, the last event of the junior rodeo, was well underway by the time Rhett and Vox joined us in the stands.

"That took a while," I commented.

"We ran into some friends, and they had to show us their new horse trailer," Vox said.

Rhett buried his face in my hair, kissed my head, and whispered, "You know us boys and our toys."

His breath on my ear sent a chill up my spine, even in the midafternoon heat.

They stayed with us for the rest of the steer riding and until the team roping ended, then they went to get ready. Rhett had to go put on his pair of bright blue chaps with black tassels off the side. I always liked the way bull riders wore their chaps—like they were made of gold instead of leather.

Though the rodeo began just like any other, with the Star Spangled Banner and the local rodeo queen loping around the arena with a flag flying behind her, this night felt different. We weren't walking around to see what guys were there or talking about which ones were cute. The only men we talked about were our own. Somehow, I became suspended between nostalgia for the good times Cass and I had together and grief for the way life had been in Austin. Things were different—not just with my job and dating situation, but also with Cass—and I started to think they wouldn't ever go back to normal.

We both stood up in the bleachers when it came Vox's turn to get on a bull, and Cass's reaction was almost as exciting to watch as the ride. She went from anticipation, to awe, to fear, to pride, to pure admiration, all in a span of eight seconds. Was that what I looked like watching Rhett?

Rhett rode toward the end of the bull riders, and I heard a group of friends behind us talking about him. That he had been coming to this rodeo for several years, that he was attractive, that they wondered if he would be going to the bars later…

Cass slipped me a pleased smile. To her, the highest form of praise was having other girls talk about her man. To me, it was disrespectful of the relationship. One time of being cheated on turned every casual admirer into a threat, and I dreaded the thought of other girls vying for Rhett while I still tried to sort out my feelings.

But, to be fair, Rhett and I hadn't defined anything. We had a relationship, sure, but even though I'd said I wasn't ready to be his girlfriend yet, we'd not said anything about our exclusivity. I hoped we weren't exclusive yet, but only because I didn't want my encounters with Hudson to ruin my chances with Rhett.

I watched Rhett adjust his hand under the strap that girdled the bull and give a swift nod to the man operating the gate. It burst open, and I stood on edge waiting to see how the ride would go. His bull bucked and spun, and Rhett's body jerked with it. Eight seconds seemed so long when waiting to see whether or not Rhett would succeed—if he would be okay.

The buzzer sounded, and Rhett sailed through the air to the ground in a puff of dirt. A rodeo clown dressed in bright socks and shorts stood between Rhett and the bull, giving Rhett the chance to run over to the fence and climb over. When he took off his helmet, I saw his smile that stretched for miles.

One of the girls made a sexual comment about Rhett and eight second rides.

"How original," I muttered.

Chapter twenty-one

MOST PEOPLE—INCLUDING RHETT'S FAN club—had left the stands by the time Rhett and Vox made it to us. We had been standing near the bleachers, talking about what we wanted to do the next day, but when they showed up, Cass stopped mid-sentence and jumped into Vox's arms like he'd been away at sea.

Rhett took me out of my cynical thoughts by wrapping me in a hug and then dipping me in a kiss like we were in an old western movie. Being judgemental about Cass and Vox's gushy behavior was hard when I enjoyed it so much with Rhett.

He pulled out of the kiss, and his eyes pored over my face.

"Good job," I said, breathless.

Lifting me out of the dip, he said, "Thanks, beautiful."

I smiled. "So, what are we doing now?"

"I'm taking my girl out to celebrate."

"And how are we going to do that?"

Freeburg's population tripled that of both McClellan and Parke. Rhett told me they didn't have a dance in association with the rodeo, but there were several bars around he wanted to take me to. The first one we arrived at had a huge dancefloor crowded with people.

Vox slipped off with Cass to get us drinks, and Rhett led me out to dance. The week before, Rhett had been disappointed, no matter how well he'd hid it, and it contrasted starkly to the joy he exuded now. As the song faded out, he held my face in his hands and kissed me, everyone around us disappearing into the next song and purple lights.

Rhett guided us through the bodies packed between us and the table where Vox and Cass sat with three beers. Cass had volunteered to be DD on the ride over, and I was surprised she'd agreed to that two weekends out of three.

Vox complained about the crowd and body heat, pulling open the top buttons of his shirt, and, of course, that was our cue to leave.

The next bar they took us to resembled what I

imagined to be a stereotypical biker bar; grungy with graffitied tables, dim lighting, and a haze that hung in the air from people smoking glowing cigarettes in the corners. Vox said not to judge it too quickly because the old barkeep made the best Long Island Iced Teas and a game of pool was free.

Several pool tables were open, so all four of us got in on a game—Vox and Cass versus Rhett and me. Cass missed just about every shot she took, except for one she accidentally knocked in when she bumped into the table. Mom had bought a pool table to help me "bond" with Dad when we were in that awkward dad/daughter-dealing-with-puberty stage, so I'd gotten fairly decent from playing against him.

After I sunk the eight ball and won the game for Rhett and me, Vox made a joke about Cass being Rhett's and my MVP. I laughed, but Cass's face turned stony, and she stormed outside. Confused about her reaction, I started to follow her, but Rhett held onto my forearm.

"Let them handle it."

"But I…" Vox was already halfway to the door, and I realized I couldn't come up with any idea how to help them, other than just by being there, so I sat back down with Rhett and sipped on my drink.

What Vox hadn't mentioned earlier about the Long Island Iced Tea was that the bartender made them stronger than anywhere else. Apparently, the bar was owned by an absentee owner, and after years of working there every weekend, the barkeep flat-out didn't give a rat's ass about giving away extra alcohol.

We played another three games of pool and had two more drinks before Cass and Vox finally came back inside.

I gave her a questioning look, but she refused to make eye contact and said, "Who wants to go to a different bar?"

Rhett agreed, even though the last thing I wanted to do was sit in the cab of a pickup with a couple mid-fight. They were scarily quiet, but at least they weren't yelling anymore.

The next place we went was a little smaller, but less crowded than the first. They needed the extra room for dancing though, because couples twisted around on the floor in swing dance moves I usually only saw on TV.

"I've got to go pee," Cass yelled over the music.

I followed her because, usually, "need to pee" meant "need to get away from this creep that won't leave me alone" or "need to plan for the night because I'm going home with this hunk." Admittedly, the latter was usually Cass, and she usually called him something other than "hunk."

Instead of pausing at the sinks like she normally did, Cass went straight into a stall—by herself—and refused to say anything about why she'd been so mad about Vox's comment or why they'd been outside so long.

"Let it go, Sav!" she said, coming out and slamming her hand into the soap dispenser.

I raised my hands in a gesture of surrender.

"And don't act like you're such a victim."

I dropped my hands by my side where they clenched into fists. The strong iced teas were making me fuzzy, and I was more than upset with Cass and how unhelpful and unsupportive she'd been about Hudson. All I wanted to do was check if she was okay, and she was treating me like crap.

When she didn't say anything else, I turned on my heels and left her at the sink.

"Savannah!" She stopped me in the hallway outside the bathrooms.

"Whoa," a teetering girl giggled to her friend. "Cat fight."

I could have smacked her flat-haired head.

"What?" I snapped.

"You shouldn't run away every time we have a little disagreement."

"I can do whatever I want to, Cass. I don't need you to tell me what to do."

She folded her arms across her chest and rested her weight on one leg so she looked like a shorter, skeptical version of my mother.

"Oh, grow up," I snapped.

"No, you grow up." Her voice rose in an imitation of mine. "Oh, Cass, what should I do? I slept with Hudson, but he doesn't give a shit about me. Should I call him?"

I knew we were making a scene, but between the embarrassment, anger, and pounding in my head, I didn't care. "You're the one who gave me shitty advice!"

Her voice stayed at the same, mocking octave. "But I think I'll just string Rhett along, because I can't stand the thought of being alone any longer."

"Says the girl who sleeps with anyone who asks!"

"At least I don't mope around waiting to be some guy's booty call."

Cass and I had fought before. Her family liked to yell, and Cass was no exception. My family never confronted each other about anything—we just let it simmer until we didn't think about it anymore and moved on. But this fight hurt more than usual because she was saying all the things I worked so hard to convince myself weren't true. And she meant them.

"Don't worry about it," I said, lowering my voice to keep from lashing out. "You won't have to put up with me after we get back."

Squaring my shoulders and taking a deep breath so Cass wouldn't see how much she hurt me, I turned and walked away.

Then she yelled the only thing that could have

stopped me dead in my tracks. "I'm getting married!"

My mouth fell open, and I twisted around so I could see her face. "What?"

Cass looked so small standing there with people walking past, and even smaller when she shrugged and started crying.

I hurried to her side and hugged her, and she hugged me back with one arm, using her other hand to wipe her eyes.

"What's wrong?" Usually if someone cried about their engagement, it was out of happiness.

"I'm pregnant."

My heart caught in my throat. "Oh, Cass."

She held me tighter, sobbing into my shoulder. "I haven't slept with anyone since my last period. It must have happened the first time I slept with Vox."

The wheels turned in my head. "Maybe you're just late?"

"I took a test Friday morning," she cried.

While I wasn't ready for it yet, I hoped my Sunday morning sleep-ins would eventually turn into Sunday morning snuggles with kids. The timing for Cass could have been better—to say the least—but she understood pregnancy was always a risk, and during one of our late night talks, she had told me she'd never even consider an abortion if something like this happened. A baby was a blessing, she said, always. And I agreed.

So, I did the best I knew how to do. "You love him, don't you?"

I felt her nod.

"And he's good to you."

"Better than anyone I've ever been with," she sniffled.

I held her at arm's length. "I'm going to be an aunt?"

A smile spread across her face to match my own, and she nodded. "But you're going to be my maid of honor first."

Although I wanted to, Cass made me promise not to tell Rhett about the baby or her impending marriage until Vox had the chance. Cass shouldn't have expected much of me because she couldn't keep a secret to save her life, but I kept my word.

Rhett and I shared a few dances, and Cass and Vox sat down at a table together, appearing to be deep in conversation. Between spins and steps, I imagined them as parents. My earlier assumption about things changing between Cass and me had been true, and realizing just how quickly our relationship would change made me unhappier than I'd ever been.

CHAPTER twenty-two

THE WEEK AFTER THE RODEO CAME AND WENT uneventfully, especially compared to the news Cass had shared. Hudson had yet to text me, and I kept my silence with him. Rhett came over on Wednesday to help me pack for our trip to the lake. We'd be leaving on Friday after work, and Cass and I agreed that no boys were allowed at this Thursday's hangout.

I sat on my bed, leaning against the headboard while Rhett dug through my dresser and closet. He drew a red lacy thong out of my underwear drawer and held it up between his thumb and forefinger.

"This is definitely going to the lake," he said, suggestively waggling his eyebrows.

I laughed and tried to take it from his hand. The fabric stretched before he yanked it behind his back and fell onto the bed, covering it with his body.

"Come and get it." He lifted his chin in a challenging gesture.

I got on top of him and started kissing his neck before unbuttoning his shirt, pulling up his undershirt, and feathering my lips over his chest and stomach.

"You do not play fair," he moaned.

I smiled against the waist of his pants. "I'm winning, aren't I?"

He reached down and undid his belt. "Maybe."

It only took four hours to pack the bag for the weekend.

CHAPTER twenty-three

THE FOUR OF US RODE TOGETHER IN RHETT'S pickup, and the only person who didn't seem to be on edge was Rhett. I felt nervous to see his family and Cheyenne, not as a friend or classmate, but as Rhett's girlfriend—for the second time.

Rhett sang along to the radio and twisted the ends of my hair around his fingers, and we all talked about what we wanted to do over the weekend. I hoped Cass and Vox would tell him about their news soon, because it was killing me not to mention it.

I kept my silence about the pregnancy until we got there, surprisingly thankful to have the distraction of Rhett's family. His parents had already arrived, having taken the day off to get the cabin set up for everyone else. They met us at the doorway.

"Hi, Mama Lane," Vox said, pulling off his cowboy hat. "Howard."

"It's great to see you, honey," Rhett's mom cooed.

"Deena," Vox grinned, his bottom lip sticking out with chew. He inclined his head toward Cass. "This is Cassidy Reddick."

Rhett's mom lit up and took both of Cassidy's hands in her own. "It's so great to see you again. You take such great care of Aunt Delpha."

Cassidy smiled. "It's nice to see you, too."

"Vox's always been like a second son to us," Deena said.

"He's pretty special." Cassidy beamed at him.

Rhett shook his dad's hand, hugged Deena, and with one arm around her he said, "Mom, you remember Savannah Dondi."

"Harleigh's classmate. Of course." She gave me a tight-lipped smile so all I could see was the dark red of her lip liner.

"Good to see you again," I lied and extended my hand, which she shook with too firm a grip.

"It's great to see you, Savannah," his dad said. He took off his cap with one hand and gripped my hand with the other. "Your folks are doing good?"

"Great," I said once I recovered from hearing

him speak so much. "Thanks for asking."

Rhett let go of his mom and put an arm around me. "We're starving," he said. "Is dinner ready?"

"Oh right!" His mom stuck a finger in the air and scuttled into the kitchen. "Howard, can you show them where to put their bags?"

The four of us were supposed to share a room, and when Rhett's dad led us to the bedroom that Rhett and I had stayed in the week before, we saw a queen-sized air mattress had been placed next to the bed.

I quickly volunteered Rhett and I to take the air mattress because I knew Cass hadn't been sleeping well. Rhett agreed, and we set our bags down before returning to the living area. Everyone else planned to arrive the next morning, so when we got back to the living room, Deena led us outside to eat.

"How long have you two been seeing each other?" Deena asked Cass and Vox after they'd finished each other's sentence in a nauseatingly cute way.

"Not very long," Vox said, wiping his face with a napkin. "But I've got something to tell ya'll."

I tried my best to make my face a blank slate.

Cass and Vox shared a look, and she nodded.

"We're getting married in August, and we're going to be parents." Vox's sentence came out in a rush, and he took a deep breath while waiting for our reactions.

Rhett's mouth fell open in what I could only

assume was a mirror image of mine from last weekend.

"Oh my Lord. Congratulations, sweetie!" Deena stood to give Vox a hug and kissed him on the cheek, leaving a red ring of lipstick. "How exciting!"

"You're gonna be a dad?" Rhett's mouth hadn't quite shut yet.

Cass nodded, her cheeks glowing.

Rhett pushed back his chair and crossed to the other side of the table where he spread his arms around both Vox and Cass. "I'm so happy for you two. Let me know if there's anything I can do to help."

"Well, now that you mention it," Vox said, "I'm gonna need a best man."

"You found him," Rhett said.

It seemed like the rest of the evening was soaked in the glow of their announcement. No one mentioned that they'd only been dating seriously for a month or that it was a shotgun wedding; everyone just seemed happy that they were bringing a new life into the world. They had as good of a chance as anyone else to make a marriage work.

I wanted to ask Rhett more about his thoughts on their engagement, but sharing a room with them kind of ruined all chances of frank conversation with Rhett—or doing anything else with him for that matter.

CHAPTER twenty-four

WHEN HARLEIGH AND CHEYENNE SHOWED UP around lunchtime the next day, old feelings of loathing bubbled to the front of my mind. Other than posts on social media, I hadn't seen them except the occasional time I bumped into (avoided) them at the local grocery store or restaurant on visits home. As they came inside and greeted Rhett's parents, I took them in.

I couldn't help judging every minute detail of Cheyenne's appearance now that Rhett and I were on the verge of a serious relationship again. She stood tall and thin, with a narrow face and green eyes. Her mouth stretched into a toothy smile as she hugged Deena. The biggest change I saw, though, her chest had filled out more since high school—or she'd learned which bras to buy—and she'd finally found a brand of jeans that fit her right. Overall, she looked better than I had hoped she would, and I struggled to shove my insecurity into the mental trashcan where it belonged.

Rhett hugged his sister, but only said "hi" to Cheyenne before coming back to sit by me at the table.

Less than half an hour later, his aunt, uncle, and three cousins pulled in the driveway. Even if I hadn't remembered Aunt Lorraine from my first time dating Rhett, I would have known she was his mother's sister right off the bat. She had the same hair and shape, but her eyes were free of blue shadow, and her mouth fell into an easy grin when she saw me.

She remembered me, too, and asked me questions about myself—how cosmetology school went, what I did for a living, and hair advice—and told Rhett to hang on to me this time. Overjoyed by her statement and the way it made Deena's lips pull down at the corners, I said I'd do her hair that evening if she felt up for it. Anything to fix at least one set of feathered bangs in the family.

After everyone had caught up with each other, we went tubing, which basically consisted of tying a string of inner tubes to the motor boat, floating around the lake, and drinking. Rhett's uncle had even rigged up a Styrofoam cooler with pool noodles so we'd have a buoyant bar. Rhett took a tube on my left, and Cass on my right, and we enjoyed the ride.

His uncle steered the boat to the middle of the lake, killed the engine, jumped in, and swam over to his tube.

"So, Savannah," Cheyenne said without the noise of the engine to drown her out, "how's cutting hair?"

The snide tinge to her voice frustrated me. "Great. How's cleaning animal pens?"

Cheyenne had gone to school to be a vet tech, but she worked at a hog farm, and I liked to think she was just a glorified shit scraper.

"Chey just got promoted to manager," Harleigh jumped in.

"Is that a good thing?" Cass asked coolly, and I barely resisted giving her a high five.

Cheyenne's face flashed from confusion to anger to defeat in a matter of seconds. "How's the rodeoing going?" she asked, ignoring Cass's question altogether.

Both guys said some version of "pretty good."

"Rhett's been doing great," I said. "We went to Freeburg last weekend, and he won the whole thing. We had a great time celebrating, didn't we?"

I tried to make the sentence as suggestive as I could. Rhett and I hadn't done more than fool around, but Cheyenne didn't need to know that.

Rhett rubbed my foot where it rested on his

tube. "Yeah, babe, it was great."

He looked like a farmer's-tanned rock star on the lake with his orange trunks and sunglasses, and I didn't want Cheyenne thinking for one second she could come in and mess everything up again.

It went on like that for a while until Cheyenne and Harleigh finally gave up and kept to themselves. So far, Rhett had been sweet and attentive toward me and utterly neglectful of Cheyenne. We'd avoided any major confrontations, and I hoped it would keep going that way because I knew how much Harleigh and Cheyenne liked to stir the pot.

Since we'd graduated high school, I'd heard of bar fights they'd gotten into with other girls—mostly because Cheyenne didn't like a man unless he had a wife, and Harleigh was too much of a crony to know when to back out of a fight that wasn't hers.

Rhett and his sister looked fairly similar; they both sported muscles only built from farm work, they both had brown hair and hazel eyes, were athletic, and sloped their heads a little to the side when deep in thought—a rarity for Harleigh—but that's where the similarities ended.

Where Rhett's muscles and masculine features made him attractive, they made Harleigh butchy. She couldn't pass freshman English after taking it twice, so she dropped out of college and worked as a pen rider for a feedlot south of Woodman. Rhett was brilliant, gifted even, but had skated his way through high school. He ended up with a diesel mechanic degree from the tech college in Austin, but all his dreams revolved around the family ranch west of town. Now he was working for the Shillings until he could buy enough cattle to go into business with his dad full-time. As far as I could tell, Harleigh's best bet was to get married.

One of Rhett's cousins—I still hadn't learned their names—began complaining about being out so long, so after some yelling by Rhett's uncle, some crying by the cousin, and some persuading by Lorraine, the boat veered back to the dock and moored to one of the posts.

The sun had started to lower in the sky to the point where I couldn't look out over the water without getting an eyeful of reflected sunshine, so I figured it must have been close to suppertime anyway. Mostly, I reveled in the coming chance to shower off the lake water and get away from Harleigh and Cheyenne.

Rhett insisted Cassidy shower first, and I agreed, which meant Vox and Cass would be in there for a while.

"Let's go on a walk," Rhett said.

I looked down at my damp bikini and sandals. "Like this?"

He smiled. "Yeah, come on."

Rhett led me outside past his family and down

what appeared to be a cattle trail near the cabin. At first, I had to watch where I stepped, but the path eventually widened and became more even. Tall oak trees surrounded us, making me feel like we were in our own shady world.

Five minutes later, we were sitting on a bench along the trail, my hand in his.

"What do you think?" he asked.

"Not much."

He kissed hair along the part. "No, really. About the trip."

"Your aunt's nice."

"She always asked about you after we broke up."

I looked at him, trying to figure out it was the truth. "Seriously?"

"I think everyone knew I'd lost something good."

My heart twisted at the painful memory, and my stomach churned with butterflies. That's what it felt like to be with Rhett Lane—like sky diving the moment before you knew whether your parachute would open or not.

"What else do you think?" he asked, relieving me of replying to his previous comment.

"Your cousin's timing is great."

"It's not bad," he agreed, laughing.

"And the view's not too bad."

"Yeah, I love it out here." He gazed over the

trail at the small slivers of lake visible through the tree line.

"I was talking about the hottie in the orange shorts, but that too."

He pressed his lips against my cheek and shook his head back and forth until I couldn't help but laugh.

"Thanks, Sav-Sav," he said when I stopped laughing.

I rolled my eyes. "Sav-Sav?"

"We have to come up with cute nicknames. What's mine?"

"Hmmm."

"Rhett Lightning?"

"Please."

"Rhettson Stetson."

"Come on."

"Sexy Rhettsy?"

"Oh my God!" I laughed. "But maybe."

He stood up. "You should think about it on the way back."

"Okay."

CHAPTER twenty-five

"SAV," RHETT HISSED. "SAVANNAH!"

I blinked open my eyes, seeing Rhett silhouetted in the glow from the night sky, fully dressed. "What time is it?"

"Two."

"In the morning?" I put my face back down on the pillow. "Why are you up?"

"Come on." He handed me a pile of fabric, which I soon learned was a pair of sweatpants and his old track sweater.

"Where are we going?" I whispered over Vox's snoring.

"You'll see." The moonlight shining through

the window danced over his eyes, giving them a mischievous gleam.

He allowed me a few minutes to rub the sleep out of my eyes and get dressed before pulling me through the house and out into the night. Crickets and bullfrogs chirped softly as if they knew it was late and they should stay quiet.

When we reached the dock, I saw a canoe waiting for us. Rhett helped me in and then nimbly climbed to the front and sat down facing me.

"This is why you woke me up at two a.m.?" I yawned.

Rhett's teeth reflected the bluish light from the night sky when he smiled. "Partly."

For a while, the stroke of his paddle against the water joined the outdoor symphony. I looked out over the lake and saw small fires flickering near the farthest shore. Trees waved in the breeze, forming a jagged black line against the indigo sky.

The sound of sloshing water stopped, and I saw Rhett had ceased paddling and was digging through a bag. He produced a bottle and a cork screw.

"White wine," he said, twisting out the cork and then taking a swig from the bottle.

"Thanks," I said when he passed it to me.

He nodded and took a drink after I handed it back to him. "Isn't the sky beautiful out here? The stars just look different at the lake."

UNFAIR CATCH

This time I nodded, enjoying the warmth of the wine spreading through my body. "Life looks different out here."

On the boat with Rhett and our shared bottle of wine, I could imagine a life with him—a happy one. I pictured us walking down the aisle after sharing our vows, him in starched blue jeans and me in a flowy dress with a headband of wildflowers. I could see him teaching our children how to care for cattle and fix equipment. I imagined us going to dances, the awkward couple pretending we weren't too old to be at a college bar. I envisioned a million more nights like this, and my heart hurt at how much I wanted that make-believe future to become a reality.

We'd been in this more-than-friends-but-not-quite-lovers dance since that first rodeo, and it was great, wonderful. He reminded me every day of all the things I loved about him… His singing, dancing, compliments, kisses that made me feel like we were the only two people in the world… But I couldn't forget our past. Was I kidding myself to think we could make it work this time? That things were different?

"What are you thinking about?" he asked.

"Us."

His eyes seemed darker, as deep and fluid as the rippling lake. "Really?"

"Why did you do it?" I knew I needed to hear his answer, the real one, before I could ever commit.

He rolled the oar over in his hands for a minute, and I could see on his face he knew what I had referred to.

"Because I could," he said finally, making my eyebrows furrow. "Because I was eighteen and thought there was no way I'd met the love of my life in high school. You wouldn't have sex with me, and you weren't going to have sex with me until we were married. I thought I wanted more experiences, but now I know what I really need is to experience life with you."

My heart throbbed at the admission and swelled knowing he also thought of a future with me.

"The love of your life?" I asked.

He smiled at me and balanced the oar across his knees before leaning forward and holding my face in his hands. "The love of my life."

He let go and reached out for my hands. I wedged the bottle of wine between my feet and when I slipped my hands into his, they felt as warm as the wine.

"Sav, I want to do this for real. No lying. No cheating. No games. Just you and me. Will you be my girlfriend?"

"Yes," the answer fell out of my mouth before I even thought about saying it. I guessed my heart moved faster than my mind.

His lips spread into a no-holds-barred grin, and, careful not to tip the canoe, he bent forward and kissed me.

"I love you," he said against my lips.

"I love you, too."

When our kiss got to be too much, Rhett pulled back and picked up the paddle.

"Are we going back now?"

Beaming, he said, "Not even close."

Fifteen minutes of gliding across the water later, Rhett was carrying me from the canoe to the shore so I wouldn't get wet. There weren't any campgrounds nearby—actually, upon inspection, there wasn't much of anything nearby except closely-packed oak trees.

Rhett led me down a narrow trail much like the one from earlier, but we quickly left it. Yellow fireflies sparkled around us, lighting our way, until Rhett told me to close my eyes.

"Seriously?"

"Just do it."

As I lifted my hand to obstruct my view, I heard grass swish under his feet.

"Keep them closed!" he called as if he could feel me spreading my fingers.

"Fine," I groused.

"Okay, open," he said.

I dropped my hand down by my side and couldn't believe what I saw.

Rhett stood by a large quilt spread over the grass with an old-style lantern, two wine glasses, and rose petals scattered about. I had to be dreaming.

His face took on that nervous look from the first time he brought me to his house. "What do you think?"

"It's perfect," I breathed.

And it was. The air smelled of grass and water, the wine kept me warm, and the breeze added an otherworldly feel to our nook. We made love for the first time that night, slow, soft, sweet, and perfect, just like he'd promised it would be.

CHAPTER twenty-six

IT WAS WELL PAST FIVE O'CLOCK IN THE morning when we finally slipped back into our beds to put on the pretense we hadn't been out all night. Rhett said that it didn't matter if anyone knew where we were, but his mom already didn't like me, and I didn't want her to think of me as just another floozy Rhett brought home for the weekend and would never see again. I still didn't know what our future held, but our nighttime escapade proved to me that I wanted to put all my efforts into finding out.

The shift between us seemed to be imperceptible to everyone except Rhett, me, and Cass.

"What happened last night?" she asked at

breakfast, her mouth half-full of scrambled eggs.

I giggled. "You're so gross."

"I'm pregnant. It's all going downhill from here."

I reached across my chair and touched her stomach, imaging the bump that would surely show in a few short weeks. "It's beautiful."

"What happened?" she pressed.

"What do you mean?"

She raised an eyebrow.

I leaned a little closer to her so Cheyenne and Harleigh couldn't hear us from across the table. "He asked me to be his girlfriend."

"What?!" she said so loudly that everyone looked at us.

"How could Jaimie possibly want a bowl cut?" she said even louder.

If she had any cover-up success, she immediately ruined it with a conspicuous wink.

"You said yes, right?" she whispered.

I nodded. "And we slept together."

Her mouth opened in a silent squeal. "Sav! Why didn't you lead with that?"

I'd told Cass about our—or rather, Rhett's—no sex clause, and she had been just as shocked as me.

My shoulders lifted in a shrug. "I'm still processing."

She leaned forward, her elbows on her knees,

buttered toast clenched between her greasy fists. "How was it?"

A small ember sparked in the pit of my stomach. "The best."

"Better than…"

She stopped like she didn't dare say his name.

I nodded.

Toast still in hand, she squeezed me in an awkward side hug across our chairs. "I'm so happy for you."

"Me too," I said, looking down at my plate. The happy flutter in my heart had Rhett's name all over it. The guilt had Hudson's.

CHAPTER twenty-seven

THERE'S NOTHING QUITE LIKE THE TIMING OF a bull rider. Every second is measured, planned, and carried out with a lot of courage, luck, and, most likely, a beer. That's what dating Rhett felt like for the next few weeks.

His rodeo schedule kept us busy every weekend and sometimes during the week. We'd quickly fallen into a routine—we'd drive to the rodeo, Cass and I would hang out in the stands until they were done competing, they would come back, we'd all go out to eat, hit the dance, and get a little bit more than tipsy but not quite drunk. Depending on which direction we came from, Rhett and I would stay at his or my house, then we'd go home, make love, and fall asleep together.

UNFAIR CATCH

It felt like a sweet dream on repeat.

Unfortunately, there was something else that kept repeating itself: I couldn't go to a rodeo without hearing some girl talk about Rhett. Usually Cass and I would overhear some rodeo bunny in the bathroom talking about a friend who had slept with him, how she'd slept with him, or how she wanted to sleep with him. I trusted Rhett to be faithful this time, but it irked me to no end.

At the Rowley Rodeo, Cass and I were making our third trip to the restrooms when we heard other girls talking about some of the bull riders. It might have made me nostalgic for all the times that Cass and I had done the same thing, if one of them hadn't shared her plan to make a move on Rhett at the dance.

I gave Cassidy a look and sat down. We'd never actually heard someone with a make-him-mine itinerary.

She rolled her eyes.

"Did you see his ass?" the girl asked.

"Please—" I started to mention his failed ride that evening, but Cass snapped her hand out and covered my mouth… with her dirty hand.

I pulled it away, but stopped talking.

"Do my boobs look good?" The girl asked her friends after getting confirmation that they had, in fact, seen and admired his hind quarters. They all chimed in about her cleavage, and I looked down at my

T-shirt, which left a lot to the imagination. A lot of imagination.

"Have you guys talked since…?" one of her friends asked.

"After tonight, we will."

They left the bathroom, a cloud of cheap perfume behind them. Fuming, I finished using the bathroom and walked to the sinks. I knew that tone in her voice, that confidence that said she'd slept with him once, and she knew she could do it again.

"Are you okay?" Cass asked.

"Why wouldn't I be?" I scrubbed my hands under the stream until the water burned, then flicked them over the floor to shake the excess water.

"Wait," she said and bent over to pull something out of her boot. She grinned when she handed me her silver flask. "A little medicine for you?"

"Cass, you can't drink…"

"Oh please," she swatted her hand through the air dismissively. "This is for Vox if he does bad."

I opened the cap and took a long swig. "You're going to make a great mom."

By the time we got into the pickup with Rhett and Vox to go to the dance, the liquor had hit me hard. At Cassidy's advice, I didn't say anything to Rhett about the girl in the bathroom, but I wanted to. We guessed she was his ex-girlfriend from the year before—a girl named Blaire who'd shared in Rhett's longest relationship since he dated me the first time. I'd heard back then that it had been an ugly breakup, but apparently that didn't stop her from wanting to get back together with him.

When we parked outside the dance hall, I opened the door, and Rhett reached over me to shut it. He smelled good, like cologne and dirt. I told him so, and he laughed.

"Thank you. Now wait for me to come get your door."

"Fine." I folded my arms over my chest and lamented my lack of endowment.

"See you inside," Cass said and patted my shoulder.

Cassidy and Vox were halfway up the steps to the building before Rhett moved from his seat.

"Let's get out of here," he said, squaring his shoulders to me.

I scrunched my brows. "What?"

He had an adventurous look on his face. "Let's go drive around. Do something."

"Dancing is doing something."

"I mean something different. We do this every weekend."

"I like going to the dances." And making your ex jealous. And making Hudson jealous. Even if I didn't want to be with him, I wanted him to know what he was missing out on.

"We can have our own private dancefloor," Rhett winked and leaned over to kiss me on the cheek.

"We can do that any night," I said, trying to make my voice sound provocative.

"Any night?"

I nodded.

"Monday?"

"Sure. But only if we go to this dance tonight."

He slipped his hat over his face and leaned back in the seat.

"Fine," he said through the fabric.

When Rhett came to my side I still hadn't undone my seatbelt, and he leaned over me again to undo it.

"I can do it myself," I muttered.

"So can I."

He slipped the seatbelt over my shoulder, leaning overt my knees.

I threw my arms over his shoulders. "Hey there, cowboy."

"Howdy," he said and tipped his hat back so I could see a faint tan line across his forehead.

I turned so my knees were on either side of his hips. "How's it goin'?"

"Better now," he put his arms around my waist, "that I'm with the prettiest girl here."

I ran my hand over the back of his neck. "You mean it?"

He dipped to put his lips on mine, soft and sweet, and I wrapped my legs around him. When we broke apart, he grinned at me. "What do you think?"

"I think it's good we're going to this dance," I said and let him help me out of the pickup.

We walked inside with his arm around my waist, and the first person I looked for was Rhett's ex-girlfriend as I remembered her from her profile picture. Then I looked for Hudson, but I didn't see either of them.

Rhett led me to a corner where he pulled out two folding chairs for us to sit. I dropped into my seat, still scanning the room, but noticed he was a little slow bending to sit in his chair.

"Are you okay?"

He readjusted his hat so it cast his eyes in shadow. "I'm made of steel."

"Of course you are." I rolled my eyes.

He lifted my legs and draped them over his lap. "What else would I be made of?"

I looked up at the ceiling. "Well…"

"Be nice now," he warned.

"There goes what I was gonna say."

He rubbed his hands up my calves and a shiver went up my spine.

"I know what you're made of," he said.

"And what's that?"

He ran his thumb over a hole in my jeans.

"Something sweet, for one."

I narrowed my eyes.

"And something tough." His hand slid back over my calves.

"And something sexy." Vack toward my thighs.

I blushed.

"And cute."

Blush gone.

"Something I want," he pushed his hat back and leaned a little closer.

"Hey, man! Tough ride today," Hudson swaggered over with a couple of his friends. One of them I recognized from another town over, but the other was a stranger.

Rhett left one hand on my legs but used the other one to greet Hudson. "Good job out there."

Hudson shrugged.

I looked at him, stared, trying to get him to at least acknowledge me with his eyes.

He didn't.

"I think I got the easier bull," Hudson said.

Rhett shrugged this time. "Luck of the draw."

"Are you going to Tighler next weekend?"

"Planning on it. You?"

"Not unless it rains. We've got to finish harvesting."

They talked crops for a little while and then shook hands again. Hudson sauntered off with his cronies, my eyes sending daggers at his back. We'd been on radio silence since our fight, and I knew the only reason he came to talk with Rhett was because I sat with him.

"What about you?" Rhett asked.

Hudson lagged behind his friends and bent over a girl sitting at a table.

"Savannah."

She stood, putting her hand in his, smiling up at him.

"What?" I asked, turning my gaze back to Rhett.

"Are you going to Tighler next weekend?"

I shifted in my chair. "I don't know. I'd have to ask Cass."

He ran his hand back and forth over my thigh until my jeans felt warm.

"Do you always do what she wants?" he asked.

My phone felt hard in my pocket as Hudson spun the girl and then tucked her back into his side.

I shrugged, ignoring the irritable tone in his voice. "She might want to do something for the wedding."

"What do you want?"

"I want to dance."

I dropped my legs off his lap, stood up, and stuck my hand out.

He grabbed it in his rough one and pulled me

back onto his lap.

"This man of steel's a little rusty," he said against my hair.

"You were dancing just fine last weekend."

"Sav!" Cassidy ran up out of nowhere and pulled on my hand. "Rhett, I've got to borrow my girl for a sec."

Rhett let go of me, but I could tell from his curt nod he was annoyed.

"What?"

"I saw that group of girls from earlier. That one looks exactly like the picture you showed me. She is pissed."

"And?"

I looked over at Hudson. He now swayed so close to this girl on the corner of the dance floor, I doubted air could exist between them.

"She's going to confront him."

"That would just embarrass her." I would sink into a floor before confronting Hudson and whatever girl he was talking up now. Even though we'd hooked up a lot more recently than this girl and Rhett…at least, I hoped so.

"She thought they were dating."

My mouth fell into a hard line as Cass confirmed my fears. "Why would she think that?"

Cassidy shook her head. "Rhett's been telling Vox how in love he is with you. There has to be some wires crossed somewhere."

I glanced back over at Rhett, where he sat with his back to the room and his cowboy hat low. "Yeah, there are."

I gave Cass a look before walking back over to Rhett and put my hand out again. "Let's dance."

"My back really does hurt from earlier."

"What happened to 'man of steel'?" I made my voice light, but my stare challenging.

His smile only dropped a little at the corners, but it fell from his eyes. "Fine."

When we got to the area for dancing, he pulled his hat even lower and gripped me close to him for a two-step.

"This isn't so bad, is it?" I asked, forcing a coy smile.

I had no idea what I was doing, but between Cass's warning and the sinking feeling in my stomach, I knew the shit was about to hit the fan. I just didn't know how.

He shook his head. "It's the best."

An involuntary swoop unrelated to the nerves stole through my stomach.

He bent his head over me and gave me a swift peck.

I wanted to dance more, to stay in as crowded of a place as possible so Blaire wouldn't be able to confront us, but he insisted that his back needed rest.

As we moved through the crowd to our table, I caught sight of two girls sitting with Cass and Vox. Rhett must have seen them too, because he said in my ear that he changed his mind and wanted to dance.

"Is that her?"

"What?"

I folded my arms across my chest, as much to seem tough as to keep myself from falling apart. "Don't play dumb with me, Rhett Lane."

Rhett sighed and looked from me to the table and back. "It's over, Savannah."

"Is it?"

I started walking toward Cass, Vox, and the girl who could crush this sand castle future I'd built in my mind for Rhett and me. Everyone's faces fell when I reached them, Rhett on my heels.

"Hey," I said.

"Hey," Cass said. Her eyes widened when she looked at me with a yeah-this-is-actually-happening face. "This is—"

"Blaire," the girl said, her voice as dangerous and unassuming as quicksand.

Even with my blood boiling, I couldn't help but notice Blaire was prettier than I remembered her. She'd obviously lost at least fifteen pounds and had put highlights in her hair.

"Rhett's girlfriend," she added, stealing my breath.

"This is not true," Rhett jumped in. "We haven't talked in weeks."

"And now I know why," Blaire's expression grew harder than the tile floor.

"Rhett, we've been dating for two months," I said.

He lowered his voice and turned his back to the table so he just addressed me. "We've only been exclusive for six weeks."

"Oh my God." Logic and anger warred within me. Hudson and I had slept together five weeks before. I had no idea what Rhett had done with Blaire, but I'd spent all this time feeling guilty when he'd done the same thing. I thought he'd changed. Believed he was better than that—better than me.

"Rhett," Blaire snapped, her hard voice taking on a sharper edge. "What is going on?"

Rhett looked at me, his eyes pleading.

"Nothing," I said over the hard spot in my throat and left it all behind me—Rhett's earnest eyes, Cass's pained expression, Blaire's life-ruining presence, and the building as quickly as my Tony Lamas would carry me.

The breeze hit my face like a soft pillow when I stepped outside. I didn't know where I was going, but I knew I had to get out of there and away from everything happening. Who was I to think that Rhett would be different for me now? That he could actually have a one-woman relationship after spending years hooking up with every pretty face in a skirt?

Like a slap in the face, Hudson's face crossed my mind's eye. Who was I to expect exclusivity when all I could think of in there was making Hudson jealous like some dumb schoolgirl?

I'd made it halfway down the block, but no nearer to ditching my unpleasant reality, when I heard Rhett call my name.

His voice shattered my heart. Of course, he followed me.

Instead of talking to him or waiting for him or having some sort of drawn-out conversation about what he'd done—or what I'd done—I sped up.

"Savannah!" he shouted.

I quickened my step.

"Come on!"

When I didn't respond, I heard his footsteps speed until the soles of his boots plodded at a jogging pace on the sidewalk.

I knew he was faster than me, that he'd catch me within seconds if he wanted to. I didn't know what made me do it, but I started running anyway.

"Sav, stop!" he yelled.

I couldn't.

Long legs and years of track meant he caught up with me with ease and shuffled to a stop in front of me just like Hudson had when we'd had our fight.

UNFAIR CATCH

I tried to sidestep him, but he gripped my shoulders and held me in place. "Damn it, Savannah. Talk to me."

The only thing I wanted to outrun now was our past, and the truth of what we'd both apparently done. "What's the point? We both know where this is going."

He dipped his chin so we were at eye level. "Where is that?"

I looked away and blinked back mist. "This was never going to work."

"Why the hell not?"

I pointed to the building we'd left. "Because of her. And Cheyenne. And all of the other girls you've been with."

"And you've never slept with other guys?"

I folded my arms across my chest and looked away, tears of rejection morphing into tears of frustration.

"I've seen you and Hudson together." My heart stopped. "He wouldn't even look at you tonight. There had to have been something there."

I ripped my shoulders from his grip and started walking back, determined to have Cass take me home so I could hole up in my house and never leave, never open the door for men who came knocking.

He reached for my arm and held it.

"Stop!" I shouted.

He let go like he'd been holding a snake.

"Look," he said, the hand that had gripped my arm rubbing up and down his own. "I didn't know if we were going to be a thing. I never dreamed you would give me a chance after everything I did. Blaire and I… I stopped talking to her that night we were in the pickup."

I remembered him asking me to give him a chance in his special spot, his eyes so full of hope.

"I promise," he added when I didn't say anything. "This is something. What we have—it's the realest thing I've ever had."

Tears slipped over my cheeks, blazing a trail down my face. I knew I had to tell him about Hudson. Now was the chance, to clear the air between us and start fresh.

"Say something," he begged.

I shook my head, and my tears wobbled on the way down. The words I needed to say caught in my throat before they even reached my tongue.

Slowly, he reached a hand out and wiped at the wetness on my cheek with his thumb. "You've got to believe me," he said.

My lips trembled with all the words I couldn't say. So, I nodded. And he drove me home.

But we didn't have sex.

He went home, and I fell asleep crying at the loss of my reason for coming home and at all the things I couldn't tell him, even though I wanted to.

Chapter twenty-eight

IN THE MORNING, I WOKE TO A TEXT MESSAGE from Rhett saying he loved me and wishing me a good day. Since it was Sunday, I rolled over and went back to sleep.

Around noon, my phone's ringtone roused me from that groggy stage between napping and waking up.

"Hello?" I mumbled.

"Savannah?" I heard the engine of what I guessed to be a tractor in the background.

"Chuck?"

"Yeah, we're kind of in a tight spot. Do you think you could come drive grain cart for us?"

"Today?"

"As soon as you can."

Though I was still tired, and the thought of spending a day in that close of proximity to Hudson made me queasy from both nerves and repulsion, anything would have been better than sitting around the house thinking about Rhett and wondering what had happened between him and Blaire.

I threw on my old pair of work boots, a t-shirt, and some ripped-up jeans I only wore when painting or helping Mom garden. Not caring what Hudson thought of me after last night's events, I tied my hair up in a knot and didn't bother putting on any makeup even though I still looked like a mess from crying the night before.

Chuck drove his combine to the corner of the field when I pulled up, and he took me over to the grain cart, explaining that his nephew had decided to go home and play in a summer sports league instead of finishing harvest. So, they were left without a grain cart driver, which meant they had to spend extra time dumping wheat directly into the semi. Spending longer harvesting just increased the risk of a hailstorm or some other act of nature damaging their wheat crop, so time was of the essence.

Chuck reminded me of the tractor controls and stayed with me so I could get warmed up to driving next to the combine again, then left me in the cab with my tote bag of magazines.

As I looked out over the half-cut field, I wondered if Chuck had any idea about Hudson. Did he know that we'd had… relations lately? Or about our fight? Did he have any idea how his son treated women now?

Then my thoughts turned to Hudson. What did he think about me helping them? Had he suggested me, or had he argued with Chuck when he'd said he planned to phone me for help? He definitely hadn't texted me or made an effort to call and at least make peace before I showed up.

The auger on the combine swayed out, and I steered the tractor alongside the combine. I felt just as nervous as the first day I learned to drive the grain cart, Hudson in the cab beside me and Chuck running the combine. Hudson knew what to do with the combine, so I just focused on driving in a straight line like he'd taught me.

Soon, the auger twisted back, and I bounced over the stubble field to dump the grain in the semi trailer.

Around two, after several trips between the combine and the semi, Rhett called me and asked how I was doing.

"I'm helping the McAllisters harvest."

His end of the phone went silent for a beat. "Hudson and his dad?"

"Yeah. Driving grain cart. I should probably get going."

"Okay. Well, can we meet up tonight?"

"We'll probably have to stay here late, and then I need to get some sleep for work tomorrow."

"Oh, how abou—"

Chuck's auger drifted out, so I cut him off. "I've got to go. Bye."

He hadn't finished saying goodbye before I hung up the phone. I knew I shouldn't be mad at Rhett—that everything before we were exclusive didn't count, and I hoped he would give me the same consideration. Still, I wondered if I would have ever known about his more recent relationship with Blaire if we hadn't gone to the dance. Or if I could ever tell him about Hudson.

The day progressed with me transferring grain between the two combines and the semi. Every so often, Chuck would power down the combine and drive the semi into the grain elevators in town, leaving Hudson and me alone in the field. Of course nothing happened. Hudson wouldn't even make eye contact with me through our cabs, much less talk to me.

Mrs. McAllister brought us supper around seven o'clock, and her cooking was even better than I remembered it. When I complimented her, she told me Chuck had asked her to make a special meal for me.

Hudson didn't say a word to me when he

picked up his food, and he kept cutting while I ate with Chuck and his wife, Linda. Chuck said he thought Hudson felt antsy because he wasn't able to go to the rodeo. I nodded, because I couldn't bring myself to tell him that might not have been the entire reason.

Chuck asked me if I would be able to drive grain cart until they were done harvesting, which would likely take another week. Although I couldn't cancel any appointments, I told him I would come by after I got off and wouldn't take on any clients later than I had already scheduled.

Around midnight, Chuck's voice crackled over the CB radio saying they were going to dump their last loads in the semi, so I drove the grain cart over to my car and headed home.

CHAPTER twenty-nine

THE NEXT FEW DAYS PASSED MUCH THE SAME. I used work as an excuse not to talk to Rhett while I tried to sort everything out in my mind.

Even though driving grain cart had kept me occupied at first, I soon fell into the pattern of harvest, and found I could only read so many magazine articles before my thoughts returned to Rhett and Hudson.

This harvest contrasted my memories of working with the McAllisters in high school because this time I didn't spend any time with, or talk to, Hudson. We used to fill the CBs with meaningless chatter, which I think Chuck only allowed because he started to get bored with harvest himself. Back then, when he got tired of our radio babble, Hudson and I would call each other and talk on our cell phones. I missed that.

Thursday night, my grain cart broke down, and Chuck told Hudson to help me fix it. That was code for me standing around to hand Hudson whatever tools he needed while he climbed all over the tractor letting out the occasional swearword.

He wouldn't look me in the eye, even when he wasn't actively working on the machinery, which was hard for me to handle. The only words he said to me, he spoke into the engine.

"It's a hose. Got one in the truck."

When the machine finally ran again without problems, I knew for certain things between us would never be good again. He tossed the tools back into his pickup, bounced back over the field, and started cutting again without so much as a goodbye.

I missed Rhett so much. I just wanted him to come and pull me into one of those Western movie-worthy kisses and tell me he loved me. Time and proximity to Hudson had worn off the sting of Rhett's relationship with Blaire. In the scheme of things, he hadn't cheated, he hadn't carried on with her, and he'd given our exclusive relationship his whole effort. It had to be enough because that's all I'd done myself.

My stupid fling with Hudson had driven a wedge between me and both of the people I cared about most. I had to miss girls' night, but only told

Cass it was because I was helping a family harvest. I knew how she would react if she found out who I was helping, and I figured I'd save me the lecture and her the stress.

Since she was sticking around Roderdale with Vox for his family's wheat harvest, Rhett and I had made plans to take the rodeo home (renamed by me) to the Tighler Rodeo. But when I called him to talk and told him I needed to stay in McClellan and harvest, he thought I was lying.

"Is this how you're going to end it?" he asked.

"End it?" Even with how upset I'd been, the idea of ending it seemed unbearable.

"You haven't been talking to me, you're finding extra work with Hudson, you're not coming to the rodeo, you're—"

"Rhett! I don't want to break up with you."

"Really?"

"Yes," I tried to make my voice soft. "Chuck told me they really need help, and I already know how to run grain cart."

"Can I at least see you before I go?" he asked.

Every bit of hard work the last week expressed itself in my tired eyes and the heaviness of my arms on the wheel. "I'm just going to pass out when I get home."

"Well, can I be your shotgun rider for a little bit then?"

"Hold on," I said into the phone and then picked up my CB radio.

"Can I have a friend come ride with me for a bit?" I asked, feeling less like 22 and more like 12.

"That gal from the diner?" Chuck's voice crackled through the speakers.

"No, Rhett."

"Who?"

Hudson broke his radio silence at last. "Rhett Lane. Rides bulls. Works on the Shilling Ranch. Savannah's boyfriend."

"Sure can," Chuck said without missing a beat. "I'll have Linda make an extra plate."

I got back on the phone with Rhett and gave him directions to the field. When he showed up, he had to wait in his pickup while I caught the grain from Hudson's combine. I dumped it in the semi, then crawled over the field toward Rhett as fast as the grain cart could go.

I apprehensively exited the grain cart as he climbed out of his pickup.

"Hey," he said.

"Hey." And then I was in his arms again, and his lips were on mine, and the last week melted away in the heat between us.

"Come on," I said, "We better get going."

Driving grain cart is some sort of checklist item to see if a kid grew up on a farm or not. I didn't, and since Rhett's family mostly raised cattle, I hoped to show off the tiny bit of agricultural knowledge I had over him. But then he started talking about harvesting jargon I had no clue about. Apparently, he'd spent a summer on a custom cutting crew and knew how to drive semis and combines, forcing me to lament the loss of the upper hand.

"So, how's 'work' been going?" he asked, holding up the heavy tote bag of magazines I'd shoved off his seat.

I glared at him. "That is work. Do you know how many people ask for hair styles that celebrities have?"

He took off his ball cap and rubbed his short hair. "What celebrity style do I have?"

"Rhett Lane," I said with a smile. "Professional bull rider slash play thing."

Time with Rhett flew by. We had a lot to catch up on from the week we'd been apart. He said Harleigh'd been seeing someone new, but she wouldn't tell him yet who it was. Probably just because any guy dumb enough to date Harleigh wouldn't be a looker, but I didn't tell Rhett that. Apparently he hadn't seen or talked to Vox all week with harvest and had been using his extra free time to help some farmers in the area work on their tractors to make some extra money.

We had to pause our conversation when Linda came to the field with supper. Much to my surprise,

Hudson sat and ate with us. After the third question he asked Rhett about rodeos and the ranch, it dawned on me he might not really care about Rhett and I dating. The thought relieved me. Sort of.

Around midnight, Chuck sent me home, and it wasn't soon enough. Rhett had spent the entire evening with me, and with the occasional rub of his hand on my thigh and stolen kisses, I was burning for him.

We barely made it in my front door before we started taking each other's clothes off. We made love on the same couch Hudson and I had on the night that started this whole big mess. As I laid against him afterward, the heat of his skin warming me from the air conditioning, the steady rhythm of his breaths drowning out every other thought, I thought maybe we could erase the past altogether and build our future on its ashes.

***

I didn't have to work at the salon on Saturday, but Chuck asked me to be at the field at eight. It had been so hot that the wheat dried out quickly, and he thought if we kept working at the pace we were going, we could be finished by Wednesday. That was good, because I kept getting panicky texts from Cass saying how much help she needed getting her wedding plans together.

Rhett got up before I did and left to buy me breakfast while I was still asleep—coffee and a packaged muffin from the gas station. I hadn't had time to go grocery shopping, nor did I usually make myself anything other than a Pop Tart or cereal for breakfast, and that was if I woke up on time.

He sat with me in the kitchen while I ate and drank and talked softly about things we could do together or trips we could go on when we had a weekend free from rodeos or wedding planning. I thought it was his way of showing me that he saw me as a part of his future. That he saw us taking trips together even after our fight.

Soon, the time came for me to leave. I kissed him goodbye and wished him luck at the rodeo, trying to forget the girls sure to be there, wanting to take my place.

CHAPTER thirty

OF COURSE MY GOOD FORTUNE COULDN'T last forever. Only an hour into the morning, my tractor broke down. I hopped out of the cab to see what went wrong and landed in a shallow hole, my left ankle twisting hard enough to make me scream.

I lay splayed on the ground, clumps of rock and straw digging into my back as tears evaporated down my cheeks, whimpers escaping my mouth.

After the initial shock had worn off, I sucked in a breath through clenched teeth and sat up, screaming with the pain of the motion. Waving at the two men and potentially having Hudson come help didn't rank high on the list of things I wanted, but I knew I couldn't climb back up the ladder by myself, and I'd left my phone in the cab.

Hudson maneuvered his combine to the semis, probably assuming I hadn't seen his auger swing out. With no hopes of getting his attention from the ground, I stood up, moving my left leg as little as possible, and waved my arms, hoping he would see me and come over.

The combine made a slow looping circle toward me, and I clung to the ladder, not wanting Hudson to think I couldn't handle a sprained ankle.

After what felt like much longer than the five minutes it probably took him, Hudson throttled the combine down, parked, jumped too easily down the ladder, and ran to my side.

Concern colored his face as he put a hand on my shoulder and asked, "What's wrong?"

"I hurt my ankle," my voice cracked with fresh tears.

"Let me see it."

I moved my leg out a fraction of an inch, choking back a cry of pain.

"I need to take your boot off," he said, his face firm.

I pulled my leg away from him, this time unable to stifle a yelp.

"Savannah," he said, looking me in the eyes for the first time since our fight. "We have to get that boot off before it swells too much, or they'll have to cut it off, and it'll hurt more."

I bit my lip and nodded.

"Sit down," he ordered and stuck out his arm so I could hold onto it.

He lowered me to the ground then sat next to my injured ankle. "Look away."

I twisted my head over my shoulder and saw Chuck's combine drawing near when my vision blurred and white spots erupted over the straw field.

Hudson made a soft "shh" sound, and pulled my sock over my foot, the fabric feeling like needles sliding over my skin.

"Oh, Sav," he said.

I looked down and saw a purple bruise flowering over my already swollen ankle.

"Do you think it's broken?" I asked, tasting salt.

He shook his head and then shrugged. "A break heals faster than a sprain."

"What happened?" Chuck yelled as he ran to us from his parked machine.

"Savannah hurt her ankle," Hudson called back.

Chuck slowed from a run to a jog, and when he reached us, he let out a low whistle and one of his curse words.

When I first started working for them, Chuck told me that he only had a limited supply of cuss words, and he made a point not to use them up too soon. "In case he needed one," he'd said with a wink.

"Take her to the hospital," he said to Hudson. "Get it checked out."

"I can't get her in the cab," Hudson said.

Chuck looked across the field. We were probably a quarter of a mile from the pickups—much too far to walk. "Well, get over there and bring the truck over."

Hudson stood up and started loping away from us, and Chuck crouched down to sit beside me.

"What happened?"

I looked toward the sky, embarrassed. "I hopped down and landed in a hole…"

"Happens to the best of us," he said.

"Because the tractor broke down," I finished.

He used another one of his cuss words and then stood up.

"Hydraulic hose again?"

"I think so."

He walked a few feet to the engine of the tractor and checked it out. Both combines and the tractor were still running, and I was grateful for their humming. Silence might have given me too much focus.

Chuck had begun banging around under the hood when Hudson pulled up. Hudson called out to him, and they served as human crutches to help me into the pickup. I had Hudson drive by my car and grab my purse, and then we flew down the country roads into town.

I told Hudson he didn't have to drive so quickly, but he said there wasn't any point of me being in pain longer than I had to. Other than that, we didn't talk. It felt like a big gray circus animal had squeezed between us in the cab, and there was no way either of us would ask it to move.

At the hospital, Hudson got out and half-carried me into the emergency room. They informed us there would be a wait, so Hudson guided me to one of the cracked leather chairs and helped me sit down. He was the last person I wanted with me at the hospital, but I didn't have a lot of options. Rhett was two hours away at a rodeo, and I knew if I called him, he'd drop everything to come back home, even though it was probably just a sprain. Cass didn't know I was working with the McAllisters, so calling her was out of the question. Mom and Dad were in Amarillo visiting Monti, and Viv would have had to drive from Roderdale.

Still, I wished for a better option. The silence between Hudson and me proved nearly as excruciating as my ankle, and I refused to be the first one to fold.

When a nurse finally came to take me back, Hudson helped me into the wheelchair and told me he would be there when I got back.

An hour and a half later, I hobbled on crutches into the waiting room where Hudson dozed with his cap over his face.

I tapped his shoulder. "Hudson."

He pulled his hat up, rested his elbows on his knees, and rubbed his face. "Hey."

"Ready to go?"

"Yeah," he stood up. "Do you need any help?"

"I got it," I said.

He matched my pace as we made our way outside, and then—for the second time since I'd been home—he opened the door for me and helped me into the truck.

"So, what's the verdict?" he asked when he got in after putting the crutches in the bed.

"Just a bad sprain," I sighed. "I have to use crutches for a few days and wear the boot for four weeks."

"I guess it's a good thing you have two."

I looked at him, a questioning look on my face, and he reached back and scratched the nape of his neck.

"Legs, I mean," he added with an impish smile.

I groaned. "Laaaame! That's the best you can do?"

He laughed hard. Really hard, and I don't know whether it was exhaustion or the relief of not having a broken ankle or what, but I laughed too. All the tension between us turned into deep belly laughs and gasping for air and tears dripping out the corners of our eyes. Soon, our breaths slowed down and the laughs grew further and further apart, and the tension that had left with the laughter got replaced by a distance between us that couldn't be spanned or ignored.

"Savannah," Hudson began and then looked away. "We've made a mess of things, haven't we?"

"I'll say."

We looked at each other, and I saw him, really saw him for the first time since I'd been home. And for the first time, I recognized him as the person he was, and not the boy that I'd loved. And then he said the words I'd been waiting to hear ever since junior year of high school when Rhett broke up with me and Hudson refused to take me back, but it was all wrong.

"I like you," he said.

My back stiffened. "No you don't."

Our "relationship" had almost ruined things with Rhett—and it still could if I ever plucked up the courage to tell him or he found out.

He looked over at me, eyes still shining from leftover laughter. "You're right. I love you. I have since we were in high school… since I first saw you this summer at one of my rodeos…since that night after the diner. I just didn't realize it 'til I saw you with him."

"And the fight?" I asked.

He looked at his lap. "I was scared. Jealous."

"Showing up at my house drunk and leaving?"

"Confused."

"Having sex with me and then not talking to me?"

He frowned. "I just… wanted to know if I could, and then I didn't think I even deserved a chance after that. Or if I wanted one after everything."

"What makes you think I'd want you to have one?"

"I feel like there's something here," he said, looking more like a hopeful teenager than the man who'd broken my heart. "I know there is."

"Hudson…" I tried to find a way to tell him that he'd ruined any chance of there being anything real between us the night we had our fight, but he spoke before I could.

"I know I screwed everything up, but when he breaks your heart—because you know he will—you give me a call."

My mouth gaped open and closed for a moment before I found my bearings. Righteous anger rose within me and threatened to boil over until I told Hudson every way Rhett had him beat. He didn't know the first thing about Rhett. "Take me back to my car."

"You know it's true."

"You have no idea what's true. All you know is this sick, little game you've been playing with me because you're still jealous that I picked him," I snapped. "Take me back to my car. Now."

"Are you fucking kidding me?" he growled,

sneering down at the floorboard.

I matched his anger with a harsh tone. "Excuse me?"

"You chase me around all summer, use him to make me jealous. You're the one who's playing games because you don't know what the hell you want."

I folded my arms over my chest and looked out the window. "You'll never be half the man he is."

He snorted then spit on the floorboard. "Well, at least I'm not a cheat."

"He's different now."

"I meant you."

I couldn't come up with anything to say, so I didn't. Hudson didn't need an explanation of when Rhett and I had established our relationship, nor did he deserve one. I could feel him fuming across the cab, but if he had anything more to say to me, he kept it to himself.

We made it back to the field around suppertime, and Hudson jumped back into the combine without a word to any of us, leaving me to sit and eat alone with his parents. They quizzed me about my boot, and I reassured them I could use my right foot to drive as long as I didn't have to get in and out of the cab. Mrs. McAllister clucked and tsked over my injury like a mother hen, making sure I felt good enough to continue.

"The real problem," Chuck said with a bashful

grin, "is that we can't keep a grain cart driver to save our lives."

"Well, if the next one is half as good as Savannah, we'll count ourselves blessed," Linda said.

CHAPTER thirty-one

HUDSON'S CONFESSION DID A BETTER JOB of distracting me from my pain than the superhuman strength ibuprofen the doctor prescribed. All I could think of was the look on Hudson's face when he told me he loved me and the way he'd called me a cheat.

Rhett had worked hard to prove that he'd changed, but I'd been so focused on following through with my reason for coming home that I never even considered Hudson might have changed, too.

But he had.

He'd gone from the sweet, nervous kid sneaking me kisses behind hay bales to a man who used me to prove a point. That was a loss in more ways than one.

I'd just gotten home and arranged pillows on the bed to elevate my leg when Rhett called to tell me about the rodeo. He had a fit when he found out first, that I'd gotten hurt, and second, that I'd gone to the emergency room with Hudson without calling him.

"I would have been with you," Rhett said over the chatter from the people in the stands and the boom of the announcer's voice.

"What were you going to do? Drive two hours to take me to the ER?"

"Well," he bristled, "I didn't even have the option to."

"Look," I said, adjusting a pillow under my head, "if I'd've needed to, I could have called Cass or my parents. But Hudson was there so I wasn't even by myself. I was fine. I am fine."

"So, you're saying you didn't need me."

"I can handle myself," I snapped, leftover stress from earlier transferring into my tone.

Even with the noise in the background, I heard him sigh. "I know. I'll just be glad when harvest is over."

"Me too," I said, but I didn't tell him why.

CHAPTER thirty-two

THE REST OF HARVEST CAME AND WENT without any more excitement, much to everyone's relief. On the last day, we had supper at the McAllisters' house to celebrate. Hudson left early, for whatever reason, but I decided to stay.

Hudson's parents had felt like my own since ever since I worked for them in high school. Even though the issues between Hudson and me added a layer of discomfort, I still enjoyed spending time with them.

I thought of Rhett's mom and how she could artfully craft an insult to sound like a compliment—a talent she'd passed on to her daughter. Every second with Rhett's mom felt like holding glass in my mouth; I had to keep it shut to keep from hurting myself or someone else. Mrs. McAllister would have made a great mother-in-law once upon another life.

"You're probably worn out," Mrs. McAllister said, picking up my empty plate.

With supper under my belt and harvest behind us, I couldn't deny how exhausted I felt.

So, Chuck cut me a check for way more than I had expected to be paid—"for medical expenses"—and told me if I ever needed a warm supper or a part-time job, I should give him a call.

Instead of driving home, I took the dirt roads out to Rhett's house to surprise him and knocked on his door.

He answered shirtless, with a big grin on his face, and carried me straight back to his bedroom.

Chapter thirty-three

"WE'RE ONLY INVITING TWENTY PEOPLE TO THE ceremony." Cass had a binder and so many random scraps of paper spread over my table I couldn't see it underneath the clutter.

"Yes." She'd already told me about the overall plans, and frankly, I thought she was getting herself worked up because she thought that's what brides had to do. Everything seemed to be set already.

"And we're going to put an announcement in the paper for the reception. It needs to say BYOB—if I can't drink, I'm not paying for other people to."

I laughed. "Good."

"And we're going to look at dresses in Austin

this weekend before the rodeo."

"Your mom's coming, right?"

She nodded. "And my dad and my little sister."

"Cool."

"We'll look at bridesmaid dresses then, too."

"I figured."

"And shoes… those weren't exactly the boots I had in mind." She inclined her head toward my elevated foot.

I rolled my eyes. "It comes off in three weeks. And the bridal shower's the fifth?"

"Yep. Is there anything I need to do for that?" she asked, scribbling something on one of her papers.

I gave her a look. "I'm pretty sure that falls under maid of honor duties."

"Okay. You have my mom's number to call about invitations?"

I pointed at the pile of pink and beige invitations on my coffee table. "I already have, and I'm going to finish addressing them and send them out tomorrow morning."

She blew her bangs out of her eyes. "Great."

"When do you want a haircut?" I asked. "We should probably do it soon to give it some time to grow in."

"What about if we do it before the bachelorette party? That is the fifth, too, right?"

Shit.

Between all the planning, rodeoing, getting injured, and the drama with Hudson, I'd totally forgotten about the bachelorette party. I guessed part of me had written off anything other than a sleepover the night of the wedding since Cass wouldn't be able to drink, and it seemed a little silly for a pregnant lady and her friends to go around to the bars before a shotgun wedding. Maybe it was just the right amount of inappropriate, given the situation.

"That's what I was thinking," I hedged.

"Where are we going, by the way?" she asked.

I made my best attempt at a coy smile and said, "It's a surprise."

Her lips puckered out in a pout, but I could see from the shine in her eyes the idea of a surprise excited her.

"Should I plan for anyone other than the bridesmaids?" I didn't even know who all would be going. I assumed her little sister would tag along, and her other bridesmaids—a cousin and a friend from school—but other than that, I had no clue.

"Nope, just me and my girls. And my sister's got a fake, so she should be good to go to the bars... if we're doing that." She winked.

So, we were going to bars. At least I knew that much.

"Are you excited for the honeymoon?" I asked. Hearing about the trip to Florida that Vox's mom had planned for them had grown old after the fifth time Cass told me about it, but it was better than thinking about my failure as a maid of honor or Hudson's predictions and accusations.

She talked on and on about the same things: what she should pack, how much seafood she would be able to eat—not much, according to the one baby book she'd read—if sunburn would hurt the baby, what they would do while they laid out on the beach…

Cass acted excited about the engagement and the baby, but part of me ached for her. It had never been in her "plan" to be a mother, or even get married young. We'd talked about trips we wanted to take when student loans were paid off, and none of them included a baby or a husband tagging along. She'd adapted so well into the role of expecting mother and wife that I wondered if she'd just been fighting it because that's what she thought she was supposed to do.

Together, we ran over every single detail imaginable about the wedding, and my list of to-dos kept growing. I had to pick up the flowers to bring them to Vox's parents' place—where they would have the ceremony—help make decorations for the reception, and finish everything bridal shower related. Plus, I had to make sure Rhett held up his end of the chores because Cass didn't trust Vox to remind him.

When I convinced Cass I had everything under control, she gathered all her materials, kissed me on the cheek, and left to get ready for work.

Immediately after she left, I called Rhett in a panic.

"I forgot the bachelorette party."

"What?" the sound of what I guessed was his TV snapped off.

"I forgot the bachelorette party."

"Just hire a stripper. What else can you do with a pregnant lady?"

"I don't know, but apparently, I'm supposed to plan something." My voice rose steadily with my guilt. What kind of friend forgets about the bachelorette party? "What are you doing for Vox's?"

"We're going out after the rodeo the twelfth."

I sighed. "What should I do?"

"Why don't you guys go on a trip?"

"Dallas."

"What?"

"Dallas. There's great bars there. It's pretty close to where her other bridesmaids live. I can get us a hotel or something."

"Well, that sounds like a great trip for us, but what about Cassidy?"

I heard the smile behind his words. "Shut up."

He chuckled.

The corners of my mouth lifted of their own accord. "I'll talk to you later. When I'm done being a failure friend."

"Love you."

"You too."

I sat down with my laptop resting on of the pile of invitations and found a way to put my harvest money to good use. Within three hours, I had two connecting rooms booked, figured out how to hire a stripper, and ordered T-shirts for each of us, because if all of the other bachelorette parties I'd seen in the bars were any indication, that was a must.

It was well past midnight by the time I finished addressing the bridal shower invitations, and I fell asleep hoping Cass would never find out about her almost-not bachelorette party.

CHAPTER thirty-four

WHEN I GOT OFF WORK THE NEXT DAY AND walked out to my car, I saw Rhett leaning against his pickup, chatting with someone through the open window. As I walked closer, I could see Cass and Vox sitting in the backseat.

At the sound of my footsteps, he looked over his shoulder and grinned.

"Hey, beautiful," he said and came to meet me.

"Hey. What's going on? We didn't have any plans, did we?"

He planted a kiss on my lips that made me want to do more than we could in a parking lot midday, and I heard Cass whistle from the pickup.

"We're going fishing," Rhett said, one arm still around my hips.

"Seriously?" Growing up, "fishing" meant sitting with a pole in my hand while Monti taunted me with worms and my parents drank beer—well, wine coolers for Mom.

"Yeah. Let's go." Rhett took my purse from me and carried it in what he called the "manly way," which was basically holding the bag away from his body with the straps doubled over.

"Don't we have to wedding plan?" I asked Cass, thinking even hearing about their honeymoon plans for the fiftieth time would be preferable to spending my evening getting eaten up by mosquitos.

"We're taking a night off," Vox said. "No saying the 'w' word for the rest of the night, unless you mean worms."

It turned out that fishing as an adult wasn't too much different from my childhood memories—except Rhett brought camping chairs so we didn't have to sit on the ground, and we were the ones drinking the beer. Unfortunately, Rhett wouldn't bait my hook for me because he didn't want his girl to be some "hoity-toity girly-girl too good to touch worms."

I told him he shouldn't have picked a hairdresser then, and he threatened to "dress up" my hair with the bucket of worms if I didn't bait the damn hook.

After much grumbling, I stuck the poor worm

and cast my line out, hoping nothing would bite.

Music spilled out of the rolled-down windows of Rhett's truck and blended with the wind in the grass, chirping bullfrogs, and clicking locusts. It would have been a perfect evening if we nixed the fishing poles and added a bonfire.

"This is nice," Cass said, lifting her feet out of her flip-flops and resting them on Vox's lap.

"The best," Rhett said, idly spinning his reel.

A different song than the one on the radio played from my phone, and my mom's name lit up on the screen.

"Hey, Mom."

"Hey. How are you?"

"Good. How are you?" My mom could make a conversation about chocolate vs. maple doughnuts stretch for over an hour, so I usually only called her when I had plenty of time to talk, or just went to see her instead, now that I was home.

"Great. Your brother got a new job."

"Doing what?" For the last five years, he'd worked as the manager at a parts store in Amarillo, and as far as I knew, he liked it.

"He's going to be managing a new branch here!"

"What?"

"Well, in Woodman. But anyway, we're having a welcome back party on Friday, and I wanted to know if you could make it?"

"In Woodman?" I asked, still wrapping my mind around the news.

"No, at home. Are you free?"

Rhett jerked his pole back and started spinning the reel as fast as he could.

"Yeah, of course, I'll come. Mom, I'm fishing, so I better let you go."

"Well, I've hardly seen you since you've been home. Who are you fishing with?"

Rhett had moved to standing, his pole bending with the weight of a fish.

"Cassidy and her fiancé and Rhett. Bu—"

"Is everything ready for Cassidy's wedding? Because if she needs any help, just let me know what I can do." I imagined my mom twirling a piece of her hair like she always did when she talked on the phone. "Lord knows it'll be a while before Monti pops the question and I can help Steph with their wedding."

"It's all good. Cass has everything planned out. Mom, Rhett just caught a fish, so I should probably get off the phone."

"Is Rhett treating you well? I honestly can't believe after last time—"

"Mom, it's great. We're doing fine."

"Well, that's good." She paused, and I imagined her running a file over a rough spot on a fingernail. "Bring him too then."

The fish flew out of the water with a splash,

and Vox got up to check it out.

"I don't—"

She'd already hung up. The one piece of phone etiquette she hadn't mastered was the goodbye.

"What'd your mom have to say?" Cass asked while Rhett unhooked the fish.

"A lot, apparently," Vox joked.

I rolled my eyes at him. "She says if you need any help with the we—"

"Hey," Vox said, pointing a finger at me.

"—very big event in your very near future, to let her know."

Cass winked at me. "I don't know what you're talking about, but I'll keep that in mind."

"Hold this," Rhett said, outstretching the perch.

I knew how to grip a fish from the trips with my parents, I just didn't want to. "Do I have to?"

"Are you pretty?" he asked.

"No."

"Yes, you are. And you're taking this guy." He pushed it toward me.

I groaned and took it from him, pressing my thumb against its bottom lip and holding it away from my body.

Rhett ran to the back of his pickup and took out an empty mineral tub, then jogged with it to the pond, filled it with water, and carried the sloshing bucket back to the tailgate.

"Well, don't just stand there. Put it in," he said.

I made my path over the grass and then gingerly lowered it into the tub where it splashed water on my face. Of course that was knee-slapping hilarious to everyone but me.

"So, what did your mom call about?" Rhett asked when we had settled back into our chairs.

"Oh, my brother's moving back."

"Wasn't he in Amarillo?"

"Yeah, but he's going to be the manager at a new branch in Woodman, I guess, so Mom's throwing a welcome home party, and she told me to bring you." I took a sip from my drink. "But you don't have to go if you don't want to."

"Of course I do. When is it?"

"Friday. At my parents' house."

He smiled, and the setting sun bounced off his eyes, making the amber colors in his hazel eyes stand out. "It's a date."

"I think I got one!" Cass shouted and jumped up, knocking her chair over.

Cass grew up in the city, and her parents weren't lake people. Fishing was rare for her, and actually catching something, even rarer.

"Hold your horses!" Vox said, bounding to stand next to her.

He stopped a little to the side and behind her, one arm around her back to steady her, and started giving directions about what to do. "Okay, jerk your line… now reel it in… keep going… hang tight on the pole… give 'im another jerk…keep reeling… There he is!"

A giant frog flew out of the water, and, in Cass's excitement, it rainbowed over their heads and slapped Vox on the back.

"Sorry!" she cried, dropping the pole and the frog on the ground where it hopped around, dragging the pole with it.

Rhett doubled over, laughing, as Vox pinned the frog down. After he'd unhooked the frog and picked the pole back up, Cass made him take a picture of her with the frog—she even held the squirming thing in her hands. If she was bothered that her catch wasn't a fish, she didn't show it.

"Vox got fish-slapped," Rhett said between chuckles.

Vox flipped him off, and even though Vox tried to keep a straight face, the rest of us were laughing too hard for him not to crack a smile.

After Vox caught a decent-sized fish, Rhett went into the stand of trees along the south side of the pond and came back with an armful of dried branches. While he gathered kindling, I felt lonely. Cass and Vox were in a world of their own, with no room for me.

Ever since I'd met Cass in college, we'd been best friends. One day standing in the cafeteria line,

Cass made some joke about the freshman fifteen, and we'd stuck together ever since. At the end of our first semester, we moved out of the dorms and become roommates. It was only after moving to McClellan that we decided to get our own places, mostly because rent cost nearly half of what we paid in Austin.

Now, she sat so close to Vox, her head rested on his shoulder, and his hand protectively held her stomach. They murmured to each other, occasionally breaking for a smile or a kiss. Cass had only called me over the last few weeks to talk about wedding plans. After how she acted about Hudson, I still hadn't told her about our conversation the day I hurt my ankle. I had hopes things would go back to normal after the wedding, but maybe this would be the new normal.

The sound of clattering wood rattled me from my thoughts, and I saw Rhett walking to the pickup and back holding an old magazine.

"Can I use this?" he asked, showing me the cover.

"Yeah, I've read it," I said. "What's the fire for?"

"You thought we were just fishing tonight?" he smirked.

My eyes landed on the black mineral tub where I knew the fish were swimming. "We're eating them?"

He laughed. "Yeah."

"Do we have time?" Dusk had settled over the pond, and even I knew it would take a while to gut and cook a fish.

"If you help me. Let's hope you're better at cleaning fish than you are at catching them."

The lighter flickered, and the magazine caught fire, throwing light against his face. The shadows made him seem older, more chiseled.

"We'll see," I said, knowing there wasn't a snowball's chance in hell Rhett would let me get out of cleaning fish.

Once the fire popped and crackled with enough strength to satisfy Rhett it wouldn't sputter out, he led me over to the bed of the pickup and tipped the mineral tub until most of the water pooled on the ground.

With quick hands skilled from years of working on the ranch, he grabbed a fish and slapped it down on the tailgate.

"What you do first is take the knife and cut its head off," Rhett said, demonstrating.

I tried to act as if the action didn't thoroughly revolt me. I knew where my food came from, I just didn't want to witness it up close.

"And then the tail," he said.

"Then you make a cut from here—" he used the knife to point where the fish's head used to be "—to here." He pointed toward the stump at the end.

For how easy Rhett made it look, I made it look just as hard. He taught me patiently, and fifteen minutes later, I had cleaned (mutilated) my first, and hopefully last, fish.

"You never made me do this in high school," I said, rinsing my hands in the stream of a water bottle Rhett held for me.

He shrugged. "My wife's gotta know how to clean a fish."

My heart leapt at the word. "Wife?"

"A guy can dream."

He gave me a smile that made me weak in the knees before wrapping the fillets in foil and slathering them with copious amounts of butter and seasoning he'd brought in a cooler. Then he put a few foil-wrapped cobs of corn and the fish into the fire.

"Might as well reel 'em in," Rhett told Cass and Vox, who were now sitting in the same chair, Cass on Vox's lap.

Cass got up and reeled her line in—less enthusiastically this time—and handed it to Vox so he could put them in the back of the pickup.

We moved our chairs to sit around the fire, and even though it had gotten over a hundred degrees that day, Texas cooled off enough at night for me to welcome the heat from the pile of burning sticks. Conversation dwindled, and I didn't know if it was because everyone was tired or because we just didn't have anything to talk about anymore except for the wedding and the pregnancy.

We ate the fish off of paper plates with plastic

UNFAIR CATCH

silverware, and I had to admit it tasted pretty good, but not as good as it would have been if I hadn't been the one to "prepare" it.

Chapter thirty-five

"WE'RE GONNA BE LATE," RHETT SAID FROM my kitchen table, where he'd been waiting for the last half hour.

"I know." I flew into the bathroom in search of my necklace.

"Well, I want to make a good second impression," he called.

My search stalled for a moment. It's not that I didn't want Rhett to see my family, but I didn't really want them to see him again. After we'd broken up, I cried for a month. Something about him coming to this party as my guest made our past and our future feel more real. Like I couldn't turn back, even if I wanted to.

I found the necklace at the bottom of a drawer and untangled it so I could put it on.

"I'm ready," I said, walking into the living room.

"You look great," he replied, getting up and crossing the room in the dramatic but not tacky way only Rhett could before sweeping me into a dipped kiss.

"I thought you didn't want to be late," I gasped when our lips broke apart.

He grinned. "For that, it's worth it."

He lifted me back to my feet and pressed his lips on mine for an extra second I wanted to turn into hours.

I grabbed my clutch off the coffee table, and we left for my brother's party.

Monti wasn't what I'd call handsome, but he more than made up for it with his personality. Monti had been popular in high school, and when he went to college he made a lot of friends who went out a lot, started balding, and gained thirty pounds, mostly in his gut.

Even though he picked on me constantly as kids, he was the kind of brother who had no problem beating up some jerk for talking about me behind my back. When he saw us walk in, he gave me one of his tight, soft hugs, and greeted me with my old nickname.

"You look great, Smelly! What happened?"

"Ha, ha," I said, then turned to Rhett. "You know Rhett."

Monti's lips dipped for a fraction of a second, but he quickly recovered and reached out to shake his hand. "Of course."

Rhett returned the handshake. "Great to see you."

Monti didn't reply, and it felt one hundred percent awkward. For the first time, I cheered internally when his girlfriend approached us, but only for a second.

"This is Steph," Monti said, putting his arm around her.

"I think we met a couple years ago." The entire time she had her hand in Rhett's, she held my gaze. "Well, isn't he a looker, Vannah."

She giggled and patted me on the arm like we were old friends. Just because she'd dated my brother for five years didn't mean I had to like her.

"We better go see Mom," I said and led the way toward the kitchen.

"Good to see you both," Rhett called as he followed me out of the room.

"We don't need your head getting any bigger," I muttered.

He paired his smug smile with a shrug.

I found Mom in the kitchen, loading empty pans in the dishwasher, a red checkered apron tied around her hips. At the sight of me, her eyes lit up, and then they slid to Rhett.

"Good to see you, honey," she wrapped her arms around me and squeezed me tight with an "ooh ooh" sound.

"How are you, Rhett?" she asked, letting me go to fiddle with her apron strings.

"I'm great. Thank you for having me over."

"Well, we couldn't leave Vannah's friend out." She hung her apron over a hook by the pantry. "That is what you are, right?"

Rhett glanced at me behind her back.

"Yeah, he's—" I jumped in before realizing I needed to finish the sentence with "my boyfriend."

"We're dating," Rhett finished.

"Well, alrighty then," she said like we'd told her the weather. "Let's go sit in the dining room. We're about to eat."

Rhett kept his hand on the small of my back as we followed Mom out of the kitchen. At the dining room table, we found my two aunts, my grandma, Monti, Steph, and my dad. Our entrance brought with it an awkward pause until my Aunt Darla, who'd driven all the way from Austin, made it worse by wolf-whistling.

"Is this your man, Vannah?"

I groaned.

"I guess I am," Rhett said, enjoying the

attention a little too much.

"Rhett's Howard Lane's son. He works for the Shilling Ranch," Dad interjected.

"You know, your dad and I dated way back when," Darla said with a girlish sigh. "We spent many a night in that '68 Corvette."

"Darla!" Mom admonished.

She winked at Rhett with a self-contented smile, but didn't press the issue.

"Nice to meet you," Rhett said.

I introduced him to Aunt Viv, who he already knew, and when I came upon my grandma, she batted her spotted hand at me.

"This is the young man I wanted you to meet," she said. "Viv and I see him at church every Sunday."

I gave him a confused look. I knew he prayed his rosary since I saw his worn turquoise beads come out before every rodeo, and he always left early Sunday mornings to go to church, but usually he was back by ten. Why hadn't I connected the dots that Grammy probably knew him?

Rhett beamed one of his brightest smiles at Grammy and nodded. "That's right. It's good to see you outside of mass."

"You too. I'm happy Vannah's dating such a fine young man."

"For the second time," Mom said.

I didn't know whether to crawl under the table

and hide or sit there and watch it all unfold. Monti started coughing over his water, and patted at his chest until he could breathe normally again.

"Wrong tube," he croaked. Then he shot me a wink, and I loved him even more.

Mom had Steph help her carry the dishes to the table, putting out a meal even nicer than Thanksgiving, and then poured champagne out for everyone.

"I would like to make a toast," Dad said, pushing back his chair and standing up.

"Dad," Monti said. "It's just a new job, no big deal."

"You're home, and that's a big deal for me."

Darla made an "aww" sound like she'd just seen a cute puppy.

In high school, Dad had been strict—more so with me than with Monti—but he always made an effort with us. Between him and Mom, they made sure we had regular movie nights and "dates" at the restaurant. After hearing some of Cass's horror stories about her dad, I counted my lucky stars mine cared enough to do that for me.

"I just wanted to say how proud I am of you. Of both of my kids. You're both exceptionally hard workers, great friends, and great children. Monti, congratulations on your job. I'm so glad to have my kids home."

"Cheers!" Steph said, lifting her glass so quickly

a bit of the drink spilled over the edge.

"Cheers," I murmured and took a drink, wishing more than anything that I had moved home on purpose.

Dinner conversation chased rabbit trails for hours—from Monti's career change to the county commissioner elections—Dad told us he had decided to run for office—to Steph's new job search, until Grammy announced she wanted to get back home "before Viv's car turns into a pumpkin."

Viv helped Grammy gather her things, and Grammy made the rounds with her grandma kisses—the wet ones on the cheek that you couldn't avoid even if you wanted to. Rhett got included in the custom, and I had to help him wipe off the red lipstick after she left.

"Talk about a spit shine," Rhett said, eliciting laughter from everyone except my brother, who politely smiled and then took a drink.

"Oh," Darla said, "I almost forgot your gift, Monti."

He waved his hand at her like he was turning down another drink in a restaurant. "You don't need to get me anything. It's great just to have you here."

"Well, you got one. Vannah, will you come help me?"

I didn't know what she could have gotten that would require two people to bring in, but I pushed back my chair and followed her outside to her car.

UNFAIR CATCH

"What is it?" I asked.

She opened her trunk like a man ready to show me a bunch of faux designer handbags, but instead, I saw a cross decoration made solely of painted horse shoes.

"Just a little housewarming gift," she said with a pleased smile. "Of course, it'll have to sit around here until he finds a house."

"Cool." I started reaching into the trunk—I could easily carry it by myself—but Darla put her hand on my forearm.

"Hold on," she said, lowering her voice. "I didn't really need your help to carry that thing."

"I was wondering if all of that product had gone to your head," I joked.

She gave a conspiratorial smile. "The opposite. I'm looking at expanding, and I want to bring someone new onto the team, young, but I haven't found the right person yet. How would you feel about moving back to Austin?"

"As a temp?"

She shook her head again, and her choppy layers fluttered with the movement. "You're the right person for the job."

"Oh… I…" I stumbled over my words trying to come up with an answer on the spot while my brain reeled at the idea.

When I graduated, I'd wanted to work with

Darla, but she hadn't had any positions open. Now that I was home, I knew I wanted to go back, but I had Rhett, and Cass had uprooted her whole life to join me here. Could I leave her and her baby here after she did that for me?

"Rhett could move to Austin with you," she said. "Stylists at my salon make quite a bit more than you do here, and I'm sure a strong, young thing like him could find a job like that." She snapped her manicured fingers.

"Well… I…"

"Is it serious with him?" she asked, her heavily eye-linered eyes alight with interest.

Again, I couldn't answer.

She gave me one of those rare, knowing smiles that made me realize that Darla was a lot smarter than she let on. "Just give me a call when you find out, but I need to know by the end of the month so I can have someone start when we open mid-September."

She lifted one end of the cross and waited for me to take the other. Everyone fawned over it when we walked in, but I couldn't get Darla's questions out of my mind.

We used the next day's rodeo and wedding shopping plans as an excuse to leave the party shortly after Monti brought the gift back to his old bedroom.

"Can we come to the rodeo?" Steph asked me before turning to Monti, as if to double check. "Can we?"

I looked at Rhett. "Well, we can't ride together because I'm shopping with Cass. You'll have to ask Rhett if he'll get stage fright."

He dipped his knees and tilted his head back in a fainting gesture. "Gosh, I just don't know if I can handle the pressure."

I smacked his hard stomach with a laugh.

"No, come," he said, smiling warmly. "I'd love to have you guys there."

"It's a plan," Monti said.

CHAPTER thirty-six

THE NEXT MORNING CAME FAR TOO EARLY, and for how exhausted Cass had been the last several weeks, I couldn't believe she'd committed to brunch with her family before dress shopping. She showed up at my house around eight o'clock, and we left in my car soon after.

"Do you mind if I take a nap?" she asked, bunching up a sweater I always left in my car behind her neck.

"Sure," I said.

I'd been excited to have a couple of hours alone with Cass without the distraction of a rodeo or boyfriends. Darla had dropped a huge bomb on me with the job offer, and I needed Cass's advice more than ever. I had no idea what I was going to choose or how to approach Rhett about it. But what could I say to a tired pregnant woman? No?

She slept for the better part of the trip until we hit Austin traffic, made worse by weekend travelers. Something I definitely didn't miss. As I drove into the city, I tried to take it in, not just the memories the skyline brought up, but as a potential future home.

Someone honked at me for driving too slowly, and Cass mumbled and turned to look at me, her head still resting on my sweater.

"Hey," she said, her voice hazy with sleep.

"Hey, sleepy head." My eyes darted from the rearview mirror to the road ahead.

Her mouth stretched open in a yawn, making her chin look nonexistent. "Are we there yet?"

"No. It's just off Canadian Street, right?"

"Yeah, right by the interstate."

"Okay. We should be there soon."

Out of the corner of my eye, I saw her take out her phone and start tapping on the screen.

"They're there already," she announced.

"Okay."

I took us across two lanes to get to the exit, and my racing heart slowed in tandem with the car. By the time we arrived at the restaurant, I felt too relieved to be done driving to be nervous about spending the day with Cass's family.

I'd only spent one holiday with them, but that was enough. If someone in my family had an issue, we usually made a comment about it and either let it go or buried it. Everyone in Cass's family had to get the last word, and that meant their fights never ended.

Everything in their home had been loud that Easter: the TV, the colors, and especially the people. If Cass and her sister weren't screaming at each other about a "stolen" piece of clothing, her parents were yelling about who forgot the ham or, ironically, whose relatives were more obnoxious. If they weren't screaming because they were mad, they were screaming because they were happy. When Cass's cousin announced his wife's pregnancy, I thought their house would implode from the noise.

Cass said I hadn't even seen the tip of the iceberg. Her parents fought, and sometimes words weren't loud enough, so they threw things. About once a year, her dad became abusive, usually around the anniversary of a car accident that had left his sister brain damaged.

Although her dad acted nice to me, it felt strange for me to spend time with him after hearing Cass's stories.

When we walked inside, I immediately knew the approximate location of their table because I could hear her sister's squeaking giggle. The sound turned into a squeal when Cass came into their line of sight.

Camdyn jumped up and gave Cass a hug, and it made me a little jealous that I didn't have a younger sister of my own.

"There's our mama bear!" her mom cried, setting her menu down.

Cass's mom looked exactly like Cass with only a few added wrinkles. She was one of those women who would look thirty until she turned sixty.

"Hey," Cass said and gave them each side hugs before sitting down.

I waved at the group and then pulled out my own chair and joined them.

"How was the drive?" her dad asked. He had a low, rolling voice that sounded like logs sliding together.

"Good, except for someone," I pointed at Cass, "slept the whole way."

Her mom pouted her lips, a slightly-aged replica of her daughter. "Gotta get some sleep before the baby comes."

Cass shot me a look behind her menu. Her pregnancy had only been public information for a few weeks, and she already bristled at the unsolicited "advice" people felt free to give anyone pregnant.

A waitress came and took our drink orders and then returned later for our food orders. One piece of advice Cass did take seriously was the old eating-for-two idea, so she ordered a big breakfast with a side of pancakes.

"You're going to have trouble fitting a dress," her mother said after the waitress walked away.

Cass blew her bangs up like an irritated horse flicking an ear back. "I'm already getting fat. Might as well do it right."

That ended that.

Listening and eating my pancakes relieved me of trying to talk over the group, a nearly impossible feat. Her family spent most of breakfast gossiping about people from Cass's hometown—who married, who divorced, who else was pregnant—and even spoke about a local drug bust. If they had changed the names, they could have been talking about any other small town in Texas.

After breakfast, we arrived at a boutique-looking bridal store with a window full of vintage and contemporary gowns on yellowed mannequins. Beside me, I felt Cass take in and release a breath when I turned off the car.

"Are you ready for this?" I asked.

Her eyes seemed wider than normal behind her too-long bangs. "I have to be."

We entered the store, which barely allowed for walking room between racks and racks of wedding dresses sealed in plastic garment bags. An older woman with scrunched hair shiny from too much gel met us at the door and asked us what we were looking for.

"A wedding dress?" Camdyn popped off.

"And it's going to need to be flattering," her mom added, sticking up a hand to hide her finger pointing at Cass's waist.

Cass narrowed her eyes and looked at them sideways. "I need a white or blush gown, empire waist. It can have straps or no straps—I don't care—but I don't want a halter. None of that one-shoulder stuff. I don't want it to look plain, but I don't want it to look like I'm going to prom, either. Lace is okay. Tulle is okay. Shiny is not."

I wondered if she'd written this all down on one of her scraps of paper and practiced it.

The lady nodded, her hair staying perfectly still. "What size?"

"Ten," Cass said without batting an eye.

"I'll see what I can find, and you guys look around to see if you like anything."

Cass stuck with her mom—or rather, her mom trailed Cass around the store—and I went on my own to scout out bridesmaid dresses. I knew a general idea of hairstyles she wanted for the bridal party, so I tried to find a neckline that would complement the style and each of the bridesmaids.

Twenty minutes later, Cass called me over, and we were sitting in front of a makeshift podium in a squadron of mismatched armchairs while the woman helped Cass into the first gown.

When she came out of the room, she looked beautiful. Her cheeks were flushed, her eyes bright, and she had a small, nervous smile on her lips.

"What do you think?" the woman asked, adjusting the small train.

"It's beautiful," Cass breathed.

And it was. It was a blush colored, empire-waist dress like Cass had asked for. The tulle bottom fell in an A-line from her waist, and small, spiraling flowers gave the bodice texture. Small jewels decorated the split between the bodice and the skirt, flattering her curves. In this dress, she didn't look pregnant, or rushed, or like anything but a girl getting married to the love of her life.

"You look perfect," her mom croaked, using her thumb to wipe away tears.

Her dad sniffed, his eyes slightly red, and nodded.

"I think it's great," Cam agreed, her eyes watering as well.

"Guys," Cass said. "You're gonna make me cry, too."

"I just can't believe…" her dad sniffed again. "You were just a baby yesterday."

Cass's bottom lip trembled, and she smiled. "I can't believe it, either."

She turned and looked at herself in the mirror, nervously smoothing the front of the dress.

"Is this it?" the woman asked, eyes hopeful.

"Maybe," Cass said. "But I want to try some more."

Of course, she wasn't going to skip all the fun.

For the better part of an hour, Cass tried on dress after dress, but when she ran out of options in her size that fit her specifications, she put on that first dress again. The woman placed a veil in her hair, and I cried along with her family.

"Which dress do you guys think?" Cass asked.

"This one's the best," her dad said.

"Are we saying yes to the dress?" the woman asked.

Cass nodded. "I think so."

CHAPTER thirty-seven

VOX AND RHETT CAME TO AUSTIN EARLY SO we could eat a late lunch together. We drove to Vox's favorite restaurant, a hole-in-the-wall barbecue joint with a lot of reclaimed wood, dim lighting, teenage waitresses, and an old chef who peered through a peekaboo window at everyone who walked in.

Cass's family seemed to like Vox, especially her dad, who, from the moment we sat down at a table, immersed himself in conversation with Vox and Rhett about vehicles.

While we waited for our food, Cass and her mom talked centerpieces, and Cass's little sister asked me about cosmetology school. We were in a good conversation about which programs were the best and how to get scholarships when a waitress delivered heaping plates of food to our table.

Apparently, Vox liked this restaurant for two reasons: it served Paul Bunyan-sized portions, and it didn't even attempt to make anything healthy. The pulled pork oozed grease and barbecue sauce, and all the sides came fried and generously salted. It was the kind of meal that would be off-limits on one of our fitness benders, but Cass dug into her sandwich like she was carrying a garbage disposal instead of a baby.

"When's your brother coming?" Rhett asked when the mechanic talk had finally died out.

I wiped some grease off my hands with my already soggy napkin. "I think they should get here whenever the rodeo starts."

He nodded and ate a fry dipped in the pool of barbecue sauce and fat on his plate, but that was the last thing he ate for the rest of the meal.

We had all planned to go to the rodeo together, but Cass's mom wanted to go look for a dress to wear to Cass's wedding. Cass and Rhett switched vehicles so Cass and Vox could ride together. I was more than happy to let Rhett drive my car in Austin instead of me.

"Is that the dress?" Rhett asked, jerking his head at the big white garment bag in the backseat.

"Yep."

He shook his head. "I never thought Vox would get married."

"Me either," I said, then added, "I mean, Cass. At least, not for a while."

"Do you think it'll work?" he asked, pulling out of the parking lot and onto the road.

I frowned. "I hope so."

"Yeah, me too, for the kid's sake at least."

We were quiet for the rest of the drive, and Rhett's jaw tightened like it always did before rodeos. I didn't see his rosary, since both of his hands were firm on the wheel, but I noticed his lips moving almost imperceptibly. Rhett easily slipped in and out of traffic, and then drove to the rodeo grounds without using a map or GPS. When we got out, he looked over at me and gave one of those smiles that softened all of his features except for his hazel eyes.

"Good luck kiss?" he asked.

I nodded and leaned across the console to touch my lips to his. Every kiss with Rhett seemed special—the way his hands left trails of fire over my skin, the firm pressure of his lips that took away thoughts of anything other than him, the spearmint breeze of his breath over my cheek.

We broke apart and he smiled at me, his lashes dreamily brushing together.

"I love this," he said. "Us."

"Me too."

He gave me one last kiss before getting out of the car and coming to my side. He wore an older pair of jeans, I noticed, broken in and fitted to his frame. My mind had wandered to what he looked like under his jeans when he opened my door.

"You look good, Rhett Lane," I said from my seat.

His smile switched from tight to a ghost of a smirk. "Yeah?"

He bent over and pressed his lips to mine, harder this time.

"Yeah."

His tongue slid over my lips, then he nipped the bottom one and tugged at it.

"Tease," I breathed.

"You just wait for tonight," he said against my mouth, sending a warm shiver through my body.

I groaned as he stepped back, took my hand and pulled/dragged/lifted me out of the car.

"That's my girl." He kissed the side of my forehead.

We walked to the metal building where check-ins were and found Vox and Cass waiting inside. As Cass and I left the men standing in line and made our way outside, I heard a familiar voice.

"Savannah."

I turned around to see Hudson standing outside with a few of his friends.

"Hey," I said, caught off guard. "You remember Cassidy?"

When was the last time Hudson actually talked to me at a rodeo? Two months ago at Roderdale's rodeo dance, if I remembered right.

"Yeah," he nodded, the shade from his cowboy hat dipping lower over his face for a moment. "Congratulations, by the way."

Her eyes sharpened as she smiled. "Thanks."

"How's your ankle doing?"

I looked down at my boot and shrugged. "Healing."

"Good. Dad worries about you."

"Your dad?" I laughed a little to mask the confusing pain blossoming in my chest.

"Yeah."

"Well, I guess you can give him a good report."

"That's good," he said, hooking his thumbs in his pockets.

"We better go meet my parents," Cass interjected. "They're waiting in the stands, and it's going to take us forever to find them."

Hudson tipped his hat at us. His smile looked as sad as I felt.

"See ya," Cass said, already walking away.

Silently, I turned to follow.

"What was that about?" she asked when we got out of earshot.

I peered around, trying to decide which side of the stands would be best to sit in. "What do you mean?"

Keeping secrets from Cass was much easier without eye contact.

"You know what I meant," she said. "What happened?"

"Well, usually we don't walk right by him," I said in a half-hearted attempt to keep from discussing Hudson. "I guess he thought he should say hi."

Usually, I talked about everything with Cass, but ever since our fight in the bar, I didn't want to tell her anything about Hudson. Especially with her impending wedding to Rhett's best friend and the comments she'd made about me.

"What happened?" she asked.

When I didn't reply, her eyes widened. "You guys didn't sleep together again, did you?"

It was like the wedding/baby fog had lifted and I had Cass back.

I shook my head. "He told me that he loved me—"

Before I could finish my sentence, she gave me a judgmental look, jarring me back to reality. Cass wasn't my go-with-the-flow, anything-goes friend from college anymore, just like Hudson wasn't the same sweet guy from high school.

"It's over," I said.

"Is it?" Her eyebrows were gone behind her bangs again.

I nodded. "That fight we had was so bad I didn't think he'd ever talk to me again."

"Until he said he loved you?"

We'd come to a standstill by the north side of the arena. "Kind of."

She dipped her head forward. "What's that supposed to mean?"

"Well," I started. "You know how I helped with that harvest?"

She nodded.

"That was for Hudson's family. And Hudson was the one who took me to the emergency room."

Shock and realization flooded her visage.

"And when we were at the hospital, he basically apologized and asked me for a second chance."

"You didn't sleep with him," she practically begged.

I glared at her. "No. I told you I haven't slept with him since Rhett and I have been an actual couple."

"You didn't even tell me you were working with him! How am I supposed to know?"

"Like I could tell you," I snapped. "You've been so judgemental."

Her voice rose half an octave. "No I haven't. You're just feeling guilty about carrying on with

Hudson."

"Give me a break." I folded my arms across my chest. "And you've been so wrapped up in Vox that the only thing we've talked about for the last month is your wedding or the baby or Vox or how he's doing…"

Between the hurt look on Cass's face and the anger I felt myself, I stopped talking because even though I knew there were a million other things I could have confronted her about, we were on dangerous ground.

"I'm about to have a family," she said, her narrowed eyes shining. "I have a wedding to plan. I can't be worried about you and your obsession with Hudson."

"Obsession?"

Her head jerked up and down. "You know he's not good for you. You have a man, a good man, who wants you, and all you can think about is high school."

"That's not true, and you know it," my voice rose.

Her hands were on her hips, and I bit back a snide comment about her trying to be mother material.

"You moved back to your hometown to work in the hair salon your aunt owns—only because your other aunt wouldn't hire you, I might add. And now all you can do is fawn over your old high school crush and you're not stuck in high school?"

"You wanted to come here!"

"Because you can't do anything on your own!" she shouted. "You couldn't even keep a job! It's like you need someone to tell you every step to take!"

"I got laid off." Unwelcome tears stung my eyes, and I did everything to stop from crying like the baby she thought I was. "And this is exactly why I didn't talk to you about any of this!"

"Good!" she yelled. "It's pathetic. And I'm sick of talking about it. Unlike you, I'm moving forward with my life."

It felt like a slap in the face, and before I could stop myself, I said the only thing I could think of that was worse than what she'd said to me.

"On purpose?"

From the look on her face, I knew I'd won, but I wished more than anything I hadn't.

CHAPTER thirty-eight

I DIDN'T LIKE SITTING BY MYSELF IN THE STANDS, but I wasn't about to call Rhett and tell him the reason I was sitting alone, so I happily met my brother and Steph in the parking lot when he called thirty minutes later.

Before they'd walk to the stands with me, Steph had to show me the curtains she'd bought earlier.

"You guys don't have a house yet," I pointed out, too sullen to just go with it.

"Well, actually," she turned to Monti and smiled, "we do."

"What?"

Monti grinned into his beard. "It was a

surprise… Grammy is giving us her house."

"Doesn't she have renters in there?" I asked.

"It was like a God thing," Steph said. "They're moving out next month. It's pretty rundown, so we're gonna have to stay with your parents while we renovate it." She made a face and did a thumbs down. "But since it's in Roderdale and only a half hour drive to Monti's work, it'll work out! And then we'll have our own house and be closer to you guys."

I did a double take at her hand that had given the thumbs down and grabbed it. "What is this?"

All the air evacuated the sky as I stared at the diamond on her finger.

She left her hand in mine and squealed. "He proposed! After five years!"

I looked from the ring to her excited face to my brother's sheepish smile, and it felt like the whole world was shuddering around me, but she kept talking like it wasn't.

"I told him before we moved here that I didn't want to move away from my family if this wasn't going to go anywhere, and he said it was, and now it is!"

I still couldn't speak.

"He got down on one knee in the living room of Grammy's house—our house—and, it was the sweetest thing." She turned to Monti. "Can I tell her?"

A blush reddened his cheeks under his beard, and he grunted.

"He said," Steph went on, "'Steph, this house has been in my family for nearly eighty years. My great-grandpa built it, and Grammy and Grandpa had a fifty-year marriage here. Will you do me the honor of continuing the tradition and being my wife?'"

The story and her sparkling diamond made my head spin and my throat sting.

"What do you think?" Monti asked.

Looking at his hopeful face broke the spell. Air flooded back into my lungs as the weight of the world pressed on my shoulders.

"It's great." I managed a smile through the growing stream of tears. "Congratulations."

I let go of her hand and stretched out my arms so I could give both of them a hug at the same time, thankful for the few moments it gave me to compose my face.

Walking back to the arena helped settle my mind, except for the fact that Steph kept nauseatingly referring to my brother as "Mr. Dondi." I didn't point out how ridiculous that was, considering, one, they weren't even married yet, and two, his name wouldn't change after the wedding.

Only after we sat down did someone make a mention of Cassidy.

"Where did you guys go to shop for wedding dresses?" Steph asked.

"Oh, 'Discount Dress.' Right off the interstate.

But I think it was more for people whose weddings are coming up sooner."

"We still have a while," Monti said. "I want to get into our house first."

Steph shrugged. "Never too soon to prepare."

"So, where is she?" Monti asked.

I frowned. "We kind of had a fight."

"About what?" Steph asked.

She had this bad habit of thinking we were best friends just because she was da—engaged to—my brother. But it looked like I would be seeing a lot more of her, so I just sighed and said, "Boys."

She rubbed her hands together like a mad scientist. "Well, that's my specialty."

Was there a political way to tell her to back the hell off?

"I'm hungry," Monti announced.

Steph looked at him, momentarily distracted. "Me too."

He shifted sideways so he could take his wallet out of his back pocket, then pulled out a twenty. "Would you go and get us something to eat, babe? I'm pretty sure there should be a concession stand somewhere."

"You guys don't want to go with me?" she asked.

"My ankle's starting to hurt," I said, grateful for my injury for the first time.

"I'll hang out with Smelly," Monti said, tucking

his wallet back into his pocket. "Is that okay?"

For a second, I thought she'd say no, but she shrugged and then nodded in a jerky movement that made her look like an awkward cheerleader. "Yeah. Want anything special?"

"Whatever you pick's fine, baby. You want anything, Vannah?"

I shook my head. "No thanks."

After she gave Monti a wet kiss and made her way out of the bleachers, Monti looked at me.

"So, am I going to have to punch preggers?" he asked.

A laugh escaped me before I knew it. "No."

"Good. What's going on?"

With the exception of the time he caught me crying over Hudson's picture in my apartment, or the time he offered to come home and beat up Rhett for cheating on me, Monti and I rarely talked about relationships. But a lot of what frustrated me about Cass had to do with Hudson, and I didn't know how to forgive her, or myself, for the mess we'd made of our friendship.

"Cass tried to give me relationship advice," I improvised.

"About Rhett?" he asked.

"Sort of."

"I didn't even know you were dating him before last night," he said.

"It's kind of recent."

"Why?"

"We just started dating after I moved home."

Monti laughed a little. "No, why are you dating him?"

The second I opened my mouth to talk, he added, "And I'm only asking because I want to know if you remember what kind of guy he is."

He was talking about the womanizing. The promiscuity. The manipulation and cheating and one-night stands that Rhett was famous for, even in high school. Before Blaire, I had been the only girl Rhett had dated for more than a few weeks. Monti was a grade ahead of Rhett in high school, and he'd been upset when he'd learned Rhett and I were dating the first time. It struck me now that he probably knew Rhett just as well as I did—the old Rhett anyway.

"He's different now."

He scoffed and folded his arms over his chest.

"I'm serious," I said, looking down at my chipped fingernail polish.

"Look," he said. "It's your life. And you're still young. But let me give you some unsolicited advice."

I held my breath, waiting. If Monti took the time to say something, he must have thought it was important… I just didn't know if I could take another rebuke in one day.

"People can change, but that old seed will

UNFAIR CATCH

always be there, and it doesn't take much water to make it grow."

Pairs were team roping in the arena, and I watched a steer desperately trying to escape the ropers until a lasso whipped around its middle. An "unfair catch," Rhett called it.

"Okay," I said.

He patted me on the shoulder. "Okay."

I tried to take in the events around me—the southern accent of the enthusiastic announcer, the old tracks that seemed to be played at every rodeo, the jaunty prancing of high-strung horses, and the swagger unique to men in cowboy boots. Dust scented the air, and I breathed it in because that was easier to focus on than everything else I'd dealt with that day.

Steph came back, bringing both nachos and her boundary-less presence. She at least took my brother's attention off me, and while they ate nachos, I scanned the stands for Cass and saw her on the opposite end of the stadium, sitting with her parents and sister. I wondered if she'd spotted me too.

Having Steph along ended up improving my night because she asked lots of questions about the rodeo, so Monti and I spent most of the evening explaining why the riders did what. Rhett had filled in my background knowledge where it had been limited, and Monti had picked up a lot from where he worked. Steph, a city girl through-and-through learned everything we knew by the time it came Rhett's turn to ride bulls.

"Up next, we have Widowmaker and a young man by the name of Rhett Lane," the announcer's smooth voice boomed. "Sounds like a country singer!"

The gates flew open, and the bull's hind legs sailed into the air.

"This young man comes from Roderdale, Texas, and let me tell you, he's taking this sport by storm!"

For eight slow, breathless seconds, the only thing I could see was Rhett and his bright blue chaps, the bull, its roan skin and long horns, and the distance between Rhett and the ground.

When the timer sounded, Rhett still remained on the bull, and a roar ripped through the crowd.

"That was awesome!" Steph said, clapping her hands together as Rhett soared off the bull, tucked and rolled, and ran to the edge of the arena.

"Not bad," Monti admitted, but he wasn't smiling.

The rest of the bull riding seemed blasé in comparison to Rhett's ride—or rather, it didn't make my heart race and my breath stall in my chest.

We stayed in the stands after most people had cleared out, waiting for Rhett to find us. We were deep in conversation about countertops—Steph preferred marble and Monti thought a butcher block would be better and cheaper—but Steph stopped talking and started clapping when Rhett approached us.

"You were so great!" she cheered.

I smiled at him. "Good job."

He came and kissed me on the cheek, then shook my brother's and Steph's hands.

"We're getting married!" Steph squealed.

Rhett's face took on a bemused expression. "What?" Then, "Oh! You two!" He waved his finger between Steph and Monti.

She nodded and stuck out her hand, which Rhett quickly examined without what I'm sure was the look of pure terror I'd had when I saw it.

"That's awesome," he said. "Wow. Congratulations."

"Thanks," Steph chirped, staring at her hand and admiring the reflection of the stadium lights in the square diamond.

"Thanks," Monti echoed.

Rhett nodded.

"Well, we better get going," Monti said after an awkward pause. "Long drive back home."

"Yeah. Us too," Rhett said, intertwining his fingers with mine.

Monti and Steph easily took the few steps down the bleachers, but I had to hold onto Rhett's hand since my boot made it so much harder to maneuver down stairs than up them.

Until we parted ways at the parking lot, we

were silent, but then Rhett asked, "So what happened with Cassidy?"

The tightness in my chest pulsed in full strength. "We had a fight."

"Vox said she was really torn up about it."

I couldn't even defend myself because I wasn't about to tell Rhett that Cass thought I was stuck in high school because I'd slept with Hudson.

"Me too," I said instead.

"What was it about?" he asked.

The long shadows cast from the stadium lights made Rhett's brow seem harsher.

"She said I wasn't growing up. That I couldn't keep a job."

Rhett walked slowly so I could keep up, but I wished we could get to the car already.

"Vox said you insulted her for being pregnant."

My jaw dropped, and I let go of his hand. Of course she hadn't told him any of the awful things she'd said to me.

"Hey, that's what Vox told me."

"Did you believe him?" I fought to keep my voice low as to not draw attention from the few people still walking around the grounds.

"I think Cassidy knows how to push buttons and get her way."

"That didn't answer my question."

He looked down and over at me for a long

second. "No."

"Good."

My stomach burned with rage and shame. I hadn't meant to imply I was anything less than thrilled about her bringing a baby in the world. I was happy for her, really, I was, but I didn't need her telling me to grow up when her decision to be a grown up wasn't her own.

But after hearing second-hand her take on the argument, I didn't know how we could get past this. We'd spent the better part of two years with only minor fights, but lately, it seemed like fighting was the only thing we could do.

Rhett and I walked in silence until we reached the car, and as I buckled up, Rhett leaned over me and kissed me on the cheek.

"I know you're a good person," he said, making all my anger and guilt liquefy and pour out of my eyes.

He squatted down and sat on the edge of my seat, holding me in the circle of his dusty arms.

"You guys will make up," he said.

I wasn't so sure. With a husband and a baby on the way, Cass didn't have room for an old friend—or her secrets. If she told Vox about Hudson and me, Vox wouldn't have any choice other than to tell Rhett. And even though Hudson and I hadn't slept together since Rhett and I became official, and I'd forgiven Rhett for talking with Blaire, I knew what I had done was different. And I didn't think we could come back from the truth.

As my sobs became weaker, he brushed my hair away from my face. He looked me in the eyes, the dome light of my car making his olive skin seem pale, gray almost. Even so, he emanated a warmth I didn't think I deserved.

With the softest voice, he said, "If she gives up on a friend like you, it's her loss."

Rhett had no idea how much I stood to lose if things got any worse.

"I don't know if that's true," I sniffed.

"That's okay, because I do."

CHAPTER thirty-nine

AT FIRST, I THOUGHT I DREAMT IT, BUT I HEARD another knock on the door and looked at my alarm clock. Six a.m.

Worrying something bad happened, I jumped out of bed and ran to the door—as much as anyone can run in a boot—and looked through the peephole I had installed after the dropped towel incident.

Rhett.

"Open up," he called, adjusting his grip on what looked like two cups of coffee and a plastic bag.

I unlocked the door and let him in.

Leaning over to balance the load, he shuffled in and set it on the coffee table.

I took a cup, and he kissed me on my cheek.

"Good morning, beautiful, how was your night?" he sang.

In the back of my mind, I saw Cass, lip quivering, staring at me in shock and hurt, then turning away. Horrible.

"Short," I said instead.

He laughed. "I know. But I had this idea on the way home."

"Let me guess. 'I'm going to wake up Savannah at a God-awful hour in the morning.'?"

"Close but no cigar. No, I thought, 'I'm gonna take that girl to church.'"

I raised my eyebrows. "Church?"

Rhett usually left every Sunday morning for church and came home before ten. I hadn't been to any church, much less a Catholic one, since Grammy asked me to take her on Easter while Viv was in the hospital recovering from a gallbladder removal.

"That's right."

"Catholic church?"

"You're a Catholic, aren't you?" he asked.

"No, I'm a Baptist. And only on Christmas and Easter."

He laughed. "You're a comic."

"Still."

"I'm sure your grandma would love to see you at church."

I couldn't deny that—or come up with an argument at such an early hour.

"My family goes there, too," he said. "Maybe it will help you and Mom bond."

"So, I'm going with your family, too?"

"We'll sit with Grammy and Viv if that makes you feel better."

"Can't I just go back to bed?"

"How are you supposed to sleep with all that caffeine in your system?" He gestured at my untouched coffee.

"Fine, fine." I took a sip and started walking back to the bathroom to take a shower.

"Thank you," Rhett called behind me.

After getting ready, I returned to the living room and saw Rhett setting the table.

"You cooked?"

He nodded his head toward the pan of scrambled eggs on the stove. "Apparently you don't. I'm glad I brought food with me."

My heart couldn't sink any lower. Would Rhett still be doing thoughtful things like this if Cass revealed my secret? He definitely wouldn't be able to if I moved to Austin.

He set a fork next to a plate. "What's wrong?"

I looked down at my floral sundress, shook my head, and tried not to cry.

"You don't have to go to church if you don't

want to," he said.

"No, I really do want to go." And it was the truth.

On the ride to the church, I finally asked him about his faith.

"So, Catholicism," I said.

He put his coffee in the cup holder. "Yeah?"

"Well, how long have you been going?"

"I stopped going with my family after graduation, but I started back about six months ago."

I crossed my legs and tucked the extra fabric of my dress between the seat and me. "Why'd you decide to go back?"

His eyes stared over the road like his memories spread out before him. "Honestly?"

"Yeah."

"After Blaire and I broke up, I was miserable. I went out to that field I showed you, and I just started talking to God for the first time in years. I told him how mad I was that I'd ruined things with the only two girls who'd ever meant anything to me. That I hated myself. Hated how I made the girls I slept with feel when I didn't call them. How bad I felt after every one-night stand."

I watched his face twist from the pain of his past to awe as he continued. "And this feeling just came over me. Like I was warm all over but still had goosebumps. I don't know how, but I just knew that I had to be different. Better. I went home, not really sure what to do, but Mom called me that night, for whatever reason, and asked if I wanted to go to church with her on Sunday. I've been going ever since."

For a moment, I reveled in his story. I hadn't put a name to it before, but now it all made sense. When he'd told me he was a different man, he didn't just mean he'd woken up one morning and decided not to stay on the same path. He'd been totally and completely changed that night, leaving all the old parts of Rhett behind.

CHAPTER forty

WE ARRIVED AT THE CHURCH TWENTY minutes early because Rhett said he wanted to go to reconciliation. I didn't know what he had to confess, but I assumed part of it had to do with me. In the Baptist church, sex outside of marriage was the first step down the wide path to fire and brimstones, and Rhett wasn't exactly a virgin.

Rhett guided me to an empty pew, and before getting in beside me, he knelt and made the sign of the cross. He got into the pew and pulled down a kneeler, getting down on his knees and closing his eyes for a few minutes before sitting beside me.

"I'm going to go to reconciliation," he

whispered.

"Can't you just sit here and pray and tell God you're sorry?" I didn't really understand the whole "confession" thing, and I had no inclination to sit alone in the pew, waiting for Viv and Grammy to show up.

"Yes, I can." He kissed me on the cheek. "And so can you."

He excused himself from the pew, kneeling and signing himself with the cross again before walking toward a door in the back of the church that had a green light above it. I saw his shoulders lift and lower, and then he walked in.

Without Rhett in sight, my mind thought freely about all I'd discovered that morning. I pondered Rhett's story and confession and apologizing to God for my sins. It had been so long since I'd been to Sunday school or even said a proper prayer, much less asked God's forgiveness for my shortcomings. With Rhett in the confessional, Cass not on speaking terms, and Hudson an unpleasant memory, I couldn't think of a reason not to pray.

I kneeled—because it seemed like the right thing to do—laced my fingers together, bowed my head, and closed my eyes so I couldn't see the crucifix anymore. And then, in a silent prayer, I confessed. I told God about Hudson, about fear, about judgement, and about my fight with Cass. And at the last part, I pressed my eyelids together so tears wouldn't fall. I knew I probably wasn't anywhere close to being on solid footing in faith, but my chest felt a slight bit lighter when I was done.

I settled into the pew and looked around to see if Viv and Grammy had gotten there yet. My eyes locked with Rhett's, who was walking toward me with my grandma and Viv in tow. He pointed at me, and I didn't think I had ever seen my grandma smile wider.

After church, Viv asked us if we wanted to get lunch with her and Grammy. Rhett said he didn't have anything else planned for the day, so we rode together to the nursing home—the only place in town to buy a meal.

At first, we talked about church and then Rhett's rodeoing, but eventually, the conversation turned to business when Grammy asked me about my work. Aunt Viv owned two salons, one in McClellan and one in Roderdale. I worked with her and another older woman at the one in McClellan. Three days a week, Viv drove to Roderdale to cut hair there, mostly for older women who couldn't drive.

I told her things were going well, and that, although I didn't get as much business as I'd like, I thought I had built up a good clientele over the last couple months.

"Have you decided about Darla's offer yet?" Viv asked.

I cringed. Of course Darla had told Viv, and

UNFAIR CATCH

I was glad because it dawned on me how much of an awkward conversation that could have been—almost as awkward as Rhett hearing about it for the first time at lunch with Viv and Grammy.

"Not yet," I said, hoping that would be the end of it.

"Well, let me know when you do so I can know if I need to start looking for someone new." Viv's business didn't depend on me—basically, I gave her a percentage of my earnings as rent for the space—but she still needed to know if she could start offering the space to other stylists.

"Looking for someone new?" Rhett echoed.

Oh no.

"If Vannah goes to Austin, then I'm going to have to replace her," Viv said, all business.

"Of course, I don't want to," she added with a smile, aggressively unaware of what she had just done.

"We wouldn't want to lose our girl, now would we?" Grammy set her napkin on her plate and patted my hand.

"No, we wouldn't," Rhett agreed with a wry smile.

The next ten minutes felt like Rhett and I were in slow motion and everyone around us was flying by in a high-speed blur. I had even less of an idea of what to say to him than when Darla had first approached me with the opportunity, but now we'd also have to discuss why I hadn't told him.

Grammy said she felt tired and needed to take her afternoon nap, so we said our goodbyes, got our Grammy kisses, and left. Without speaking, Rhett led me out to his truck, opened the door, and then walked to his side of the vehicle.

While he started the ignition and turned down the radio, I looked at him, trying to gauge his thoughts. Was he mad? Hurt?

My seatbelt dug into the bare skin around my sternum, so I reached up and slipped my hand between my chest and the strap.

"When were you planning on telling me?" His quiet voice stung.

His chin flexed, and his eyes stared straight ahead like looking at me for even a second would send us careening off the highway.

"I don't know," I said.

"Were you even going to tell me?" His lips stayed pressed together after he said "me."

His calm seemed so scary, like he was a snake coiled to strike and I had to back away slowly.

"I just found out Friday at the party, and I was going to talk to Cass about it on Saturday, but after our fight, I couldn't even think about it."

"What's the deal anyway?"

"About the job?"

He gave me a sidelong stare, then nodded.

"Darla is expanding her salon, and she has a space for me if I want it."

"Do you want it?" he asked, finally looking at me.

Again, I couldn't answer as my love for Austin and my love for Rhett battled each other in my chest. "I don't know."

He cast a scowl at me that made me wither into my seat. "What exactly do you know?"

"I love you."

A staccato smile found his lips. "Why didn't you tell me about it on Friday?"

"Because Darla asked me if it was serious with you… and I didn't know how my decision would affect our relationship."

"Are you leaving me?" he asked, his voice tripping over the word "leaving."

"Of course not." I reached out and touched his leg, rubbing my hand back and forth over the starched denim. "I love you."

He breathed in shakily then blew out a breath before putting his hand on top of mine, squeezing it, and lifting it to hold it against his chest.

"Good," he said, "but we've got to talk about this."

"I know."

He glanced in his rearview mirror. "Is this what your fight with Cass was about?

"I haven't even told her yet."

A low whistle flew from between Rhett's lips. "We've got a pickle here, don't we?"

"You don't know the half of it."

He snorted, and it wasn't as mirthless as his earlier smile. "So, what do we do?"

"I probably just won't go."

"Why not?" he asked, one hand on the wheel, the other now holding mine in the middle seat. "You loved it there."

"I don't know. When I came here, I wanted to go back so bad, and I couldn't, so I kind of gave up on it… But now it's an option, and it would be cool to work there, but I have a home here. I have a job. I have a friend—had a friend," I corrected, "and I have you."

A little warmer smile. "I won't ask you to give up your dream for me."

"And my family's here. My brother just moved back."

He swiveled the wheel and turned us into my driveway. Although he put the truck in park, he didn't turn it off.

"But it's a chance I might not ever get again," I said.

"Or, at least, not for a long time," I added.

"Do you like it here?" Rhett asked, turning his torso so he could lean his back against the door.

I'd never even asked myself that question.

UNFAIR CATCH

Things had gone downhill with Cass ever since we moved, and running into Hudson would be inevitable in a town this size. And then there was Rhett. With everyone getting engaged around me, I had to think about my future—our future.

What would I be doing in Austin, anyway? Living in a shoebox apartment? Going out to the bars? Being lonely because my best friend lived two hours away? Dating city boys who didn't even know what a callous was?

"I do," I answered finally. "Like it here."

His white teeth shined against his tan skin for the briefest flash of a smile. "Sav, I know we've only been dating for a couple months." He paused.

My heart bullfrogged in my chest.

"And I'm not going to propose today, but I think we both know this is going somewhere." He took both of my hands in his. "I don't know how far it can go if we live that far apart."

So this was it. An ultimatum, no matter how gently portrayed, was still an ultimatum. Three months prior, my answer might have been entirely different. So much had changed since I moved back. Including myself.

At that moment, I felt my decision with every bit of who I was. And who I was, was his.

"I want to stay," I said.

A relieved grin landed on his face and stuck

this time. He spanned the gap between us and pulled me into a conversational kiss.

"That's"—kiss—"the best"—kiss—"news"—longer kiss. "I love you."

He ran his hands over my shoulders and knotted his fingers in my hair. Inches apart wasn't close enough, and I pulled his shirt out of his belt so I could reach underneath and touch the warm skin on his chest, shoulders, feel the rawest version of him. The cab of the pickup couldn't contain our passions, and he carried me inside to the one place that could.

CHAPTER forty-one

ON MONDAY, RHETT TOOK CASS'S WEDDING dress to her house.

On Tuesday, he brought me to the nursing home to visit with Great Aunt Delpha.

On Wednesday, the shirts for the bachelorette party came in the mail.

On Thursday, instead of girls' night, Rhett and I had plans to eat in Woodman then go to the store because he wanted to get me a cowboy hat to wear at the next few rodeos.

While we ate supper, I tried to get him to budge on the whole cowboy hat shopping trip. I knew girls who wore cowboy hats around rodeos, and

I thought they looked ridiculous. Everyone knew I worked in the salon and not in the fields, and I already toed the rodeo bunny line by wearing my cowboy boots around.

"Every cowgirl should have a hat," Rhett said.

"I'm not a cowgirl."

He grinned at me and gripped my hand across the table. "You're my cowgirl."

Which was all it took for me to agree to the hat. Apparently, he had some sort of power over me to get me to agree to whatever he wanted—some call it love. I called it annoying.

His phone vibrated on the table, and he picked it up and started texting. Usually, Rhett was a great date—totally kind and attentive. This was a new one for him.

"Is that your other cowgirl?" I teased.

He finished typing a message and set his phone on the table. "I don't know. Vox wouldn't look as cute in those jeans as you do."

"What's he up to?"

Rhett shrugged and took a bite. That meant it had something to do with Cassidy, and I couldn't drop my pride enough to ask.

"What are we doing this weekend?" I asked.

"Aren't you going to Cass's bridal shower?"

"Umm. Are you crazy?"

His phone vibrated again, and he thumbed the

screen. "Didn't you plan the thing?"

"Yeah, but I'm sure her mom and sister can take care of it." Maybe not without a huge, screaming fight, but they would handle it.

"Well, I have a rodeo and Vox's bachelor party this weekend."

"Oh." I had assumed this weekend wouldn't be different from any other, but I'd totally forgotten his plans. "Right."

"What about the bachelorette party?" he asked. "Isn't that this weekend, too?"

I took my time chewing my food and glared at him. "Can you let it drop?"

"Hey." He gripped my hand again. "I know this sucks."

My stomach felt heavy, and I couldn't keep eating. "You know it's just as much her fault as it is mine."

He set his fork down beside his plate and wiped his hands with a napkin. "No, I don't know that. You haven't told me anything about your fight other than it was bad. All I know is what Vox heard from Cass."

"Well, it wasn't pretty." I pushed a piece of salad around my plate.

"You know Delpha said that it's more important to be kind than to be right."

I froze. "I'm not going to say sorry if I don't mean it."

He rested his forearms on the table and leaned forward, looking me straight in the eyes. "I don't know what you could have said to her or she could have said to you that would be worth throwing away your friendship."

Yeah, but I knew, and that was bad enough.

"Rhett. This is really hard for me. Can we just try to enjoy our night?"

The set of his jaw told me he wanted to argue, but he must have thought better of it because he only said, "Okay."

We left the restaurant, and Rhett took me to the only western store in Woodman. It had just about everything a country person could need: tools, clothing, boots, and, in the very back corner, a modest selection of cowboy hats.

Half an hour later, Rhett made me the proud owner of a cream-colored Stetson hat. The brand didn't mean too much to me, but Rhett swore Stetsons would last through a "shit storm" and stay on in a hurricane. In Texas, both were just as likely.

I just didn't know I was in store for a shit storm until an hour later when Rhett took a detour to Cassidy's house.

She lounged on her front porch with Vox, a glass of iced tea in her right hand. The moment we came close enough to see her expression, I wished I hadn't. Her eyes turned into slits and her mouth formed a hard line. We—I wasn't welcome there.

"What are we doing here?" I demanded, anxiety roiling in my chest.

Rhett appeared sympathetic, but firm. "She's your best friend."

"Was."

He dipped his head down along with the corners of his lips.

"Is," he corrected, putting the truck into park and switching the ignition off. "Now, go make things right. You owe her that much."

I looked from him to Cass in time to see her get up, walk inside, and slam the door.

"Even if I wanted to, she doesn't." I jerked my head at the porch where Vox sat alone, looking just as resolute as Rhett.

Vox signaled us to wait and followed Cass inside the house.

"Rhett, take me home."

He shook his head, and I let out a whiney groan like I had when I was a sixteen-year-old and Dad wouldn't let me stay out past ten.

"Savannah," he snapped, making me feel like I really was sixteen. "Get your ass out of this pickup, go inside, and make up for whatever the hell you two fought about."

"I don't—"

"Damn it, Sav. Go. This has gone on long

enough."

I gave him the harshest glare I could muster, got out of the truck—without his help—and marched to the front door. Cass didn't think I could make a decision on my own? Well, maybe she was right, but if I was here, I at least intended to tell her exactly how I felt about how she'd acted lately.

Three quick knocks later, Cass and Vox stood behind the screen door. Vox kissed her on the cheek, opened the door, and walked out toward Rhett's truck. Cass stayed behind the screen, arms folded over her chest.

For a moment, we stared at each other.

"What?" she said, not making eye contact.

I couldn't bring myself to give her a tongue lashing with her looking so guarded. Cass had stuck with me through it all—boyfriends, the loss of a job, a move—and Rhett was right. I owed it to her to make things right. Whether that meant continuing our friendship or not, I didn't know.

"Rhett's… a jackass," I managed.

She didn't smile.

I looked down at my feet and then up at her through the fraying screen. I'm sure we were a sight—me in my cowboy hat that still had the tag dangling from the back, and Cass, slightly pregnant in a stained tank top—separated by a beat-up screen door.

"And I'm sorry," I said, "for everything. I really

am happy for you for… making it. You know? Falling in love… starting a family… Basically everything I've ever wanted, and you have it."

Her expression softened. "Why didn't you tell me?"

"That I'm happy for you?"

She shook her head. "No, about the job in Austin."

Of course Rhett had told Vox.

"I guess I didn't think you'd care."

She didn't say I was right, but she didn't deny it either. "What about Hudson?"

I turned around to make sure Rhett and Vox were still in the pickup, and they quickly became interested in the radio.

I turned back to her. "I was… afraid."

"That I'd judge you?"

"Yeah," I sighed, "and that you'd tell Vox."

Her mouth fell open like that was the most appalling thing that had happened between us. "I would never do that."

I raised my eyebrows. "Come on, Cass. He's your best friend now. And he's Rhett's best friend. And you haven't exactly acted like yourself lately."

She gazed down at her hand and picked at the cuticle of her thumb with her index finger. "Yeah. I know."

"I really like him, Cass."

Her eyes shifted from her hand, to the pickup, to me, and she met my eyes without a hint of anger, but with more than a touch of sadness.

"I mean, I love him," I went on, words pouring from my mouth. "And I don't know what I would do if he ever found out. If he ever left—" Tears drowned out the words, and I studied the hole in the screen until my bottom lip stopped trembling.

"I won't tell," she said, and I felt five-years-old again, making a spit shake with my best friend.

But it was different now—now that I knew friends could break sacred promises. Now that I knew people changed and a friend who promised forever could become a stranger.

My lip trembled again when I asked, "Am I going to lose you?"

Her eyes were getting red and bright, and her bangs fell into her lashes when she shook her head no.

The screen door came open, and Cass buried me in a hug—the one thing a Stetson hat couldn't withstand.

CHAPTER forty-two

ALTHOUGH WE'D MADE UP, DRIVING TO Cass's bridal shower in Oakridge felt like taking a trip with a friend I'd just met. How are you doing? That's a nice dress. Where did you get it? Is it okay if I turn the radio on? How's Vox? What do you think about this song?

If things kept going that way, the bachelorette party was going to be really awkward.

Seeing her mother proved even more uncomfortable than the ride there. After Cass found a chair to rest in, her mom had me join her to help set up the cupcake tower. Between cupcakes, she said, "I didn't think we'd be seeing you around again."

"Excuse me?"

"After the way you treated our Cassidy?"

My mouth fell open. I'd been wrong, but Cassidy wasn't without fault either. "Friendship is a two-way street, Mrs. Reddick."

"Yes, it is. So, you better stop driving on a one-way road."

She must not have noticed my sardonic expression, because she put the last of the cupcakes on the stand and then left to sit by Cass. I wondered what Cass had been telling everyone. Surely I wasn't the monster she'd made me out to be.

Her sister played some music over the small speaker system, and I let the mix take me out of my thoughts. I had just enough time to do a final check that everything was in place before people started showing up. We were in a hotel basement, but with the decorations and music, it felt more cozy than claustrophobic.

In the next fifteen minutes, women filtered into the party. I met Cass's Grandma Mildred, who had wild, curly hair and talked like everything was a secret; her old math teacher, who's back stayed ramrod straight; Vox's grandmother, who seemed more pleased to see me than Cass; and a host of children sprinting circles around the room.

People drifted in for the better part of an hour, setting gifts on a bowing folding table, then snaking their way to the cupcakes and punch. I'd enlisted Mom's help to make a scrapbook with snapshots of Cass and Vox, from selfies to the impromptu engagement photoshoot they'd done only days before our big fight. Luckily, I'd conspired with the photographer to get a few prints early. Mom had the great idea to leave blank areas for her friends to write advice and well wishes. Everyone in attendance lined up to leave a note while we played a "find the guest" scavenger hunt.

As the game dwindled down, I poured myself another drink. I dropped the ladle, making punch splash over the table when I felt something brush against my arm. Cass's mom stood within two inches of me.

"Oh my gosh!"

"We should go ahead and get started with the gifts," she said, then took a sip from her drink that smelled strongly of vodka.

"Okay." I slowed my breathing and began walking to get Cass from where she sat, deep in conversation with one of her teenage cousins, but Cass's mom let out a loud whistle, and everyone quieted and stared at her.

"Savannah's got something to say," she slurred.

"Oh." I cleared my throat. "First off, thank you all for coming. It's been great to meet so many of the people who helped make Cassidy the awesome friend I know and love." Grandma Mildred clapped loudly.

"Now, it's time to let our girl open her presents."

Cass made eye contact with me and I waved her over. Then I located her sister and gestured that she should come, too. With only a few snarky comments from her mother, some tears from Vox's grandma, and a stack of everything Cass could possibly need for her home with Vox, we had successfully finished the bridal shower.

CHAPTER forty-three

WE LEFT FOR TOWN IMMEDIATELY AFTER bringing the gifts to Cass's parents' house. The original plan had been to stay and eat lunch with them, but her mom was three sheets to the wind, and her dad had left to hang out with some of his friends without telling anyone.

    I felt bad for Cass, but didn't mind the change in plans. Even though I didn't like fighting, I didn't know how much longer I could keep my mouth shut with the stream of shit her mom had been slinging.

    All the bridesmaids were excited to see what I had planned, and I hoped they wouldn't be disappointed when they found out. I gave Cass's cousin the address to the hotel, but other than that, I'd kept things on the down low.

Cass ended up riding with her friend and cousin, and her little sister came with me. I felt relieved I didn't have to make small talk with Cass again, but another part of me cringed at the thought of hearing Camdyn's nonstop chatter for an hour straight.

Ten minutes into the drive, Camdyn told me she had decided which hair school to attend—the same program I had—and she planned to start the week after the wedding. Twenty minutes later, I learned about all the drama between her and her boyfriend, and that she didn't know if she would keep dating him after she moved away. Thirty minutes in, she had told me about the pill giving her acne instead of clearing her skin up, and forty-five minutes in, I was glad we only had fifteen minutes left to go.

The other half of our group arrived earlier than we did because I refused to drive more than three miles over the speed limit, and Cassidy's cousin sped like Clyde's getaway driver. I checked us into our two connecting rooms with four beds in a hotel right downtown.

We had supper at a Chinese place Cass had once mentioned was her favorite restaurant in the world, and then we went back to the hotel, pre-gamed—well, everyone but Cass did—and spent some time getting ready.

Tension still existed between Cass and me until I showed the bridesmaid and bride shirts, which made tears build up in her freshly mascaraed eyes.

"I'm sorry," she cried, reaching her arms out for a hug. "It's this pregnancy! It makes me cry all the time."

I hugged her back, glad we'd used waterproof makeup.

Ready to hit the town with our new shirts on, we heard a knock on the door.

Cass perked up. "Did someone order a snack?"

"Something like that," I said with a coy smile.

I went to the door and opened it to see an astonishingly fit and young… janitor, the top of his jumpsuit unzipped, one muscled arm up against the doorframe.

He slapped a mop head against the side of his thigh. "I got a call that there were some dirty girls in here."

I pushed him out of the room and shut the door behind me. "Are you kidding me?"

He readjusted the mop head in his hands, his chiseled features pulling into a frown. "What?"

"A janitor? Why didn't they send a cop? Or a cowboy? Or a firefighter? Or a sexy butler, for crying out loud."

He smiled and looked at me through his lashes, confidence practically seeping through his pores. "You want a preview before I go in there?"

"Oh my God."

"Look," he said. "It's a good bit. Trust me. I've been doing this for a while."

He hardly looked like a seasoned pro, since he couldn't have been more than a year or two older than me.

I don't know what it was. Maybe the whiskey, maybe the nerves, maybe the fact that I'd already used up my harvest money/stripper budget, but I led him into the room, mop bucket and all.

"Who was it?" Cass called from the desk where she was examining her makeup in the mirror.

Camdyn's jaw dropped at the sight of us, and she nudged her sister on the arm. Cass let out a giggle the second she saw him.

Unfazed, Mr. Janitor stepped past me into the room, pulling a small speaker out of his mop bucket, and started playing music.

"Someone in here is a dirty girl," his voice sounded smooth and low, "and I think I know who."

I hid my bright red face in my hands, but I couldn't look away from the train wreck in front of me for more than a second.

He adjusted his mop and slapped it against his thigh.

"You," he pointed at Cass, taking slow, deliberate steps toward her.

UNFAIR CATCH

"Sit down," he ordered, pointing the mop at the bed closest to him. "Now."

With another incredulous giggle, Cass got up and scuttled to sit down where he told her.

Things took a stranger turn after the first dance, when Cass and Camdyn traded off slapping the "janitor" with the mop head and letting him dance on them. That went on until he'd either had enough, or the hour I'd paid for was up, and he slipped his jumpsuit back on.

"You girls behave," he said, nodding at us, "and don't make a mess."

"What was that?" Cass burst out laughing after he shut the door behind him, and we all fell into fits of giggles.

"They didn't tell me it was going to be a janitor," I groaned.

She gave me a hug and put her forehead against mine. "Thank God I'm only getting married once."

I smiled. "At least there's that."

Camdyn jumped up and left the room, and Cass shrugged. "Encore?"

Twenty minutes later, we made our way to the bar, Camdyn and the fake janitor in tow. Apparently she had decided whether to keep her boyfriend or not.

Much like Cass's life the past few months, the night didn't go as expected. Cass demanded we stay in the bar that had a big dancefloor because it was more fun for her since she couldn't drink. Her sister, on the other hand, drank enough for the both of them. I'd never planned on getting a fake ID until Cass bought me one our second semester of college, and even I knew not to drink enough to draw attention to myself.

Less than an hour and a half into our night out, Camdyn's face sported black mascara tracks from crying so profusely. I wanted to remind her there was a reason I'd suggested waterproof makeup, but it didn't seem like the right moment for an I-told-you-so.

"I miss my boyfriend," she blubbered between words, her pouty lips pulling her features down so she looked like one of those paintings of clowns with melting faces.

I tried to guide her to the bathroom, being the self-appointed babysitter of the night, but failed. She fought away from me and stumbled to the dancefloor where Cass was two-stepping with a chubby cowboy who more than made up for what he lacked in appearance with his dance moves.

They paused when Camdyn poked the man's bulky shoulder, but Cass pointed her toward me, looking comically furious in her plastic tiara.

Camdyn literally stomped her right foot, but turned around. Halfway to me, she burped, brown liquid spilling out her mouth, darkening the pink bridesmaid shirt.

"Oh shit!" One guy who had seen pointed her

out to his group of friends, and she shot them a Cass-worthy glare, even with vomit dripping down her chin.

I ran to her, took her elbow, and dragged her to the bathroom, careful not to stand too close. We just barely made it to a stall before she spewed chunks all over the toilet.

Of course, the janitor was nowhere to be found.

I swore everything she'd eaten that day came out of her mouth, and when she finally stopped throwing up, she took off her shirt and rested her head on the toilet seat already covered in vomit.

"No, no, no!" I said a little too late.

She swatted a hand at me. "Just let me puke in peace."

I wanted to snap at her and tell her this was exactly why they didn't let people under twenty-one drink, but I knew arguing with a drunk—especially one related to Cass—wouldn't solve anything.

"Fine," I said after flushing the toilet, annoyance sharpening my voice. "I'll be back."

When I stepped out, she slammed the stall door shut, but it bounced back and hit her on the ass. It took all my strength not to cry and laugh at the same time.

She slid the latch shut, and I saw puke splatter on the floor as she missed the toilet.

So now she was sick, shirtless, and locked inside a stall. I hoped this would be enough of a lesson for her before she went to college. Cass had always been my wing woman, but I'd heard of other girls going out and waking up in a guy friend's bed without knowing what had happened—or having something even worse happen.

"Cam?" I peered through the crack.

She spat. "What?"

"I'll be right back, okay?"

She spat again, and it landed in the toilet with a splash. "Fine."

I stepped past some girls entering the bathroom and hoped Camdyn would stay in there with the door closed.

"Hey there," a slow drawl came from my left.

He looked younger than me—barely eighteen I guessed—but cute... tall with a baby face he would probably grow into in a couple of years.

"Hey," I said, but kept walking toward the dancefloor, panning the room for Cass or one of the bridesmaids. I needed backup.

"Can I get you a drink?" he asked, trailing behind me.

Still wet behind the ears.

I was about to tell him I had better things to do than flirt with some guy who just wanted to not be a virgin anymore, but the wheels in my head started turning.

"Maybe," I looked up at him and put on my

flirtiest smile. "What's a stud like you doing here by yourself?"

"Girlfriend couldn't make it?" I added, pushing my lips out to a pout like I'd seen Cass do a million times before.

The lights from the dancefloor revealed his full cheeks turning red. "Don't got one."

"You wouldn't tease a girl, now would you?" I asked, putting a hand on his arm.

Okay, maybe I was laying it on a little thick.

He chuckled, and his eyes glanced over me, starting at my boots and lingering for longer than necessary on my chest. "Now, why would I do that?"

I shrugged. "You tell me."

He shook his head and put his hand low on my waist. "I wouldn't. Now how 'bout that drink?"

"Okay, you wore me down." I smiled at him brightly, like I wanted nothing more than the cheap mixed drink he'd surely get me, and then frowned. "But I have a problem."

He looked almost like a confused puppy. "What's that?"

"It's my friend." I gave an exaggerated frown. "She's really sick," I leaned in and whispered. "Threw up all over her shirt."

He made a face. "That's the shits."

I nodded. "Uh huh. I was wondering if maybe she could borrow yours?"

"Please?" I added, batting my eyelashes, just like I tried to bat away how ridiculous I felt.

"Oh," he frowned like he didn't want to.

"And then we can see about that drink." I winked at him.

I saw his resolve falter. "Promise?"

"Yep." My voice went an octave higher with the lie.

"Okay, hold on," he said, fiddling with the buttons on his shirt.

He took it off and then his undershirt, and handed me the sweaty white t-shirt before slipping the plaid button up back over his arms. I couldn't help but notice his muscles weren't quite as soft as his face.

When I made it back to the bathroom, Camdyn was out of the stall and had her head stuck under a running faucet, guzzling water and then spitting it out.

I stifled my gag reflex and handed her the pilfered undershirt when she came up for air.

"Thanks," she said, taking it from me.

A vessel in her right eye had popped, mascara smudges covered her face, and I was pretty sure I saw a chunk of leftover vomit high on her right cheek. She looked like the half-naked child of a drunk Barbie and a troll doll.

I pulled some paper towels from the dispenser and got them wet to help clean up her face, then pulled the undershirt over her head, since she was finally accepting my help.

"I'm sorry," her voice cracked and she let out a whine, tears brimming in her eyes.

"Shh," I rubbed her shoulder. "Are you done throwing up?"

She nodded, looking every bit of her eighteen years young.

"Okay, let's go back to the hotel."

The waterworks kept coming. "I ruined Cass's party," she whimpered.

At that moment, Cass burst into the bathroom with her cousin.

"We're ready to go," Cass said. "Are you okay?"

Camdyn nodded and pulled Cass into a hug.

"You stink." Cass scrunched up her nose and disengaged herself.

Camdyn let out an involuntary laugh, and that was enough for all of us to laugh and do a group hug in the bathroom. I imagined we were in a movie where everything ended happily ever after, throwing up was a bonding moment, and the maid of honor didn't keep secrets from her lover.

But life wasn't like a movie.

Cass gave her sister a shower when they got back, and then they ended up sleeping in the bed together, Cass holding her sister tight, making me forget the part of me that was glad I didn't have a sister.

In the morning, Camdyn had a raging hangover, so Cass and I packed her things. We checked out of the hotel, and her cousin introduced us to her hangover restaurant from the year she went to school in Dallas—a breakfast joint that served plate-sized pancakes, heaping piles of fluffy eggs, and crispy bacon dripping with grease.

Cass shared her food with me since morning sickness had started in full force along with her second trimester, making it hard for her to keep much of anything down, but everyone else ate most of what they ordered.

After the meal, Cass's cousin and friend got into their car, and Cass and her sister piled into mine. Cam would be staying with Cass the week leading up to the wedding to help with the preparations since I couldn't take off work all week to help. Personally, I thought Cass had it planned out well enough that she didn't really need either of us except for moral support.

Rhett came to see me as soon as we got home, and we spent the afternoon lounging around, watching movies. Our relationship seemed to be even better now that we had committed further; me by giving up my job opportunity in Austin and him by asking me to stay.

There would always be jobs for me, but there was only one Rhett Lane, and I didn't want to give him up.

Chapter forty-four

I TOOK OFF WORK THE FRIDAY BEFORE THE wedding, and Rhett insisted I eat lunch with his family who were all in town for the big day—aunts, uncles, and sister, horrible tag-along friend included. Rhett told me Harleigh planned to bring her boyfriend over.

The second I walked through the door, my eyes snapped to the pair sitting together on the love seat.

Hudson.

Their fingers intertwined loosely, comfortably, and she had her legs draped over his lap. Even seeing Cheyenne a few feet over on the couch didn't disturb me in comparison to this unwelcome discovery.

Hudson made it look so easy, like seeing a

person he used to sleep with was nothing. Like he wasn't dating someone who made me want to simultaneously yell, puke, and punch something every time I saw her.

He lifted his free hand in a carefree wave and said, "Hey."

Hey. Hey. I could have screamed. Just a week ago this dirtbag managed to tell me he loved me, insult Rhett, and call me a cheater, all in a span of five minutes, and he had the nerve to act like none of it had happened.

"Hey," Rhett said, returning the wave like it wasn't at all strange to see them together.

Keep it cool, Savannah. "I didn't know you two were dating."

Okay, almost.

Harleigh grinned wide. "Going on a month now."

My mental calendar organized itself in my mind. "Right after harvest."

Hudson's gaze met mine. "Yep."

Rhett crossed the living room and sat as far away from Cheyenne as he could on the couch. She looked bored, staring at her phone screen and swiping her thumb up every so often. I stayed in the entryway, still dumbfounded.

"How's your ankle healing?" Hudson asked.

How could we be making small talk?

"Just got my boot off this morning."

"Good," he said.

"Yeah… Rhett, I'm gonna go see if your mom needs help with anything in the kitchen."

His face lit up. "You're so sweet, baby. She'll really like that."

Of course she wouldn't—the galley kitchen barely fit one person, and she could hardly share the state of Texas with me—but I would take any opportunity to get out of that room. It felt like the walls and ceiling were getting closer and closer, threatening to crush me every second I saw Hudson holding Harleigh's manly hand.

When I reached the kitchen, Rhett's Aunt Lorraine greeted me with a hug, a kiss on the cheek, and a concerned interrogation about what had happened to my ankle. I explained that I hurt it during harvest, which inevitably led to more talk about Hudson, and what a "heartthrob" he was. Gag.

Rhett's mom immediately refused any help in the kitchen and suggested I go spend some time with her son. And she said it like that—like he was her son and not my boyfriend.

Still unable to bring myself to return to the living room, I stepped onto their back patio and settled into the porch swing. Rhett's dad's and uncle's voices carried over the air from the shop, but I couldn't make out what they were discussing. Judging by the intermittent booming laughter, it was something funny.

I listened to the indistinct warble of their conversation and breathed deeply while attempting to make sense of why I felt so upset. Of course Hudson could date anyone he wanted, including Harleigh. I had turned him down and was in a serious relationship with Rhett, loved him enough to turn down my dream job.

For the better part of ten minutes, I stayed lost and confused in my thoughts until the screen door slid open, and Lorraine stepped outside.

"Mind if I join you?" she asked.

"Of course." I gestured at the open spot beside me on the bench.

She plopped down, making the seat swing back and forth. "Thanks."

"Yeah."

We were quiet for a moment, and then she said, "It's not bad out here with the breeze."

"And the shade," I added.

Cottonwood trees surrounded the backyard, casting broad shadows and giving a spotted view of the family's feedyard about half a mile off. The smell of hot silage wafted over them in the wind, enveloping us in the scent of sweet, most grain. Everything smelled different in the country; even though McClellan was a small town, it never smelled as purely of dust or silage or fresh rain.

"You don't need to worry about Deena," Lorraine said.

"What do you mean?"

I didn't want to act like "poor me" because Rhett's mom didn't like me. She hadn't been crazy about me when Rhett and I dated in high school, and I didn't expect things to be different the second time around. She'd probably be thrilled if he ended up with Cheyenne instead.

Lorraine gave me a practiced, no-nonsense look she usually reserved for her husband and children.

"Okay," I said, because I didn't know what else to say.

She pulled her right foot up across her lap, slipping out of her sandal so it landed with a thud on the cement slab. "You know why she doesn't like you, right?"

"Because Harleigh doesn't?"

She threw her head back and cackled like I'd said the funniest thing she'd ever heard. "Harleigh doesn't like anyone that her little friend doesn't tell her to like."

At my shocked reaction, she covered her mouth and said, "Sorry, I shouldn't talk about my niece like that. She's just got a lot of growing up to do yet, and Cheyenne doesn't help."

"Tell me about it." I couldn't agree more, but I didn't think growing up would help them any. They'd probably still be snots in the nursing home.

"No, Deena doesn't like you because Rhett likes you."

"She didn't like any of his other girlfriends?" I asked. Surely he'd brought one or two home that Deena got on with.

"No, she loved Blaire." Lorraine pressed her lips together so she looked oddly similar to a child's drawing of a smiley face. "But Rhett didn't."

"And his other girlfriends?"

"What other girlfriends?" She patted my knee and then got up to go in the house. Before sliding the door open, she said, "You better take care of his heart."

I stayed on the porch by myself, thinking about what Lorraine had said and wondering if I was fit for the task.

My lower back started to sweat in the heat, so I got up and went inside to find Rhett in the armchair, talking to Harleigh and Hudson about the upcoming rodeo—or rather, the rodeo they were going to be missing for Cass's wedding.

Cass refused to have her wedding on any day but a Saturday, and she didn't want to be hugely pregnant when she and Vox got married, even if the entire town knew it was a shotgun wedding. So, she gave Vox two options: miss the rodeo or not have the wedding at all. He'd made the right choice.

"Hudson wanted to go," Harleigh simpered,

UNFAIR CATCH

"but I told him he couldn't miss out on our first wedding together."

She nuzzled her nose against his.

I deserved a medal for keeping my breakfast down.

Hudson didn't seem at all disgusted by the display, which made me even angrier. I couldn't even get him to stay the night after we had sex.

Not wanting to share a couch with Cheyenne, I slid onto Rhett's lap.

Hudson's smile faltered for a second.

"Where were you?" Rhett asked.

"Just getting some air outside," I said. "Your mom said she had it handled."

"I could've come out with you." He wrapped his arms around my stomach and hugged me.

I leaned my head back on his shoulder. "That's okay. Aunt Lorraine kept me company."

Harleigh whispered something into Hudson's ear, and he let out a deep, slow chuckle.

Rhett made a face at me. "Is lunch done yet?" he yelled toward the kitchen.

"Just about!" his mom shouted back. "Come and get your plates!"

Rhett easily lifted me off his lap and onto the floor, then led me to the kitchen where his mom busied herself sticking serving spoons onto the platters. She'd made finger sandwiches and a variety of salads—pasta salads, lettuce salads, an egg salad, and a potato salad.

"Go ahead and dig in, honey," she said to Rhett and rubbed his shoulder.

We plated our food, and Rhett pulled a chair out for me at the edge of the table before taking his own seat. His other family members decided to eat at a picnic table in the shop, and, of course, Harleigh insisted she, Cheyenne, and Hudson sit at the table so that we could all hang out together.

"So, how's work going?" Harleigh asked Rhett.

"Eh," he said through a mouthful of egg salad.

"What's that mean?" she pressed.

"I'm just not making as much headway as I thought I was," he said.

"Headway on what?" I asked.

"Well," he wiped his fingers on a paper napkin. "I'm trying to save up enough to lease out some land and run some cattle."

I nodded. "And?"

He had already told me all about his plan to take over his dad's ranch, piece by piece, until his dad retired—not that cowboys ever really retired. But until then, he had to get business of his own so the ranch could support two families.

"Well, the price of land's going up because of the corn market. People are plowing pastures that shouldn't ever be busted up so they can get in on the corn subsidies."

UNFAIR CATCH

"You can't blame people for wanting to make some extra cash," Hudson bristled.

"Yeah," Rhett said, "I can. We're losing all of this topsoil, and the market's gonna crash, and it'll take decades for the grass to grow back right."

"Prices are gonna keep going up," Hudson said, "and we're getting in early."

A muscle in Rhett's jaw twitched, and his hand got tight on my leg.

"We'll see," Rhett said, his voice as light and sharp as a dart.

"But," Rhett said to me, "all it means is I'll have to save twice as much as I thought I would."

"What are you gonna do?" I asked.

With eyes staring hard at the wall, he said, "I'm going to eat this supper," he said, turning to look at me, a sad smile on his lips, "and I'm going to go to this rehearsal dinner with the love of my life."

Even with that hard look on his face, he sent butterflies dashing through my stomach—their wings were just a little more leaden than usual.

After lunch, Rhett took me out to check cattle, and I was glad to be free from the confining, wood-paneled walls of his parents' house.

A breeze played in through the open windows on his pickup as we bounced through the pasture, and I took in the smell of dust and dry grass as my open hand caught the wind.

"Can I tell you a secret?" Rhett asked over the sound of the engine, the wind, and the country song on the radio.

"Sure," I said.

He glanced my way and smiled at me, one hand on the steering wheel, the other slung over the back of my seat.

"We didn't really need to check the cattle."

I laughed, feeling as light as the tufts of cotton floating from the cottonwood trees. "I didn't think so."

The sky seemed to go on forever, like we were flecks on a sliver of land in a snow globe and could go falling into the blue oasis at any time.

He squeezed my shoulder. "This will be mine someday—ours."

Did he mean that?

Every day with Rhett felt better than the one before it. We'd had a great few months, and if it weren't for my colossal mistakes, I would call it perfect. Everyone around us was getting married, getting engaged, starting families... How soon would that come for us?

He parked at the top of a hill so we could gaze out over the land and the cattle that dotted the green and yellow pasture, only differentiated from the background by their red color and occasional movements.

When he killed the engine, the radio seemed so much louder.

UNFAIR CATCH

"I can't stand that guy," Rhett said.

I knew he meant Hudson, and I felt the same way. Of course, I couldn't bring myself to tell him why.

CHAPTER forty-five

BEFORE GOING TO THE RECEPTION HALL FOR the rehearsal dinner, we met at Vox's family farm and walked through the ceremony. It was supposed to be short, sweet, and to the point. They didn't practice their vows because Cass insisted they write their own, and she wanted them to be a surprise.

After we finished, we went to the reception hall in McClellan, which Cass and her sister had decorated throughout the week. I'd offered to help in the evenings, but Cass said it would be good bonding time for them before the baby came, and I'd agreed because stress and pregnancy hormones didn't suit Cass very well. We'd made up, but I wasn't about to risk another fight the day before the wedding if I didn't have to.

They'd done beautifully with the decorations. Cass's taste shined through the twinkling lights, pale pink tulle, and pearl beads that rested on burlap ribbons. One small table had been covered in food catered by a local restaurant, and we helped ourselves. Our families all came, Cass's and Vox's, mine and Rhett's.

A clear division between the four families existed, and even though it wasn't hostile, it was awkward and uncomfortable. Vox's family was the personification of southern Baptist—very prim and proper. Cass's family laid it all out there, crass jokes, oversharing and all. If they noticed how uncomfortable their off-the-wall comments made Vox's family, they didn't care.

Mom had never liked Deena or how she treated me, and even though she was polite, she made more of an effort to spend time with Vox's mom. But, as the night progressed and the boxes of wine got lighter, conversation eased.

"Hey," Cass tapped me on the shoulder.

My head felt pleasantly warm, and I reached up and gave her a hug.

"Are you ready for your toast?" she asked.

Her sister was supposed to give a speech at the wedding reception, but Cass had asked me to speak at the rehearsal.

"Yeah," I said.

"Good," she gave me a thumbs up and gathered

the hem of her white maxi dress to walk back to her seat.

I nudged Rhett. "Can I have my speech?"

"What? Yeah." He tapped on his shirt pockets until he found the paper and handed it to me.

"Hey," I said, standing up.

No one heard me.

Rhett whistled, and everyone went silent, except for Camdyn, who quickly quieted at Cass's glare.

"Hello, everyone," I said, my knees quivering under my own maxi dress, which I'd worn at Cass's request. "I'd like to make a toast… if there's enough wine left."

That elicited a polite chuckle from Vox's side of the table.

"Don't worry," Cass's Grandma Mildred raised a silver can. "We brought beer!"

That got a laugh and cheers from Cass's side of the table.

"Anyway," I said, "I haven't been to a lot of these things, but I get the idea that I'm supposed to give this sappy speech that makes people laugh and tells embarrassing stories about the bride-to-be, and I'm probably supposed to tear up by the time I'm done."

I took a deep breath.

"I know there are a million stories I could tell about Cass, and she'd have twice as many to tell about me from last weekend alone."

UNFAIR CATCH

Rhett snorted beside me—I'd told him about the janitor/stripper and the stolen shirt, both of which he'd found utterly hilarious.

"But," I went on, "I think there a lot better things I could say about Cass instead. Like how she's unbelievably smart. When I had trouble in algebra, she double-checked my homework for me, even after she came back from working a night shift at the nursing home. Or, I could talk about the way every time Camdyn called, she dropped everything, went to her room, and laid out on her bed so Cam would have all of her attention. I could go on and on about how every time she talks about Vox, she gets this far-off look in her eyes like she's imagining them in rocking chairs staring at the sunset, or how when anyone mentions her baby, she cradles her stomach like it's already here."

My voice faltered, and moisture pooled in my eyes. Was this goodbye?

"Or how she's the best friend I've ever had."

A fat tear rolled down my cheek, and I rubbed it away with the back of my hand that wasn't holding the speech.

Rhett rubbed the side of my thigh.

"Cass," I looked at her and raised my glass. "You're going to be a great wife and an even better mom. Vox, you're lucky to have her."

He nodded at me, and I felt like, in some small way, he understood what I was doing—passing the torch.

"To Cass and Vox," I said and tipped back the remainder of my wine.

Vox's older brother, who already had a wife and three children of his own, stood up next and gave a comical speech about how Vox grew up and some of the foibles he'd had as a child and young adult. He even cried a little bit as he wished Vox good luck. His speech lasted longer—and was probably better—than mine, but I'd said what I needed to say, and I figured that was enough for me.

After the reception, Cass, Camdyn, and her two other bridesmaids came to my house to stay the night. My couch folded out, and Mom had loaned me two air mattresses. We made s'mores over the gas stove, sat around and played truth or dare, and then, when Cass got tired, we called it a night.

I fell asleep next to Cass with the sight of her blush dress hanging in the corner of my room.

CHAPTER forty-six

THE NEXT AFTERNOON PASSED IN A FLURRY OF hair, makeup, and camera flashes. Aunt Viv had come over to help with hair and makeup, so she did two of the bridesmaids' and my hair, and I did Camdyn's and Cass's hair and makeup.

Since late July brought with it more days over 100 degrees than under, Cass opted for curly up-dos. She also insisted we all wear light eye makeup with lipstick so we would still look done-up without ruining our faces when we sweated or cried. With Camdyn's face at the bachelorette party still fresh on my mind, I couldn't have agreed more.

Cass's mom flitted in and out, bringing snacks

and supplies we requested from the store, all while attempting to do the extensive wedding day checklist Cass had given her.

Even though we'd spent most of the day getting ready, when the time came to leave for pictures and the ceremony, we had to rush around like we were in some sort of bridal preparation sweatshop. Everyone seemed to be anxious except for Cass. An odd calm had settled over her, and a serene smile played over her bright red lips.

We arrived at the ceremony on time, and I realized Cass had really meant it when she'd said family and close friends only. The few people there consisted of just about the same crowd at the rehearsal dinner and a few select friends from the community.

The intimacy of the wedding suited the small crowd. When it came time to read the vows, Cass's dad patted around his pockets as Rhett had the night before, just long enough to make me worry he'd lost them, before handing her the slip of paper.

"I've spent most of my life searching for love," Cass began. "I know I'm only twenty-one, but it's true. I've been to bars, to rodeos, classes, restaurants, and had more dates than I'd like to admit… We haven't known each other long, but," her voice cracked, and she took a deep breath that didn't do anything to stall her tears, "I didn't know what real love was until I met you."

And then I was crying.

"I know I'll never measure up to what you or our baby deserves, but I promise to try," she said. "For the rest of my life, I'll never stop trying. I love you."

"I promise to be faithful to you and our child," Vox said through his shaking jaw. "I promise to provide for you and our child as a husband and a father and to be everything you deserve. But most of all, I promise to be yours through everything; good times and bad, happiness, sickness—everything. I promise to love you as long as I'm here on this earth and probably even after I'm gone."

Rhett caught my gaze across the aisle, and his eyes softened as he turned his lips up in a secret smile.

The pastor sealed their union, and when they faced the crowd as man and wife, I saw them both sporting the biggest smiles I'd ever seen. Cass had pulled it off—and I didn't just mean the wedding.

After taking pictures, Cass and Vox rode together to the reception. Camdyn went with her parents because she wanted to "console" them. Cass's dad had started crying harder than the baby in the back row during the vows and muttering sentiments that smelled like whiskey since throwing the rice. Rhett took me and the other bridesmaids, and we made small talk on the thirty-minute drive into town.

I was eager to let loose a little bit at the dance, have a good drink, and eat some of the pork roast that Vox's uncle had made, but I quickly learned that wasn't in the cards. Upon arrival, the DJ whisked the wedding party into a pseudo huddle and laid out the plans for the night. We shouldn't have called it a reception so much as a choreographed production with background music.

They had to bring Cass's dad back inside for the father-daughter dance because he had left to drink whiskey on the back steps. One of Rhett's cousins threw a cupcake at his brother, starting a mini food fight, but other than that, it went smoothly. I was glad, though, when we got to the last hour.

I finally got a chance to sit down and rest my feet—my ankle ached from standing in cowboy boots all day. Rhett was dancing with his sister, Cass and Vox swayed together out of step with the song, and I was sipping lukewarm champagne from a plastic glass. It all felt like the happy ending in a movie.

Then Hudson took the seat next to me.

"Hey," he said.

I took a long swig from my glass.

"What do you think?" he asked, nodding toward the dancefloor.

Was he talking about the wedding? Or him and Harleigh?

"It was perfect," I answered, taking the safer option.

He pulled a flask out of his pocket and drank deeply. It smelled like ethanol.

"What is that?" I asked.

"This?" his voice slurred.

I raised my eyebrows and nodded.

He held it up and looked at it. "Everclear."

"Seriously?" I sputtered on my champagne. "Are we in high school?"

He chuckled and took a swig as easily as if it had been orange juice. "I wish."

As I looked out over the floor, knowing how much had changed in the man sitting beside me, I had to admit a part of me, no matter how small, felt the same way.

"You look sexy tonight," he said.

"Hudson," I warned.

With a squinty-eyed look over my body, he emptied the flask and got up.

"You do," he said and staggered toward Harleigh.

Rhett came off the dancefloor when the song ended and sat where Hudson had seconds before. When he kissed me, his mouth tasted like spearmint gum.

"You're sexy," he said.

It felt a lot better coming from him. "Look who's talking."

He smirked, and his eyes pulsed in the reflection of the DJ's strobe lights.

"Can you believe I'm the guy who gets to take

you home?" he asked.

Only a few months prior, I would have been mad at myself for letting it happen—for taking a risk on Rhett. In that moment, though, I couldn't have been happier. "I can't believe I get to go home with you."

Lying in bed with him that night, our skin still charged after being as close as two people could be, I felt more in love with him than I ever had with anyone. My heart might as well have beat right out of my chest and rested next to his. He had me, all of me, and I didn't ever want to have it any other way.

"I love you," I said, resting my cheek on his chest.

He picked his head up and kissed the top of my tousled hair. "I love you too."

CHAPTER forty-seven

IN THE MORNING, THE RECEPTION HALL DIDN'T look nearly as glamourous as it had the night before. Cass and Vox had already left for Austin to catch their flight to the Florida Keys, and we'd all agreed to help clean up.

Her dad carried the folding chairs back to the racks with one hand, a travel mug of Irish coffee in the other. Camdyn and I picked up the centerpieces and brought them out to the back of Rhett's truck, and everyone else made themselves busy taking out trash and washing the floors and tables so Vox could get his deposit back.

With no more wedding to plan for or look

forward to and my best friend a thousand miles away, married, it felt kind of like the day after my twenty-first birthday, hangover included. I couldn't imagine how Hudson must be feeling after drinking Everclear the night before, but I stopped thinking or caring about it when I remembered we'd made our choices. Mine didn't involve worrying about him.

Over the next week, I got a few calls from people asking me to do wedding hair and one from Darla checking to see if I was one hundred percent sure I didn't want to go work for her—she needed to start interviewing candidates and was "as sad as Santa looking at the scale the day after Christmas" because I wasn't going to go work for her.

Mostly, I was happy with my decision, but a small part of me lamented the missed opportunity. I hoped it would fade over time, especially since it looked like I would have plenty of business around McClellan now.

On Thursday, I had a date night with Rhett instead of Cass, but on Saturday, I got my girl back when they met us at the rodeo for registration.

"Cass wanted to extend our flight, but I wasn't about to miss more than one rodeo," Vox said.

She lifted a hand and whispered to me, "I had to go back to work anyway. Just don't tell him that."

I hugged her tight, glad to see her again, even if she was a tanner, more married, and more pregnant version of my best friend.

Like old times, we left them to register and hang out with the other rodeo-goers, and went to the stands to settle in for the show.

"So," I said, lifting my feet onto the seat in front of me, "how was it?"

She grinned. "The best, Sav. We have to go sometime after V-Key comes."

I raised an eyebrow. "'V-Key?'"

"Well,"—her tan cheeks flushed—"that's what we're calling it until we know if it's a boy or a girl. It's 'v' for Vox and then 'key' spelled with a C for Cassidy and for our new favorite spot."

I made a gagging motion. "You know that sounds like your baby is the key to your vagina, right?"

She leaned forward and giggled. "I guess it kind of is." She laughed even harder. "Because"—she gasped for air—"it's really going to open up the passage, if you know what I mean."

"Cass!" I squealed and lightly shoved her shoulder. "I don't even want to think about that part of you under normal circumstances."

"Pregnancy is normal," she said, her face still red.

I rolled my eyes. "Not that part."

Her look turned serious, and her eyes went wide. "What if it tears? You know—" she pointed below her belt line "—down there?"

"You're the nurse, Cass."

One corner of her mouth pulled up like she'd smelled something bad. "It could happen."

My face mimicked hers. "That's disgusting."

"That's not even the half of it." She motioned for me to bring my face closer. "I could shit, like, while the baby's coming out, and the doctor"—a laugh burst from her lips—"the doctor could be like"—she put on an Indian accent—"'Oh, congratulations, it's a giant turd.'"

We laughed so hard people stared, but I couldn't stop until the tears that rolled out of the corners of my eyes had evaporated under the hot Texas sun. I knew we couldn't act like this forever—young and immature and carefree—so I cherished it now.

After we quieted, she told me all about their vacation. Then she asked, "So, are we going to talk about Hudson dating Harleigh?"

"Oh, thank God," I said. "I wanted to talk about it, but I didn't want to seem like I was obsessing or anything."

"No, no, no," she said, tucking her hair behind her ear. "I mean, come on. Rhett's sister?"

"I know! He could have anyone he wanted, and—"

Cass gave me a look, and I hurriedly added, "except me—and he picks her?"

She looked down her nose at me like she used

to when I couldn't solve an especially easy algebra problem. "You know why he went for her."

"I do?"

"To make you jealous. Obviously."

I scoffed. "Come on."

She gave me a sad smile. "That's how he works. He wants to rub your nose in it that he's dating someone else. Do you really think it's any coincidence that he started dating Rhett's sister basically the same day you told him he doesn't have a chance anymore?"

"He called me sexy at your dance," I blurted, then covered my mouth.

For a moment, I couldn't see her eyebrows behind her sun-streaked bangs, and her eyes were more white than blue. "He told you what?!"

I shared the whole story, and she rolled her eyes. "What a child."

"Okay, Mama Cass."

"Sorry, just… Don't fall into his games, okay?"

I felt a little indignant, but I couldn't quite bring myself to blame Cass for thinking the warning was necessary.

"I won't," I promised. Losing Rhett was the last thing I wanted.

Midway through the rodeo, Deena, Harleigh, Cheyenne, and Vox's mom showed up and sat by us. Apparently Vox's mom liked Cass more than the rest of Cass's family, or at least didn't hate her, because she gave Cass a side-armed hug and started asking her about the honeymoon. Rhett's mom gave me a stiff "hello," but only after I'd waved and said "hi" to her. Harleigh and Cheyenne pretended I didn't exist, and I liked it that way.

When it came Rhett's turn to ride, I watched his mom instead. In her lined face, I saw every emotion I felt waiting to see if he'd be alright. For the briefest of moments, I felt like even though we didn't like each other—might never like each other—we were kindred, at least in our love for Rhett.

He rode the full eight seconds, and when we cheered, I pretended Deena and I were where Cass and Vox's mom were now: mother- and daughter-in-law standing in companionship, rooting on a man they both loved. But I realized Deena and I supported two different people—she was cheering on her past, and I was cheering on my future.

We all stayed in the stands afterward, waiting for our men. Unfortunately, Hudson got to us before Rhett and Vox did.

"Well, hi there, Mr. McAllister," Rhett's mom practically fell over herself, and I did well to keep a scowl off my face.

"Ma'am," Hudson said, taking her hand and shaking it.

Harleigh gazed up at him like he was a boy on one of the stupid, half-naked posters she'd hung all over her room in high school.

"Great ride earlier," Deena gushed.

"Almost beat Rhett," Harleigh added.

Had they noticed the frown that glanced across Hudson's face at the mention of Rhett?

"Almost," I said, and I hoped he knew Rhett had him beat in and out of the arena.

"He can take all the wins he wants." Hudson put his arm around Harleigh and kissed her. "I got the girl."

While Harleigh, Cheyenne, and Deena fawned over him, he looked directly at me and almost imperceptibly lifted an eyebrow. A challenge.

Don't fall into his games, I heard Cass say.

"Congratulations," I said and kept the sarcasm to myself.

When we saw Rhett walking up, we cheered, and he waved his chaps around like a trophy.

"Who's that good lookin' cowboy?" I called.

He put a hand over his brow like he was searching through the crowds. "Where's my girl?"

"Ooh! Here!" I called.

Cass giggled and slapped me on the butt. "Go get 'im cowgirl."

Carefully, I stepped down the bleachers, but Rhett ran to meet me and pulled me into his chest.

"Well, hello there," I whispered.

He kissed me, hard, and I leaned into him,

knowing the only person whose opinion mattered held me in his arms.

CHAPTER forty-eight

RHETT AND I RODE TO THE DANCE TOGETHER and then found a spot at a table with Cass and Vox. Thankfully, Harleigh, Hudson, and Cheyenne stationed themselves across the room, but I didn't trust that would last long.

"What did you think about the show?" Rhett asked.

"What?" I asked, too distracted by Hudson and Harleigh. Was Cass right? Did Hudson just date her to get at me?

Hudson and Harleigh got up together and walked toward to the dancefloor. If Hudson was willing to carry on the charade for this long just to make me jealous, they made a good match. They deserved each other for sure.

Rhett pressed his lips between my eyebrows. "Always spacing off."

Hudson spun her around and then gripped her low around the waist.

"I am not," I said.

Rhett's chuckle was low. "Okay. So, what did you think of the rodeo?"

I ran my thumbs over the callouses on his palm. "You were great."

"I have a buckle and a nice little wad of cash to prove it." His eyes shone.

"I lost you at 'wad.'" I winked.

He laughed a little louder. "Let's save that for later," he said in a seductive whisper.

We turned back to Cass and Vox to see them playing a thumb war. Cute.

After Vox won, he sucked Rhett into an argument about who would win in a thumb war between Yosemite Sam and Elmer Fudd, which was probably the most ridiculous thing I'd heard in a long time, but it gave me a chance to watch the couples.

Hudson and Harleigh had sat down, and Harleigh drank slowly from Hudson's flask. He looked right at me, and our eyes met in a gap between the crowd of moving bodies.

He didn't stop staring, and I refused to look

away, refused to let him win—until he winked. I was so appalled I couldn't keep looking.

The song switched to a slow one, and Rhett asked me if I wanted to dance.

"It might be ugly," I said, my heart still puttering around at a jaunty pace. "I'm still shaky with my boot off."

"Come on." He stood up. "All we have to do is rock in a circle."

Nervously, I rose and followed him to where the other couples swayed to a Johnny Cash-era country song.

I rested my head against Rhett's chest and enjoyed the way the music blended with the steady thrum of his heartbeat.

"Rhett!"

I jerked my head off his chest to see his sister storming toward us, the heels on her boots thudding against the wooden floor.

"What?" he asked, an annoyed tick in his voice.

Cheyenne skidded to a stop beside Harleigh, whose fists clenched and unclenched like the dangling claw in one of those games that ripped kids off.

"You get away from him," Harleigh said over the music, pointing a meaty finger at me.

The music didn't stop with a scratching record sound like in the movies, and aside from a few of the couples closest to us, everyone kept dancing.

"I know you don't like it," Rhett said, "but I love this girl, and if you can't handle it, you're the one who needs to leave, not her."

At Harleigh's speechless, dumbfounded look, Rhett took my hand back up and spun me away from them.

"I don't know what their deal is," he said, but I did.

Hudson had told.

I felt Harleigh's grip on my arm, and she pulled me away from Rhett. I barely kept my balance.

"Harleigh. What. The fuck. Is. Going. On?" Rhett snapped, steadying me.

"Why doesn't she tell you herself?" Cheyenne jumped in, her head cocked, bony hands firm on her hips.

"You stay out of it," Rhett snarled.

She folded her arms across her chest, and I thought one of her breasts might fall out.

"Tell him, Savannah," Harleigh growled, her big hoop earrings bobbing with her head.

"Are you insane?" Rhett's fingers clenched into my side as he yelled at her.

More people stared openly at us.

Cheyenne used one of her hands to point at me and then Hudson. "She's sleeping with him!"

Rhett's jaw flexed. "Shut the fuck up, Cheyenne."

"You're gonna trust a trailer trash rodeo bunny over your sister?" Harleigh shouted, her words slurring.

"Back off," Rhett said and started to lead me away, but I felt a splitting pain in my head.

Harleigh ripped at my hair, and I fell back on the floor, beer and spit instantly soaking the back of my shirt.

"Stop it!" I screamed and grabbed the base of my pony tail so she wouldn't rip it out.

Rhett caught her wrist, and the pain ebbed when she let go.

"What the fuck is wrong with you?" he yelled at her.

As I stumbled up, I saw his fists locked around her wrists.

"She fucked him!" Harleigh shouted and tore away from his grip. "While she was dating you."

Rhett turned to me, a pissed expression marring his features. "Tell her you didn't," he said.

"Would that make you happy?" he growled in her face. "Would it?"

Cheyenne went to stand by Harleigh, and they both stared at me, waiting.

I wiped a bottle cap away from where it had lodged in my arm. "Not while we were dating."

No one danced now, and the music seemed to stall while I waited for Rhett to say something… anything.

"You have to believe me," I begged.

He didn't. I could tell from the look on his face he didn't. And it killed me.

I spun, and as quickly as I could, walked out of the building, every bit of liquid on my back boiling under their glares.

Cass caught up to me halfway out and wordlessly put an arm around my shoulder.

We were down the stairs before Rhett caught up.

"Wait. Wait!" he roared.

We stopped at the sidewalk, and Cass kept her arm around me as we turned to face him.

"You slept with him?" Rhett asked. His voice was acid—nothing like the sweet drawl he'd used only minutes earlier.

"It was before I said I'd be your girlfriend," I said, wishing I could do something—anything—to erase the hurt look on Rhett's face.

"When?" he yelled. "Tell me right now."

My heart stuttered, and I shivered as the wind hit my wet back. "The last time was the Monday after the Parke Rodeo."

"The last time?" he ripped his fingers through his short hair and paced in a circle. "There was more than one time?"

"It was before we were exclusive!" I cried, a sob forcing its way out of my chest.

UNFAIR CATCH

"Exclusive?" his face came within a foot of mine. "I dropped Blaire the moment you told me you would give us a shot!"

He pulled at his shirt and one of the buttons flew off. "When were you exclusive? Whenever Hudson decided he didn't want you?"

"Rhett," Cass interjected in a warning voice.

He held his hand up. "Was this just some sick game to pay me back? Because you won. You won! Now we're both cheaters."

"Rhett," I cried. "It was never like that! I stopped when I knew this was real."

"How many times?" he asked. "How many times did you have sex with him since you said you'd give us a chance?"

"Two," I whispered.

"You fucked him two times in two days? What? Did he just show up after I drove off?"

My face must have showed the truth because he let out a strangled yell. I'd never seen him like this, not once.

"Rhett!" Cass cautioned.

"Oh, shut up!" Rhett bellowed.

People were filing down the stairs now. One of them yelled something, but I couldn't hear it over Rhett's rage and the blood rushing through my ears.

He stuck a finger in Cass's face. "You probably put her up to it. Jesus fucking Christ. She does everything you fucking want her to!"

"Rhett," Vox said evenly. "Leave my wife out of it!"

"Oh, you're on her side now?" Rhett said, the hurt on his face barely masked by his anger. "You probably knew all about it."

"I didn't know anything," Vox said, sticking his hands out like he was approaching a wild animal. "Just let Sav have her piece."

I looked at Cass, and she squeezed my side.

I opened my mouth to point out that Rhett had done nearly the same thing, and I'd forgiven him. I wanted explain to Rhett how sorry I was. That Hudson and I were over—that we were never even really a thing. I loved Rhett with everything that I was, and I needed him to know that if I could take one thing back in my entire life, it would be this.

But he talked first.

"Go to Austin."

"What?"

"You heard me," his chin trembled for a half a second. "Go to Austin."

"Rhett, I—"

"Go!" he shouted. "GO! FUCKING GO!"

"Come on," Cass said, turning my immobilized body away from the shouting stranger and leading me down a sidewalk, off a curb, into the backseat of a truck.

UNFAIR CATCH

The door closed.
I curled into a ball.
Someone stroked my hair.
And my chest ripped in half.

Chapter forty-nine

I WOKE UP IN CASS'S BED. MY EYES BURNED, my hair lay in matted tangles down my back, and my nose was too swollen to smell anything. Incoherent voices faded in and out from the other side of the door, and pink light panned into the room through the curtains.

I looked at my phone, hoping to see something—anything—from Rhett. But only one message waited in my inbox.

Hudson: Ur welcome. 1:08 a.m.

The door of the bedroom opened, and I felt Cass's hands sweeping my hair off my face. She murmured something, letting me know I would be okay, that Rhett would come around. But all I could see was the hurt on Rhett's face, and all I could feel was the sting of Rhett's words burning with the dying embers of my broken heart.

"How are you feeling?" she asked.

Fresh tears stung my eyes.

I shook my head.

"Oh, Sav," she pulled me into a hug. "He loves you. I know he does."

"I don't think that's enough."

She fell quiet and returned to stroking my hair.

"What are you going to do?" she finally asked.

I rolled to my side and slowly pushed myself up. "I have to go back."

"What?" She adjusted herself so she could rest her back against the headboard beside me.

"I'm going to Austin. Like…" His name stuck in my sore throat. "He told me to."

"Sav." She rubbed my shoulder. "He'll get over this. He just needs time to cool down. Vox is going to talk to him today, and I'm sure he'll—"

I shook my head and closed my eyes against the stinging tears. "He's not going to get past this. You saw the way he looked at me."

"Because he loves you," she said. "He'd never let you go."

I wished I could believe her, but I knew Rhett. How stubborn he was. How carefully he guarded his heart. He'd never trust me again.

"Cass, it's over. There's nothing for me here." Fresh tears spilled out my eyes, soothing the sting of crying the night before. "You have Vox. My brother has Steph. My parents have their own life… and I can't see him with other girls. It would kill me."

"But didn't your aunt already fill the position?"

"I don't know." I pulled my knees to my chest and bent over them just to keep myself intact. "Probably."

"Maybe you should wait to ask her until this all calms down?" Her arms rubbed slow circles over my leg. "'Til Rhett's had a chance to think things through?"

I shook my head again, then picked up my phone and dialed Darla. Not calling her now just increased the odds of her finding someone else for the job, or me losing my nerve.

"How's my favorite niece doing?" she answered on the second ring.

"I'm wondering if that job's still available," I unsuccessfully tried to make my croaking voice sound normal. "If you'll still have me."

Pop music spilled over her phone speaker. She must have been in the salon. "Are you okay?"

"Yeah. I will be."

"Can you start next Monday?" Darla asked.

Cass's hand froze on my back.

"Of course."

"You'll stay with me 'til you find a place?"

"Sure." The only detail I cared about was the distance between Austin and all the mistakes I'd made.

Darla said goodbye and hung up, and I let my phone drop to my lap.

"Oh, Sav," Cass said and pulled me into a hug that kept me from shattering into even smaller pieces.

CHAPTER fifty

AUNT VIV WAS DISAPPOINTED ABOUT MY decision, but she hid it well. She told me all I had to do was take on as many appointments as I wanted over the next couple of days and call and cancel the rest or hand them over to another stylist. It took time, but staying busy helped me more than anything else.

Word had gotten around town, and Mom came over to my house Tuesday night with a tub of butter brickle ice cream—the kind she always used to give me when I had to stay home sick from school. She didn't ask me any questions about the fight or what I'd done, but instead let me lay my head on her lap as we watched movies from the couch.

UNFAIR CATCH

Hudson had started sending me apologetic text messages, but I blocked his number. The one person I did want to hear from stayed utterly silent. I must have called and texted him a million times to apologize and beg him to talk with me, but I didn't get any calls, texts, or even run into him anywhere in town. Cass said Vox wouldn't tell her anything about Rhett, and that Vox was actually mad at her for keeping the secret from him.

I apologized to her a million and one times for causing a fight between them, but she said she had been my friend first. That if she and Vox had been married at the time, it would have been a different story, but she was looking out for me. Vox would have done the same for Rhett.

This time around, I didn't have a month to mourn our relationship. I only had three evenings left to box up my barely unpacked home, and it took all of the help I could get. Cass brought food each night, Mom and Steph stayed and packed while I was at the salon, and Monti and Dad even came after work.

Steph surprised me by renting a storage unit in Austin for my furniture so I wouldn't have to worry about it.

"Of course I'd do it… for my maid of honor," she added hopefully.

I nodded and burst into tears. Mostly, I was sobbing because I was tired, overwhelmed, and sad that I'd never get to plan my own wedding with Rhett. Even though I hadn't admitted it to myself until after our fight, Rhett was the one. If I hadn't messed everything up, we would have gotten married. Not soon, but someday. And I'd turned someday into never.

By Friday night, I had all my things packed and ready to go to Austin. I spent the last night laying in my bed in the house I'd only been able to call my own for a few months. All around me were memories of Rhett: him cooking me breakfast before church. Him making love to me and whispering that he loved me. Him curled up with me, watching movies on the couch. Him knocking on the door while I soaked in the bath, totally unaware of where it would lead.

I couldn't leave without telling him how I felt. Without seeing if he would give me another chance.

I got in my car and drove down the familiar dirt roads to his house with the radio off because I couldn't stand hearing the country songs he used to sing to me. I didn't know what would happen once I got there—what I would say other than I was sorry—but I had to hope that would be enough.

When I arrived at his house, I saw two vehicles in his driveway. I didn't recognize one, but I would tell him how I felt in front of the whole town if I had to.

Slowly, with a shaking fist, I knocked on the door and said a silent prayer.

Rhett came to the door, shirtless in his

sweatpants. It took every bit of strength I had not to reach out to him and melt into his arms—until I watched the way his face changed when he saw me. Like a curtain closing, his expression hardened and darkened.

"What do you want?" he asked.

Shocked by his greeting, I stayed quiet for a moment while I gathered myself. "I'm moving to Austin tomorrow. And I just"—my throat got tight, and I swallowed—"I just couldn't leave without coming to see you. See if… if there was any way…"

Tears flooded my eyes, and I hunched over as sobs wracked my chest. But he didn't reach out to comfort me. He didn't say a word. He just waited until I could talk again.

"Rhett, I love you."

His jaw flexed. "I loved you, too."

"You don't anymore?"

He closed his eyes and shook his head. "I—"

"Rhett?" a woman's voice called from his room. "Who's there?"

The shards left of my heart twisted.

"Hold on," he yelled over his shoulder.

"Rhett…" I could barely make myself say the words. "You have a girl here?"

"Savannah, you should go." He crossed an arm over his chest and rubbed his shoulder. "I hope you find what you're looking for in Austin, because you're not gonna find it here."

The door closed in my face, blurring in and out of focus as tears drowned my eyes and I struggled to breathe. As I got in my car and turned it on, I gave a final look at his house. All the sunflowers that had been in front of his porch were gone.

CHAPTER fifty-one

DAD AND MONTI HELPED ME LOAD ALL MY things into a moving truck on Saturday morning.

"Let's go by the house," Dad said when we were done. "Mom said she made brunch."

I didn't argue, even though I wanted to get out of town as soon as I could. We all got into his pickup and rode together to the house. Looking at the place where I grew up, I realized this goodbye felt so much more final than when I had left for college. I walked through the door, ready to say goodbye to my past.

"Surprise!"

Everyone was there: Mom, Steph, Grammy, Viv, Cass, and Vox all stood in the living room decorated with streamers.

Mom's brunch consisted of sandwiches and salads, similar to what we'd had at Rhett's the day of the rehearsal dinner, which only added to my somber mood. I'd been doing fine with not crying until Grammy hugged me.

She put a withered hand on my cheek and looked into my eyes with her cloudy blue ones. "If you ever miss him, go to church," she whispered. "That's one of the beautiful things about our faith. No matter where you go, you'll hear the same scripture, get the same blessing. God will take care of the rest."

Grammy used the pad of her thumb to wipe away the tear that fell down my cheek and then kissed the spot where it had been.

"It's been great having you home, sweetie," she said. "Come back when you're ready."

Cass and Vox said goodbye to me after Grammy, and the waterworks flowed. It would be the first time since we met that Cass and I wouldn't live in the same town.

"I'll visit soon, okay?" Cass said through tears of her own. "And call me on Thursday."

I nodded into her shoulder, staining her shirt with wet mascara. "I'm only a drive away."

She nodded and released me from the hug.

Vox was next in line, and I didn't know what to say to him. We hadn't talked since my fight with Rhett,

UNFAIR CATCH

and I knew he wasn't on my "side."

I wasn't even on my side.

I put my hand out so he could shake it, and he took me into a clumsy hug. "Good luck out there, kid."

The rest of my family embraced me, one by one, and then Dad, Monti, and I left.

Monti drove us back to my house where I left my keys in the mailbox for my landlord who'd been nice enough to let me out of my lease. Dad led us in the moving truck, Monti followed in Dad's truck, and I trailed behind in my car.

Before leaving town, I stopped at the gas station. While I filled my tank, I took out my phone and dialed Rhett's number for the last time.

He didn't answer.

I cried for the first part of the drive and tried to listen to music on the second part. Eventually, I turned off the radio and attempted to get excited about moving back to Austin, back to the city I'd never hoped to leave only months ago. Now, all I could think of was what I was leaving in the rearview mirror.

Dad, Monti, and Darla helped me fill the storage space with everything I owned except for a few duffel bags. We ate lunch together with Darla at Vox's favorite restaurant and then stood in the parking lot to say goodbye.

Dad put a hundred-dollar bill in my hand.

"Just in case," he said and wrapped me in a

hug that cocooned me from the world, but only for a second.

Monti held my shoulders in his hands. He searched my face for a moment, and I felt naked, like all my pain shined brighter than a neon sign for him to see.

"You're better off without him, Vannah," he said. "Go have an adventure."

CHAPTER fifty-two

ON MONDAY MORNING, I RODE WITH DARLA to the salon. She showed me the stall that I would be taking over, helped me set up my supplies, and taught me how to schedule and accept payments on the automated system.

Everything was a little newer and nicer than the salon in McClellan, but a pair of scissors was a pair of scissors, no matter where they were.

Darla told me I needed to get in at least forty hours a week and had to alternate weekends with another one of the stylists to accommodate walk-ins, but other than that, I was on my own as far as work went.

She warned me that it might be a little slow for at first, but told me I could stay with her until I could make enough to handle rent on my own and find an apartment I liked.

It turned out that I didn't need to worry too much. With her salon being situated right next to a busy store, we had more walk-ins than we could handle. Some of the stylists only wanted to do girls' hair because they would get paid more, but I took on as many of the male clients as I could because I could cut their hair quickly and they usually tipped bigger and came back more often.

The hardest part of my first week came on Friday when a young man in cowboy boots come into the salon. As soon as he walked through the door, he took off his hat—a Stetson—revealing short blond hair, a tan line from his hat, and a wide, crooked smile. And I was supposed to cut his hair.

"So, what's your story?" he asked as I switched guides on the clippers. "I haven't seen you around here."

"I'm new."

"I know." He shot me a million-dollar smile in the mirror. "I've been here before, and I think I would have remembered you."

A few months ago, my heart would have leapt at the handsome cowboy, but now it wrenched in pain remembering the last one. "I hope you liked your haircut last time."

His eyes crinkled a little as his smile widened. "I think I'll like this one better."

He had charm going for him.

"I'll do my best," I said and turned the clippers on.

I wasn't quite ready for another boyfriend, let alone another cowboy, but after he paid, he insisted on taking a card with my number on it in case he needed another haircut—or someone to take to dinner.

He wrote his name and number on the back of one of my cards. Maverick. But I threw it away after the door shut behind him.

For the first month, I left for the salon early and went back to Darla's place late. More often than not, I cried myself to sleep before doing it all over again. My third week in town, I started going to the Catholic Church closest to Darla's house. I didn't consider myself Catholic, but hearing the same verses Rhett was hearing each Sunday made missing him hurt a little less.

Midway through the second month, I started working out, too. My runs became the only time of the day I felt like I was getting stronger.

My third month there, I rented a new apartment in an enormous complex near the salon. My house in McClellan had been bigger, but the new place was big enough for me, and I could afford it.

Cass called every Thursday to replace our date

nights. The second she told me she was having a girl, I went online and ordered a pink camouflage tutu for the baby shower.

Rhett never called me, though. And after a while, I deleted his number from my phone, even though I knew it by heart, just so I wouldn't have to see his name.

Four months in, I still worked well over forty hours a week, except for the times when Monti and Steph came to Austin to shop for their new home or wedding supplies. I took a weekend off to go home for Christmas, and even went to mass the morning of with Grammy.

I didn't know whether I hoped to see Rhett or not, but when I saw him walk through the church doors with his family, it felt like the light of Jesus himself shined over me. He wore a dark red, almost maroon shirt that made his dark brown hair almost black. In the winter months, he'd lost most of his tan from the summer. Oh, how I ached for him, even with the time apart.

Grammy waved her hand at him in the aisle, and his face lit up as he waved back at her and smiled. I watched as his eyes slid over me, and then collided with mine as he recognized who I was. His mouth fell open and then he closed it, giving a nod to Grammy and sliding into the pew between his mom and dad. He didn't give me a second glance the rest of the

UNFAIR CATCH

service, and left right after communion, so I couldn't talk with him, even if I wanted to.

Chapter fifty-three

MY FIRST DAY BACK AT WORK AFTER Christmas, the cowboy—Maverick—came in for an appointment. Ever since the first cut I gave him, he'd been persistent, coming for haircuts twice a month and asking me out each time.

This time, I said yes.

"Just dinner," he promised, echoing Rhett's 'just coffee' deal.

Maverick had always said that he knew the best steak joint, or barbecue place, or even a seafood restaurant if I "was into that kind of thing outside of Galveston."

That night, he picked me up after work and

took me to the barbecue place, and I couldn't hide my shock when we pulled up to Vox's favorite restaurant.

I put my hand over my mouth and looked from him to the sign.

"You've been here?" he asked.

Slowly, I nodded.

His bright green eyes studied me, and a look of understanding crossed his face. "Who broke your heart?"

I met his eyes, feeling vulnerable under his gaze, but stronger than I'd ever been.

"I loved him," I said, "but I'm ready to move on."

"I'm glad to hear that. Just let me know if you ever need more time." He squeezed my hand in his for a second. "Now let me get your door."

After a perfect first date with Maverick, he walked me to my apartment door and gave me a soft kiss that was sweet enough to make me feel safe, and spicy enough to make me wonder what could be in store.

I called Cass afterward to tell her about it.

She acted happy for me, and I tried to feel the same way.

Maverick called the next morning, and for the next few weeks, he took me out every Friday. Always dinner at a new place, always a kiss at the door, and I could always count on him for a good morning text.

He made me feel like I could have a second chance at love, but every time I stared in his green eyes for too long, they turned hazel, and I had to choke back all the regret and loss that came with any memory of Rhett Lane.

Chapter fifty-four

A MONTH AWAY FROM CASS'S DUE DATE, I took off work to go to her baby shower in Oakridge.

I couldn't believe how big she'd gotten, or how beautiful pregnancy made her. Her cheeks glowed, and even with a full belly, she walked with a bounce in her step she'd never had before. It suited her—made her look more maternal. Cass's mom said that if she would have been having a boy, Cass wouldn't look as good as she did. Cass rolled her eyes.

Vox showed up to the baby shower, too, because, as Cass said, "We didn't have children the 'right way' so why would we do this any different?"

He didn't seem as happy to see me as Cass did,

though. Only sad.

"Hey, kid," he said.

Usually, I'd be annoyed at someone only three years older than me calling me 'kid,' but I let it slide.

"Hey. Are you getting excited?" I injected as much cheer and anticipation into my question as I could, but it fell flat.

He gave me a charitable smile. "Yeah. How are you?"

We were standing in our own in the corner of the same hotel basement where we'd had Cass's bridal shower. I couldn't keep my lip from trembling as I remembered how different things were from then.

Since I couldn't speak, I shook my head, stared at the short blue carpet, and took in a rattling breath.

"How is he?" I finally plucked up the courage to ask.

Vox shrugged and waved his head from side to side. "Good. I think. Works a lot. Trying to save for the ranch. Hasn't had much time to hang out since the rodeos wound down, and we're busy getting ready for Miss Ally."

"Do you think"—a burning lump in my throat blocked my words, and I swallowed—"Do you think that there's any… that he'd be…"

Vox put a heavy hand on my shoulder and the sad smile returned to his fleshy lips. "Savannah… You should enjoy Austin. It's a great city."

UNFAIR CATCH

He patted my shoulder, then left to join Cass's dad at a table. I went to the bathroom to compose myself before Cass started opening presents. There was only room for one baby at the party, after all.

I drove home the same night and called Maverick up. He said he wasn't busy, and I invited him over to my place.

"I get to move past the front door?" he asked, a smile in his voice.

"If you want to," I said. "What movie should I rent?"

We settled on a new rom-com that had recently released, and Maverick showed up about half an hour after I did with movie theater popcorn, milk duds, and a case of hard lemonade.

"You don't like that, do you?" I asked when he set the drinks on my counter.

"Isn't this what you and Cassidy always had with movies?"

The thoughtfulness soothed my frayed nerves, and instead of saying anything, I hugged him. It felt warm and comfortable and safe. "Thank you."

He spent his first night at my place, and all the time he was there, I heard Vox's voice in the back of my mind saying I should enjoy Austin.

CHAPTER fifty-five

THE NEXT THURSDAY, AS I MICROWAVED popcorn for my phone date with Cass, her name came across the caller ID.

"Hey, girl! You're early," I said.

"Two weeks, actually. Sav, I'm going into labor. Vox is taking me to the hospital in Woodman."

I dropped the bowl I'd picked up, sending popcorn across the kitchen floor, and clutched my phone with both hands. "What?"

A small groan escaped her lips. "I think you can make it here in time if you leave soon."

"Of course. I'll be there."

Before I hung up, I heard her barking orders at

UNFAIR CATCH

Vox. From the sound of her voice, he needed backup just as much as she did.

I threw the few pairs of clothes I had sitting in the drier into a duffel bag, scooped up my hair and makeup supplies and dumped them on top, then flew out of my apartment, only pausing to lock the door.

The city lights quickly gave way to the stars and headlights of other drivers. When traffic eased, I called Darla to tell her that I wasn't going to be at work until Monday. I'd warned her and my coworkers that I planned to leave when Cass went into labor, and she'd told me it wouldn't be a problem—that she had a stylist who had retired, but offered to come in during clutch situations.

The hour drive to Woodman seemed to take days, even though I broke my rule of driving only three miles over the speed limit.

Finally, I pulled into the hospital parking lot, slammed my car into park, and jogged inside through the emergency entrance.

A bleary-eyed security guard and a locked pair of double doors stopped me.

"Who are you here to see?" he asked, rubbing his eyes.

"Cassidy Reddick—I mean Cassidy Cearny."

He stared at his computer and clicked on the mouse at an infuriatingly slow speed.

"She's having a baby!" I cried so he'd understand

the rush and hurry up.

"Ah," he said, "there she is. Do you know where the maternity ward is?"

I wanted to curse when I realized I didn't. "Where is it?"

He leaned his hefty chest over the counter between him and me and pointed toward the hallway beyond the double doors. They made a low humming sound as they inched open. "Go that way, take a right, then follow the signs for obstetrics."

"Thanks!" I called and took off down the hall.

As I jogged by the waiting area, I saw familiar faces out of the corner of my eye. Vox's mom, his brother, and his sister-in-law. Cass's family wasn't there, but I hadn't expected they would be yet since they only had an hour and a half longer drive than I did.

"Hey, Savannah," Vox's mom said as I came to a stop.

"Hey," I sucked in a breath. "How's she doing?"

She smiled, her eyes crinkling behind her narrow reading glasses. "Good. She's only dilated to six."

"Is everything looking okay so far?" My freshman health class knowledge came back, and I remembered that she would have to be at ten centimeters before the baby made an appearance.

"She looks good so far," she said. "Wanted us to send you back when you got here."

"Where's her room?"

She pointed beyond the nurse's station. "Third door on the right."

As I got closer, I heard Vox's soothing tones and a moan of pain from Cass.

A contraction.

I stood outside the door until she quieted and then knocked and went in.

"Hey," I said.

Cass was lying on her side, one hand gripping the plastic bedrail, the other rubbing her stomach. Vox stood behind her, his ball cap pushed back on his head.

Cass's eyes watered, and her face scrunched up. "Sav."

I went across the room and hugged her, careful not to uproot any of the tubes she had protruding from her body.

"How are you feeling?" I asked, taking her un-stuck hand in mine.

"Contractions suck," she said.

A small, relieved laugh escaped my lips. It felt so good to see her. "Sounds like it."

She squeezed my hand and then took hers back so she could massage herself.

"So, what do you need me to do?"

"Just hang out here," she said. "The nurse said I'm only six centimeters dilated, so it might be a while."

"Okay."

"And Sav?" she asked. "Will you keep my mom busy in the lobby when the time comes? I don't want her in here."

"Anything you want." Figuring out how to get her mom out of the room—and make her stay out of the room—would be no easy feat.

"Okay."

"Vox, will you put on some music?" she asked.

Vox took out his phone and a country song Rhett used to sing to me played low over its speaker.

Cass closed her eyes and took slow, deliberate breaths. When her contractions came, she squeezed my hand and breathed through them. We stayed quiet, listening to music and waiting for the baby to come.

"Oh, honey." Cass's mom came into the room and moved between Cass and me to give her a hug. "How are you?"

Camdyn stood in the corner of the room by her dad with eyes as wide and dark as the night sky.

"The contractions are horrible," Cass said.

Her mom nodded. "How long are they?"

"You've got a crowd in here." An Indian doctor stepped into the room, rubbing his hands back and forth with the hand sanitizer.

"Tell me about it," Cass muttered.

"We ask to limit it to two," he said.

Cass gave me a look. "I only want my husband in here."

Her mom's mouth dropped like she wanted to protest, but Camdyn came and took her arm, leading her out of the room. It looked like my job might not be so difficult after all.

I leaned over Cass and kissed her on the forehead. "You're gonna do great."

She smiled at me, and as I left, I heard the doctor telling them he was going to check her dilation.

When I got back to the waiting area, the amount of people had more than doubled. There, on a hard hospital bench, deep in conversation with Vox's brother, was Rhett Lane.

My feet, my breath, and my heart stopped as I laid eyes on him. Sure, I'd seen him across the aisle at church on Christmas, stared at old pictures of us—I even kept a print in my nightstand for nights when it was especially hard to be in bed without him—but no photo could ever compare to the man sitting across the room from me.

For a moment, I observed him—the curve of his muscular shoulders, the long lines of his legs, his hazel eyes shadowed beneath his hat—before he saw me. I missed him so much.

Camdyn called my name, and Rhett's eyes snapped up and locked on mine.

I hoped to see something—anything—in his hazel gaze, but his face was a mask, hard and flat, like I was Medusa and he a statue. He looked away from me and returned to his conversation with Vox's brother, not even giving me a second glance. My carefully reconstructed heart teetered at the edge of the abyss I had tried so hard to climb out of.

"Savannah?" Camdyn repeated.

"Hey," I said, thankful that my feet were carrying me to her without too much thought on my part.

"You look great," she said. "I mean, you've always looked good, but you've been working out, haven't you?"

"Running."

"Totally noticeable. You're so pale, though. I bet if you got a spray tan, you'd be, like, Sports-Illustrated-swimsuit ready."

I forced an airy laugh through my teeth. "Thanks, girl. That's so sweet."

"Oh, yeah, of course."

"How's school going?"

Her hair had the typical beauty-school cut and color that didn't look bad but could be improved.

"I love it," she said.

"How do you like Austin?" I asked.

"Great!" She leaned a little closer and whispered, "Thank God I haven't ran into that janitor, though."

This laugh wasn't as forced. "At least there's that," I agreed.

"So, when are you going to come out with the

girls and me? Cass said you're dating a total hunk, and I want see him for myself."

Out of the corner of my eye, I saw Rhett's back straighten, but he didn't look our way.

"I think you party too hard for me," I hedged.

She blushed. "I promise I've gotten better since then."

"That's good. You can come over for dinner some night if you want. Just give me a call, and I'll have Maverick come over and cook something. He's a lot better at it than I am."

"That'd be awesome. I can't believe I haven't even seen your apartment yet."

"It's all set up," I said. "My brother's fiancé even came over and decorated for me."

"My roommate decorated our dorm, and she did such a good job. I feel like I live in a catalog or something."

For the next few hours, I listened to Cam talk about everything under the sun, nodded occasionally, and waited nervously for periodic updates from the nurse. She didn't come back again after she told us Cass had reached nine centimeters.

Vox did.

His cheeks were slick with tears, but his smile stretched across his face.

"She's here," he said. "Ally Rose. Five pounds, eight ounces, eighteen and a half inches."

Both moms stood up and followed him, like the waiting group had established some kind of unspoken agreement about baby visitation schedules.

Vox's brother and sister-in-law went next.

Then Cass's family.

And then it was just Rhett and me in the waiting room.

I looked at him, urging him to say something, to at least acknowledge me, but he didn't say a word. It upset me how much my body reacted to his. How my legs wanted to carry my body to him, how my entire body wanted nothing more than to be wrapped in the muscular home that was his arms.

"I missed you," I said. I couldn't stop the words from falling out of my mouth, but then I felt like I had stepped into a bear trap.

He didn't look up from the magazine on his lap, but he froze, not even moving a muscle to breathe.

"Are you two ready to see Ally?" Vox called from the hallway.

Rhett set the magazine down and started walking to Cass's room. I followed.

Ally slept swaddled in a pink hospital blanket. Vox took her from Cass's arms and passed her to Rhett, whose eyes glistened upon seeing the tiny girl.

"She's beautiful," I breathed and went to hug Cass.

She lifted an arm around me and smiled a

weak, exhausted smile.

Rhett stepped closer and handed the pink bundle to me. Our eyes met for the briefest of seconds over Ally, and for a moment, I didn't see the hardened man that had been sitting in the waiting room; I saw the love of my life staring back at me—but it ended in a flash.

I cradled Ally in my arms and ran a finger over her plump, smooth cheek.

"Looks like she wanted in on girls' night," I said.

CHAPTER fifty-six

RHETT SAID GOODBYE AND LEFT, SAYING HE had to get home in time for work, and I gave him a five-minute start before leaving myself.

I imagined he'd be in the parking lot, waiting for me, telling me the past few months had been a mistake, but when I got to my car, it was just me. I drove the hour to my parents' house, let myself in, and fell asleep in my old room.

Cass went home from the hospital the following afternoon. Her mom stayed in McClellan so she could help Cass with the newborn, and I dropped in and out of Cass's house, helping where I could, hoping Rhett would stop by. When it started getting late on

UNFAIR CATCH

Sunday, I hugged Cass goodbye and kissed Ally on the cheek.

Seeing Rhett again would have been too painful, I reasoned, but I never imagined I'd run into Hudson at the gas station on my way out of town.

He pulled up to the pump next to mine, and upon seeing me, did a double take. "Savannah?"

My heart was too overwhelmed from the weekend to be anything but sad.

"Yeah."

He walked over to me, but stopped about a few feet away, apparently thinking better of it.

"How's your ankle?"

I glanced down at my feet, both clad in a worn pair of knockoff Uggs. He didn't need to ask about my ankle—it was my heart he'd broken.

"It's fine," I said.

Half a tank was enough, I thought, and pulled the nozzle from my car.

"Savannah?"

I put it back on the pump and squared my shoulders to him. "What, Hudson?"

He looked at me, a shadow passing over his unshaven face. "I'm really sorry… about everything."

"Me too."

I didn't start crying until I hit the city limits.

Chapter fifty-seven

AT HALF PAST EIGHT ON MONDAY MORNING, I could already tell it was going to be a long day. A client who insisted she wanted to go from waist-length hair to a pixie cut and wouldn't listen to any of my suggestions to go shorter in increments, left the salon in tears.

Several of my Friday appointments had rescheduled so I could do their hair instead of the fill-in, which I found both flattering and very uplifting after the weekend. Unfortunately, it meant my schedule had back-to-back appointments until eight p.m., with only forty-five minutes for lunch. Usually I enjoyed the busyness, but after staying up all night at the hospital

UNFAIR CATCH

Thursday and the emotional turmoil of seeing Rhett, all I wanted was to fall into bed and sleep until the world made sense again.

I entered into autopilot, cutting hair according to my client's needs, taking a drink of water between appointments, and sneaking away to use the bathroom if I had a chance. My feet ached and my arms felt like lead pipes, but by the time Maverick, my last appointment of the day, walked into the salon, my pocket was heavy with tips.

"Hey," I said, letting him hug me.

"What's wrong?" he asked. "I've hardly heard from you all weekend."

My shoulders slumped. "Just tired."

He gave one of those bright smiles that made me wonder how anyone could be so perpetually happy. "Well, I'm glad to see you."

I returned his smile with a muted one of my own. "You too."

"You know," he said, "I don't really need a haircut. I just wanted to see you."

I wished for the millionth time I would have met him before I left Austin the first time. Before I had the chance to mangle mine and Rhett's hearts and ruin any happy memories I had with Hudson.

"That's sweet of you," I said, "but I don't mind."

He smiled and held his hat over his chest, revealing slightly grown out blonde hair. "Only if I can take you out for ice cream after. Looks like you need it."

"More like a glass of wine and a long night's sleep."

"I can take care of that too," he said, sitting in the chair.

I cut his hair in less than fifteen minutes, and then he waited while I locked up the store. He led the way to a Cold Stone not too far away and opened my car door for me when we got there.

We held hands on the way inside, and he let me order first.

"I'll have vanilla ice cream with—"

"—peanuts, hot fudge, and KitKats," he finished, rubbing my back. "I remembered."

Tears pricked at my tired eyes, and I blinked them back. His thoughtfulness felt like being hugged by someone when you're about to cry.

He ordered his cone and paid for both of us. He didn't notice my expression until he started to hand me my dish of ice cream.

"What's wrong?" he asked, bending down so he could meet me at eye level. His face practically dripped concern.

Right there in front of the teenage cashier, I broke down bawling. My vision blurred with tears, and I put my hands over my eyes.

"Hey, hey hey." He gently took my wrists

and pulled them away from my face. "What's this all about?"

"I don't deserve you." I looked out a window at the dark parking lot, unable to bring myself to do what I knew I had to.

"Is this about him?" he asked softly. "I know you probably saw him this weekend."

Closing my eyes, I nodded. Tears still seeped out my eyes, and I took in a jagged breath.

"I can't do this anymore," I said. "I'm still in love with him, and I know he'll never want me back, but I can't be with you when he's all I can think about."

His brows furrowed further. "Do you just need more time?"

I shook my head. "I'm sorry."

He looked from me to the cashier and rubbed his brow. "Me too."

Chapter fifty-eight

I DROVE TO MY APARTMENT FEELING MORE alone than ever, but determined to stand on my own. Cass had been right in our fight all those months ago.

I hardly ever made a decision someone else hadn't suggested. I only went to school in Austin because Darla told me too, had moved in with Cass the second she asked, and everything that happened over the summer I'd let Hudson or Rhett dictate.

I knew what I wanted now—Rhett—but I hadn't been lying when I told Maverick he'd never take me back. I had to learn to deal with the consequences of my actions and to practice making my own decisions.

UNFAIR CATCH

That week, I took care of myself every night—other than just by running. I got my nails done Tuesday, hair done Wednesday, bought some new pairs of jeans that fit better than my old ones on Thursday, and planned to go to McClellan and visit Cass on Friday right after work.

I was drying my scissors of the alcohol solution I used to wash them at the end of the day on Friday when one of my coworkers tapped me on the shoulder. "You have a walk-in."

I put the pair back in my drawer. "Can you take it? I just cleaned up."

"You were requested."

I looked over to the entrance of the salon, and then gripped the edge of the counter to keep from falling over.

Rhett.

On shaky legs, I made my way to the counter. "What are you doing here?"

He scratched the back of his neck and studied the black and white tiled floor. Then he met my gaze with his wide hazel eyes.

"I was hoping I would catch you here."

"Rhett," I looked around and saw the other stylist trying to look busy. "What's going on?"

"I came to see you."

My hands shook like my rattling heart.

"Really?" I asked, trying to squash back the

hope blooming in my chest. "Because last time I saw you, you didn't want anything to do with me."

A frown tore his smooth face in half. "That's not true."

"You didn't act like it." I was stronger now, I reminded myself. I could handle this—had to handle this.

"It scared me how much I wanted to see you… Hell, I'm still scared shitless."

My eyes widened at the profanity, and the professional in me hoped no one had heard him say it.

"Rhett," I warned.

"Sorry," he mumbled, rubbing his shoulder.

I looked at him expectantly. "Why did you want to see me again, then?"

"I'm moving to Austin."

The square pattern of the floor started to bend and swirl in strange ways. "What?"

"A guy from the vo-tech called me a few weeks ago and offered me a job… I just filled out the paperwork."

I couldn't let myself believe what he was saying. Didn't even dare to hope… "What about the ranch?"

He shook his head. "I wasn't gonna make enough money piddling around there."

"Oh." He'd come for the money. Believing that he had come to warn me that I had to share the city with him was easier than letting myself dream he wanted me. "Well, if you wanted a haircut, anyone else can do it."

Seeing him hurt in so many ways. I walked back to my station to pick up my purse, before I could cry. My whole plan to win Rhett back seemed so childish now, so futile. But Rhett was right on my heels.

"Sav, that's not why I'm here."

I spun to face him. I couldn't take it. After all the nights spent crying myself to sleep. After all the times I'd closed my eyes to kiss Maverick and saw his face. I knew what I wanted now, and I had to at least try.

"Can I tell you something?" I asked.

He nodded. "Anything."

Before I could think more about what that meant I started talking. "When I lost my job, Monti told me I needed to come up with a reason for coming home. And I told myself that I needed a second chance with Hudson after everything that happened. And I told myself that I couldn't fall in love with you again. Anything short of that and I'd be a failure, just coming home because I lost my job."

He opened his mouth to talk but I interrupted him.

"Wait," I said. "I need to say this."

His eyes softened, and he looked at me. "But the thing is, that plan failed before I even set foot in McClellan. I couldn't fall in love with you again because I was already in love with you. I've been in love with you from the first time you came over to my parents' house in high school, and I couldn't stop my heart when I saw you at that rodeo. No matter how much I wanted not to be in love with you"—my voice cracked—"I can't make myself not love you."

"Why stop now?" he asked.

I closed my eyes, and I wasn't in the salon anymore—I was under my covers, clutching at the tearstained picture I kept in my nightstand.

"I'm not going anywhere," he said. "Ever again. As long as you'll have me, I'm here."

I looked at him, examining every plane of his perfect face to look for some hint that I'd heard him wrong.

"Just give me a chance." His gaze was steady, but his voice wavered. "Please."

I couldn't think, couldn't speak, just knew what my body told me to do. I lurched into his arms, holding so tightly around his waist he let out a huff of air before he wrapped his arms around me. I cried into his chest thick, fat tears of pure happiness.

My home had come to me.

ONE YEAR later

Want to see where Rhett and Savannah are one year from now? To get a free, exclusive novella, visit https://www.kelsiestelting.com/unfair-catch and click "Anything But Yes."

SPECIAL
thanks

It takes a village to write a book, which, to me, feels a lot like an actual child. There are a lot of people who helped me get this story from an idea in my head to the book you're reading now, and they deserve all the appreciation I can give them.

First and foremost, I'd like to point to the man upstairs, who for whatever reason, gave me the inclination toward writing. God's pointed me back to writing time and time again, and without His gentle nudges (okay, sometimes shouts) I wouldn't have brought any of my books to publication.

Next, I'd like to thank my husband, who, let's be honest, probably deserves way more than the few sappy sentences I'm about to write. He is the most supportive person I've ever met. When I'm struggling with anxiety, or a bad day, or imposter syndrome, he's always there to talk me up and offer me a dish of ice cream. That means more than I can say. He's also the first person I let read my work nowadays, and I feel blessed that he's able to sift through hundreds of pages of romance and then tell me he loved it. Ty, I love you. Thank you.

My family. My crazy, rambunctious, wild, loving family. Thank you for supporting me on all my ventures. I know it sometimes seems like I'm dreaming big, but they always are there to offer a word of support or wish me luck, and that means more than you'll know. My mom's my second reader, and I'm glad we can share books with each other, even as I move into adulthood.

Back to the part about the village. I have a

small group of beta readers who mean the world to me. Mom, Cathy, Katie, Carol, and Cassidy, thank you so much for reading this book and sharing your insights with me. I loved bonding with you over the characters and the story, and *Unfair Catch* wouldn't be what it is today without your help. Thank you for taking a chance on a new author, and I'm excited to see where this journey will lead us!

I like books with good grammar and storylines just as much as anyone else, and my editors, Theresa M. Cole and Yesenia Vargas, helped make that possible for *Unfair Catch*. If this story is my baby, you were two great babysitters. Thanks for taking care of it.

I wouldn't exist as a writer without my readers, who let me know my words actually mean something to them. To the readers who have reached out to me on social media, by email, or in person, your words inspire me and drive me to be the best writer I can be. And to you, the person reading these words, thank you for taking the time to share in my imaginary world. I hope it brought you peace, happiness, and freedom, if only for a minute.

AUTHOR'S
note

When I first started writing this book, I thought it would be a great escape. I thought it would be a place I could vacation to—to create a world free from struggling marriages, illnesses, worries, and basically any pain I was feeling in my life. But every time I tried to write a story like that, my characters wouldn't let me. It wasn't real.

I knew these characters deserved a story, but was nervous to write something like *Unfair Catch*. First, I hadn't written a novel-length work of fiction since I was in high school. Second, did I really want to write a book where the characters have *whispers* sex?

The first fear I could overcome, but the second I struggled with. As a twenty-something married Catholic, I'm no stranger to sex—yikes, am I allowed to talk about this?—and the characters in my book aren't either. Savannah finds herself in an uncomfortable situation with two love interests, Cassidy isn't a virgin to say the least, and neither is Rhett.

My characters could just fall in love, remain abstinent until marriage, never lie or use people, have minivan loads of perfect babies, and live happily ever after, but how could I relate to that? Where's the lesson in that? Isn't one of the greatest parts of life looking back on a challenging time and seeing how much you've changed and improved since then? I don't want to get into an existential rant about joy without sadness, but I think you get the point.

I love this story so much, and I'm so attached

to it because it's authentic. And just because something is fiction, doesn't mean it can't be real. In *Unfair Catch*, you see characters doing their best, and failing, time and time again—something I can relate to. The great thing, though, is that it works out. Life might not be pretty or happy all the time. No doubt there will be tragedy and heartbreak deeper than Rhett Lane's beautiful hazel eyes, more insurmountable than the roughest bucking bull. We'll shove the ones we love most away. We'll cling more to our past dreams than our present realities. People we used to be closest to will become distant strangers. But, in the end, we'll learn and grow and become more fully ourselves, which is always the greatest gift we can give anyone else.

ABOUT THE author

Kelsie Stelting is a perpetually curious writer who loves learning from others, traveling, and making the world a better place. She writes real stories for real people in the contemporary romance and historical nonfiction genres, as well as on her blog at https://www.kelsiestelting.com.

She loves connecting with readers, so be sure and drop her an email at kelsie@kelsiestelting.com!

WHAT now?

Reviews help other readers find the stories right for them. If you'd review this story on Amazon and Goodreads, I'd really appreciate it.

Read further in the Texas Sun Series or check out my Texas Star Series for books about rural high school students learning about life and love.

Connect with me on social media. You can find me on Facebook or Instagram and Twitter.

Visit the Texas Sun Pinterest board. Email me at kelsie@kelsiestelting.com if you want to be a contributor!

Want to be entered to win prizes each month? Take a picture with this book and share on Facebook, Twitter, or Instagram. Be sure to tag me and use the hashtag #KelsieSteltingAuthor or #TexasSunSeries so I can see it. I'll pick a winner at the end of every month and send you a special gift!

Check out my other books: *All the Things He Left Behind* and *Always Anika.*

SPREAD
the love

to   from

to   from

to *from*

to *from*

to *from*

to   *from*

to   *from*

to   *from*

Made in the USA
Columbia, SC
18 September 2017